HEART
QUEST.

## PRAISE FOR *SUMMER'S END*

"In *Summer's End*, Lyn Cote skillfully weaves together the threads of small-town life, big-city crime, and a love that surpasses both. This story draws you in and won't let go. I love it!"

› **Lois Richer** ›

*author of* Blessings in Disguise

"A page-turning blend of romance and suspense with memorable characters bound by faith and love against an unknown enemy. Lyn Cote's ability to bring the heart and soul of a small town to life shines in *Summer's End*."

› **Linda Windsor** ›

*author of* Along Came Jones

"In *Summer's End*, Dr. Kirsi Royston chooses between the fear of man and the power of God; between the burdens of the past and the possibilities of the future. It's a journey we all travel, a lesson we all need to learn."

› **Nancy Moser** ›

*coauthor of* The Sister Circle

"Lyn Cote has crafted a wonderfully enjoyable romantic mystery with great characters and a fast-moving plot. There is enough suspense in *Summer's End* to keep the reader reading until the final page."

› **Linda Hall** ›

*author of* Steal Away *and* Sadie's Song

"A colorful heroine and intriguing secondary characters create conflict and interest in this romantic intrigue, and only when they allow God, in His infinite wisdom and mercy, to heal wounds and provide answers to the mystery can love and peace come to Steadfast. The fast-paced ending will keep readers on the edge of their seats. Lyn Cote has another winning story for her readers."

› **Gail Gaymer Martin** ›

*author of* The Christmas Kite

# "Lyn Cote's writing flows

wonderfully from one emotion-deep scene to another, and breathes with the Lord's comfort and love from beginning to end."

› **Maureen Pratt** ›

*author of the novella "Dear Love" and nonfiction books on health and spirituality*

*romance the way it's meant to be*

HeartQuest brings you romantic fiction
with a foundation of biblical truth.
Adventure, mystery, intrigue, and suspense
mingle in these heartwarming stories of
men and women of faith striving to build
a love that will last a lifetime.

May HeartQuest books sweep you
into the arms of God, who longs for you
and pursues you always.

# SUMMER'S End

## LYN COTE

HEART
QUEST®

*Romance fiction from*
Tyndale House Publishers, Inc., Wheaton, Illinois
*www.heartquest.com*

Visit Tyndale's exciting Web site at www.tyndale.com

Check out the latest about HeartQuest Books at www.heartquest.com

Edited by Lorie Popp

Designed by Kelly Bennema

**Library of Congress Cataloging-in-Publication Data**

Cote, Lyn.
  Summer's end / Lyn Cote.
    p. cm. — (HeartQuest) (Northern Intrigue)
  ISBN 0-8423-3558-7 (sc)
    1. Women physicians—Fiction. 2. Inheritance and succession—Fiction. 3. Stalking victims—Fiction.
  4. Wisconsin—Fiction. I. Title. II. Series.
  PS3553.O76378 S86 2003
  813'.54—dc21                                                      2003011746

Printed in the United States of America

07  06  05  04  03
7   6   5   4   3   2   1

*To my dear friend Jacque,*
*Your support has been an invaluable blessing.*
*I wish you God's greatest blessings now and always.*

*Many thanks to Harry Daugherty, chief of police of Marion, Iowa,*
*for his information about meth-drug traffic and law enforcement.*

*Thanks to the great staff at Marengo Hospital in Marengo, Iowa,*
*for giving me fantastic input on a small rural hospital.*

*Also many thanks to my doctor, Mary Ann Nelson,*
*for her help on all things medical.*

*Finally, in memory and with gratitude to my agent,*
*Jane Jordan Browne, who did so much for me.*

*"Honour thy father and thy mother."*

EXODUS 20:12, KJV

# CHAPTER ONE

*HOW DID I get myself into this?* Kirsi Royston turned onto the state highway toward Steadfast, Wisconsin. Breezes played with the unruly hair that had escaped her long ponytail. Usually that was a carefree feeling. Today it was just irritating.

She'd flown into Minneapolis two nights ago from Los Angeles. Yesterday she'd bought this used Jeep Wrangler. Today she'd driven across the wide Mississippi River and up the Great River Road, overlooking the bluffs. Now late May sunshine warmed her, but that didn't ease her taut nerves.

*Well, things change. Situations change. Mine has, and the clinic will just have to understand that.*

Kirsi's churning stomach didn't buy that, and she turned back to watching Wisconsin roll by her window. Mile by mile, the scenery along the lonely highway continued to astound Kirsi. She was accustomed to rocky Pacific beaches, soaring mountain slopes, green canyons.

Wisconsin had sounded so tame, so dull. But it had turned out to be unexpectedly beautiful—like the Rockies, without any mountains. Just thick forests, meandering rivers, and small, clear lakes.

Grandfather had tried to prepare her. "Don't under-estimate the Midwest, Kirsi. This is a beautiful country. Every part has its own splendor."

*You were right, Gramps. Sorry I doubted you. I should know better.* Thinking of her grandparents gave her a warm yet lonely feeling. How circumstances could change in only six months! She'd never expected her grandparents to offer her such an opportunity, one that carried so much impor-tance for her mother's well-being. Kirsi frowned. She still didn't know if she agreed with her grandmother's hopes. But she couldn't deny that the idea appealed to her also.

A sign snagged her attention: State Park, Stalker Lake. Her Jeep turned off the highway as though on autopilot. *Hey!* Kirsi scolded herself. *This is just plain stalling and I don't do that!*

She drove into the wooded park over a gravel track and followed the sign to Stalker Lake anyway. She found the parking lot, got out, and left her Jeep. It wouldn't hurt to make a brief stop. Her legs could use stretching.

*Excuses. I'm just putting off facing Dr. Erickson. Why can't life ever be easy?*

The lake was bigger than she'd expected and had a wide sandy beach. She pictured families on the sand and kids splashing in the water. She shivered though. Wisconsin's May wind had a chill to it, especially here in the shadows of the pines.

The breeze rustled the evergreen boughs, and a bird she didn't recognize called in the stillness. She shivered again. Feeling suddenly as though someone were watching her, she glanced around. No other cars were parked nearby, but the eerie feeling persisted. Her complete isolation dawned on her. This was something else she rarely experienced in California. By design. Experience had taught her not to be in vulnerable situations.

Could someone be watching her from the dense pine forest? She tried to push away the irrational fear yet couldn't. *Leave it behind you, Kirsi! It's long past.*

She folded her arms around herself and jogged back to her car. Turning on the ignition, she backed out and returned to the highway. Unhappy memories tried to take over. She fought them off.

Then, before she knew it, the main street of the town of Steadfast zipped by her. She slowed, U-turned, and drove the length of it again. Black Bear Café, the *Steadfast Times* office, Steadfast Community Church, Foodliner, and Harry's Gas Station—she let the quaint names sink into her mind, hoping they would calm her nerves.

With a ragged sigh, she turned at the sign that said Erickson Clinic. From the road, she noted the one-story, L-shaped, cement-brick building ahead. It had looked larger in the photos they'd sent her. But any rural clinic would look small compared to the clinics in LA.

She drove around Erickson Clinic, which was more like a small hospital than what she'd thought of as a clinic. According to the letters she'd received, the clinic had an emergency wing with one basic operating room, a small lab, and a radiology room; one wing of patient rooms; and a helipad to airlift cases the clinic couldn't handle.

Completing the circle drive around the clinic, Kirsi parked in the lot by the emergency entrance, which was nestled in the crook of the L, and glanced around. Only a few vehicles were parked nearby—not a busy place on a Friday afternoon.

Pushing down her hesitation, she jumped out and headed straight inside the ER entrance. *Time to face the music.*

The reception area, immediately inside, appeared deserted, but she could hear sounds . . . voices from down

3

the hallway. She noted that there were two curtained suites off to her left in the ER wing, which made up the shorter base of the L. In the other direction, she glimpsed a nurses' station at the start of a hallway of rooms.

From behind the counter, a gruff voice spoke up, "Hi." An older woman's gray head appeared. "I was picking something up off the floor. Didn't see you there. Do you need help?"

"Not really." The moment had come. Kirsi had to declare herself. Hesitating still, she offered her hand to the plump woman.

Eyeing her, the woman took Kirsi's hand and gave one strong shake. "You're a stranger. What can we do for you?"

Kirsi sized up the woman's no-nonsense face. *Get it over with*. "I'm Dr. Kirsi Royston—"

"The new doc?" The woman reached over the counter and claimed Kirsi's hand again, giving it another firmer shake. "I'm Ma Havlecek. I'm volunteering today, answering the phone. We're expecting an ambulance any second—"

The sound of an ambulance siren cut off the woman's words. Out of the nearest ER suite hurried a nurse with short, golden brown hair. A tall doctor with dark wavy hair followed her, rushing past Kirsi toward the doors.

From the opposite direction, a teenage boy—strapped on a gurney—was being pushed through the ER entrance. Struggling against the restraints, he spat out a string of curses.

Kirsi sized the young patient up. His agitation was all too familiar to her, but surely not here? He couldn't be suffering from . . . not in rural Steadfast, Wisconsin.

Well past Kirsi, Douglas Erickson, M.D.—she recognized him now from a photo of the clinic staff she'd been sent—paused and looked back. "Dr. Royston!" he blurted out, looking surprised. But immediately, he moved on, calling back, "When did you get here?"

"Just a minute ago. I drove over a day early." *To have a day to get acquainted with you before I tell you what's changed.* She hurried to catch up with him. "I wanted a chance to look around—"

"My grandfather will be delighted that you're so eager to get started." He reached the wheeled gurney and began questioning the EMTs.

Well, yes, she was eager to get started—in spite of everything.

As the new patient was wheeled to an examining area, Kirsi trailed Dr. Erickson. "I'll just observe you," she said, "if that's all right."

"Fine." The doctor's attention was on the writhing patient. The EMTs hovered, waiting to release the incoherent and thrashing boy from the restraints so they could leave with their gurney. The nurse tried to soothe the patient. No success.

The teen became frenzied. Screeching. Twisting. When Dr. Erickson tried to examine his pupils, the kid managed to butt the doctor's chest, nearly knocking him off his feet.

Erickson grabbed the youngster and thrust him back down. "Wendy, did the school say anything about what this kid was doing before this came on?" The doctor bit out the words, interspersed between the teen's yowls.

"The principal said he was found in one of the rest rooms." The nurse, Wendy, raised her voice. "From the odor in the room, she thought he'd been smoking marijuana."

With violent twists, the teen bucked against the gurney. It rocked, tipped. Wendy yelped.

The gurney flipped on its side and hit the floor. Erickson stumbled and nearly fell. The EMTs surged around the patient, righting the gurney.

"What's wrong with him?" From behind them, the receptionist shouted, "He's havin' a regular fit!"

Kirsi waited for Erickson to give the obvious answer, but he was too busy helping the paramedics lift the patient onto the ER examining table.

"This looks like meth to me," Kirsi said above the noise. "He probably soaked the marijuana cigarette in it first."

Both Erickson and Wendy cast worried looks toward her. "We've never had a meth overdose here—"

The teen jerked and went limp.

Erickson yelled, "He's coding!"

Automatically, Kirsi turned to the wall dispenser and pulled out a pair of plastic gloves and put them on. Without waiting for an invitation, she helped Wendy hook the kid up to the cardiac monitor.

"Pupils—dilated!" Erickson pronounced.

Wendy rolled the crash cart to the side of the gurney. Kirsi began an injection to stimulate the heart. All her own worries vanished as she fell into the familiar routine.

Wendy finished hooking up the blue bag and pumped air into the patient's lungs. Frantic moments—Kirsi worked with the other two trying to get the teen's heart beating again. Without luck.

"Clear!" Erickson shouted, paddles in hand.

Kirsi and Wendy stepped back, their gloved hands suspended in air. The jolt jumped the teen's limp body. Kirsi stared at the monitor. Still flat-lined.

"Clear!" Erickson shouted again.

"Wait!" Kirsi held up a hand, her focus on the monitor. The welcome beep . . . beep started. "We have a heartbeat."

"Thank God," the petite nurse breathed.

Kirsi echoed the thought. Her own heart pounded with adrenaline. That had been a familiar response. It gave her confidence. Things weren't really so different here in Wisconsin.

With his eyes tracking the etching line on the monitor

screen, Erickson put the gray paddles back in their racks on the sides of the red metal crash cart. He looked up at Kirsi. "Methamphetamine? You think this was a meth overdose?"

"It didn't have to be an overdose. That stuff can kill a kid like this the first time. It's lethal." Then she felt it. Her words released it, a pall—spreading, hanging over them like a funeral drapery. Crack, crystal meth—deadly poisons. "Meth's everywhere nowadays."

Erickson nodded, shedding his soiled gloves into a biohazard container. "You're right. This is just the first case like this with a teen that we've had."

"But that doesn't mean," Wendy agreed, "it hasn't been around." She turned to Kirsi. "Dr. Royston, I'm Wendy Durand. We're glad you're here."

Uncomfortable with this attention, Kirsi smiled at Wendy. What would their reaction to her be after her news? "Thanks." Trying to switch the focus from herself, Kirsi took a step closer to the patient and glanced down at him. "We'll have to see if he comes around soon. This isn't over." She peeled off her own gloves and discarded them. She waited by the curtain to ask Dr. Erickson for an informal tour. Now that she was here, she was intensely curious about the place.

"Ma," Erickson said, "call Weston's parents—though the school probably already has done that. Then call the hospital in Eau Claire. We may need the medi-vac chopper later."

"Is Eau Claire the closest, Dr. Erickson?" Kirsi stepped outside the curtain with the doctor.

Erickson nodded. "The helipad is out that door." He guided her down a short hall. "Let me show you around. And please call me Doug." He smiled broadly. "My grand-father realized in the early fifties that our county needed an anchor to keep doctors and the health care they provided in this rural area. That's why he opened this mini-hospital out in the middle of nowhere. You've seen our ER wing except for the operating and delivery room. That's here."

She paused beside him and peeked through the windowed door at a tidy, very stripped-down OR.

"We are fortunate that we still have two semiretired surgeons in the county. They do a few emergency surgeries such as appendectomies, and we can continue to deliver babies since one of them is always on call in case an emergency C-section is necessary."

Kirsi knew most of this from the senior Dr. Erickson, but it was revealing to hear the young Dr. Erickson's pride as he continued the tour.

From the photo she'd seen of the clinic staff, she hadn't been particularly impressed with Doug Erickson. But she found that he was one of those men who had a presence that a photograph couldn't convey. It wasn't just that he was good-looking. He had an aura of competence and personal force that was instantly appealing. His square jaw had a determined look to it and he had a lean, muscular build—a natural athlete.

"Now," Doug went on, "I'll walk you through the patient wing."

Trying not to appear to study him, Kirsi heard the opening swish of the automatic doors behind them in the reception area. Another patient? Already?

A woman's voice screamed, "Is Dr. Doug here, Ma? It's Rachel. I think she's having convulsions!"

Dr. Erickson headed toward the voice. As though pulled by an identical string, Kirsi followed him.

Their pace quickened at the sight of a distraught woman holding a little girl shaking in her arms. The doctor took the child from her. He ran toward the other examining area. "How long has she been like this?"

The mother jogged behind him, trailed by a little boy. "I was driving home, and she just started gasping and then this! I drove right here! What is it?"

The question went unanswered as the doctor laid the convulsing child on the examining table.

Grabbing fresh gloves from the wall dispenser, Kirsi handed Doug a pair and donned one herself. She began hooking the toddler to the monitor. The sound of an ambulance cut through the intense examination.

The doctor let out a sound of impatience. "Not another emergency! What's going on?"

"I'll get it." Kirsi swung around, ditched her gloves, and headed toward the emergency entrance. She met the EMTs at the ambulance. "I'm Dr. Royston," she announced in a firm voice.

"The new doc?" One of the men looked up. "We wondered—"

Kirsi nodded. "Who's the patient?"

"Veda McCracken." He and another EMT exited the ambulance with a large older woman on the gurney between them.

"Go on," Kirsi prompted them.

"Her heartbeat is erratic. She's semiconscious—"

The patient railed at them in an angry mumble.

The EMT continued, "The postman saw that she hadn't picked up her mail for the past two days, so he looked in the window—"

"She lives alone?" Kirsi asked, wondering where to take her. The two emergency suites were already occupied.

"Yes."

"And he waited two days to check on her?" Kirsi asked, letting her disapproval come through her voice. *This isn't LA! Don't people in little towns look after each other?*

"It's rural delivery, just a roadside mailbox. Today he

got out of his car and looked in the window," the EMT said, ignoring her comment, "and saw her on the floor of her living room."

"Let's get her into that examining room." Kirsi gestured toward the area where the teen and nurse were. It would be tight, but the teen was unconscious, and the nurse could help her with the new arrival. Kirsi could tell by the woman's sunken eyes that she was probably severely dehydrated.

Kirsi nodded to Wendy as she entered. "I want this patient's vitals, and we need to hook her up to an IV—stat."

The EMTs obeyed her but filed out of the room as soon as they moved the older woman onto another examining table against the wall.

Pulling on fresh gloves, Kirsi looked up. She was alone with the patients. Where was the nurse? Why had Wendy left?

Kirsi called out, "Nurse?" She pulled an IV pole toward the patient herself and began locating a vein in the woman's arm for the IV needle. But the woman was so dehydrated Kirsi knew it would be difficult to find a usable vein.

Wendy reentered but hesitated just inside the door. "I've paged a nurse from the patient wing. She'll be right here."

This confused Kirsi. The nearby teen was unconscious and stable for the moment. And Dr. Erickson shouldn't need a nurse for his case in the other ER suite. But Kirsi couldn't waste time with questions.

Since the cardiac monitor was already hooked to the drugged teen, Kirsi located a vein. "You're not the only nurse in ER today, are you? Please get this patient's pulse."

Wendy approached the older woman as though she might explode and gingerly took her wrist. "No, but we are having trouble with scheduling—"

The patient, who had been staring at the doctor, now

turned to Wendy. Veda started yelling and thrashing inef-
fectually on the table, attempting to pull her arm from
Wendy's grasp.

"Veda, you're going to be all right." Kirsi spoke clearly
and with authority. "You're at the clinic. We're—"

The woman managed to throw out her foot and nearly
kick Wendy, who evaded the attack. She continued trying
to take the woman's pulse even though Veda fought her
efforts and flailed on the table like a landed tuna. Incompre-
hensible words and cursing came out in spurts.

"We better restrain her," Kirsi said, setting Veda's hand
at her side and reaching for the straps at the sides of the
table.

"No," Wendy said, "this is about me. She wants me to
get away from her. Her pulse's elevated." Wendy dropped
the woman's wrist, went to the teen, and without further
explanation, wheeled him, his IV, and the monitor out into
the hallway.

Dumbfounded, Kirsi looked after Wendy. Her patient
moaned and contorted herself more. Kirsi grabbed both of
Veda's hands. They were large boned with dry, roughened
skin.

Kirsi squeezed them and leaned close to the woman's
face. "Veda? Veda? I'm Dr. Royston." She repeated this until
the woman finally stilled and met her eyes.

"I'm going to take good care of you," Kirsi continued.
She repeated this reassurance two more times. "Do you
understand me? I'm the new doctor here at the clinic. I'm
going to hook you up to an IV and take your vitals. If you
understand me, can you squeeze my hand?"

Kirsi waited patiently while urgent sounds floated to her
from where Dr. Erickson was still dealing with the little girl.
Where had Wendy gone?

Finally, Kirsi felt a slight pressure on her hands. She

gave the patient a warm, encouraging smile and squeezed Veda's hands back. "Don't worry. I'm going to take good care of you."

Veda sighed, relaxing limply on the table.

Taking the woman's faint pulse, Kirsi began to murmur reassurances and explanations of what she was doing as she went about taking care of Veda. But no new nurse came, and Kirsi fought her increasing frustration at being left alone in an ER new to her. There had to be some logical reason for Wendy's leaving her and for no other nurse to arrive. But she couldn't think of one.

※ ※ ※

As the crisis with the toddler Rachel eased, Doug's thoughts split between preparing his patient to be admitted and dealing with the arrival of Dr. Kirsi Royston. The new doctor's East Indian heritage had been obvious in her long black hair, tan skin, black eyes, and swallow-wing eyebrows. Her exotic appearance had taken his breath away—literally. His heart had felt like a cartoon character's—nearly bursting from his chest!

Of course, he'd seen a picture of the new doctor and spoken to her over the phone. But his grandfather had handled the face-to-face interview six years ago. That was when Kirsi Royston had answered their ad about receiving financial help to pay for her medical-school expenses. In return for the money, Kirsi was to practice medicine in this county for six years—now after she'd finished her residency in California.

Would Dr. Royston, fresh from a California residency, fit in here, in isolated, very-small-town Steadfast? He'd been praying so for over a year now. But he had no peace about it. Would he be able to help the new doctor adjust? Or would she resent being here as his . . .

"Will Rachel be all right?" Penny Weaver, the local pastor's wife, asked him. She stroked her little foster daughter's dark curls. Little Rachel looked wan, weakened.

Doug brought his mind back to his young patient. "I think Rachel experienced a febrile seizure. It's not uncommon in childhood. Usually due to high fever. But I want to keep her here overnight just to be sure."

Penny nodded. "I'll stay with her."

Doug touched Penny's shoulder. "Of course. I'll ask Ma to call your husband to come and get Zak for you. Wendy will be in soon and take you through admitting Rachel."

In the midst of trying to smile, Penny bit her trembling lower lip.

"Rachel will be fine." Doug squeezed Penny's slender shoulder. "I want to make sure the fever is going to stay down."

"I believe you. It just scared me."

"Don't be scared, Mom," Zak, Penny's five-year-old son, spoke up. "Jesus will take care of Rachel."

Just outside the ER suite, the new doctor was waiting for him. Doug took a deep breath. Before long, he'd be accustomed to her alluring and unusual looks. But right now he needed to remain professional, guard how he showed his reaction to her.

She stepped close to him. "I need to talk to you in private—now." Her voice was laced with irritation, or was it confusion?

He'd been so busy with Rachel that he had only been aware that she was handling Veda McCracken. What had the old woman done to upset the new doctor? Veda was capable of anything. "Certainly." He nodded. "Let's go into the doctors' lounge. This way."

He led her down the hall to the room that was used by the doctor on overnight duty and included a table and chairs, a bed, and a full bath. He switched on the light and closed the door behind them. He motioned her toward a chair at the table. "I'm sorry you had to face Veda McCracken alone—"

"I want to know—" Kirsi looked directly into his eyes—"what happened to the nurse."

"Happened to her?" He cast back in his mind. "She was taking care of the teen—"

"That's right, but I asked for help with my patient, and she just up and left me!"

Doug frowned. He wasn't surprised that Veda had upset everything. That was her singular talent. But how could he explain Wendy and Veda McCracken and . . . everything else right now? This wasn't the opening conversation he wanted to have with Kirsi Royston. He stalled. "You admitted Veda?"

Kirsi nodded. "Yes. She was seriously dehydrated. But you're not answering my question. Wendy left me and said another nurse was coming—"

"Sorry. I did get that message but didn't have a chance to pass it on. We had another patient here who needed the other nurse." He took a deep breath. "We are spread kind of thin today. And Wendy—"

A knock sounded at the door. At his word, it swung open to reveal Wendy. She stepped inside, her expression downcast. "Dr. Royston, I apologize for leaving you like that." Wendy's voice quavered. "But you didn't understand that my being in the room was what was upsetting Veda."

Doug nodded, but he knew this didn't satisfy the new doctor. Her expression was full of doubt.

"Why would she be upset?" Kirsi asked, looking up at Wendy with a furrowed brow.

"It's a long story, Doctor," Wendy replied, obviously holding back tears. "But Veda is an angry woman, and I've been a target of that anger all my life." She drew in a ragged breath before her eyes met Kirsi's. "I didn't leave because I wanted to get away from her, but because she would only have gotten more agitated if I'd stayed."

Doug's heart went out to Wendy. She was deeply embarrassed to have to expose this to the new doctor on her very first day at the clinic.

Wendy gave an apologetic shrug. "My shift is over now, so I'll be going. Welcome to Steadfast, Dr. Royston. We're very happy you've arrived." She left them, closing the door behind her.

Kirsi looked at Doug. "I don't get it. What's going on here?"

# CHAPTER TWO

DOUG RETURNED KIRSI'S steady regard, her dark eyes puzzled. How did one explain Veda McCracken to a stranger? But he didn't want Dr. Royston to get the wrong impression. He owed it to Wendy to try to explain. He studied Kirsi's face with its smooth skin. Its color reminded him of toasted coconut or butterscotch candy.

Her troubled expression needed an answer. Why wait? He began, "Wendy is one of our best nurses. If not the best—"

"Then why would she leave a new doctor alone with a patient right in the middle of an emergency?"

"Small-town medicine is different because of the closeness of the community—"

"I know that, but—"

"People here have joint histories; sometimes these histories are generations old."

Kirsi's forehead crinkled. "I don't see what you're driving at. Did Wendy and Veda argue about something?"

He frowned. "I don't like to gossip, but you need to know this. Veda hates Wendy, and it was in your patient's best interest for Wendy to leave the room."

"Hates? What did Wendy do to the woman?"

His frown deepened. He hadn't hit the mark yet. "That's just it. Wendy has never done anything to Veda."

"You're not making any sense, Doctor."

He read skepticism in Kirsi's honest face and became aware of her subtle fragrance, with a hint of cinnamon. "It's a long story," he said, stalling, wishing he could postpone it forever.

As her dark, delicately arched eyebrows drew together, Doug struggled to come up with a palatable but truthful explanation for her. He didn't want to give Kirsi a dislike of small-town life in general and Steadfast in particular. This had worried him from the start when his grandfather had come up with the idea of paying a med student's tuition.

Not everyone loved living in a small town, and not everyone was suited to it as he knew only too well. . . . He pushed aside bitterness. *That has nothing to do with this woman.*

But it was so important that this woman, the doctor he'd be working with for the next six years, settle in and be a good fit. This stranger, his new colleague, was from Los Angeles, a teeming metropolis, where neighbors didn't know—didn't need to know—the life history of everyone they met. *But you're in Steadfast now, Dr. Royston.*

He could only hope she would take to it here. Her help was important to them all. No one understood that better than he did. He looked across the table and wished he could smooth her wrinkled brow with a touch. He was better at doing than talking. "Okay." He sat back in his chair. "I might as well spell it out for you."

Kirsi eyed him.

"Veda is Wendy's grandmother's only sister."

"A family feud?" She looked troubled, her full mouth crimping.

"Just on Veda's part," Doug hurried to explain, forestalling more doubt on her part. "Veda and her sister didn't like it when Wendy's parents married. They didn't think Wendy's mom was good enough. This is according to my granddad."

"Why didn't they like Wendy's mother?" Kirsi asked him.

He felt his face harden. If only she didn't need to know this. He clenched his jaw.

The new doctor merely gazed at him, waiting.

"In the past, Wendy's mother had a drinking problem." He wouldn't add any more to that.

Her brow clearing, Kirsi nodded as though taking his words in deeply. "Poor Wendy."

Her immediate sympathy gave him confidence. "Anyway, Wendy's dad died in Vietnam. And within seven years, Wendy's grandmother died, too. But Veda—"

"Keeps up the family feud." Kirsi looked down at her hands. "That's a shame. Families in conflict . . . I hate that. My own . . ." Her voice trailed off. "Why do people who should love each other decide to hate instead?"

Gazing at the way her hair parted in the middle and flowed back to a casual ponytail, he knew he should go on. He couldn't let Dr. Royston think that the conflict between Wendy and Veda stopped there. "Veda is antagonistic to more than just Wendy."

She looked up. "She has a lot of enemies?"

*Only most of the county.* "I'm afraid so. Veda seems to delight in causing trouble. I don't think there are many people who are even on speaking terms with her." Kirsi's obvious concern for Veda touched him.

"So that's why the mail carrier didn't check on her until her mail piled up for two days?"

Doug lifted an eyebrow at her starchy tone. *So she also demands justice.*

"That's who found Veda," Kirsi was saying. "The mail carrier looked in her window after two days."

"Veda has earned that kind of . . ." He closed his mouth, not wanting to put into words Veda's petty larceny. But this new doctor deserved to hear the whole truth. "A few years ago—" he watched for her reaction—"Veda was caught stealing money from one of the fund-raisers for you."

"Stealing?" She sounded shocked.

"Yes. She skimmed some off the profits for . . . maybe three years." He looked away, severing his focus on her.

"Was she ever prosecuted?"

"No. She returned the money. She's an old woman on a fixed income. That could explain how she got so run-down physically that she ended up here today without anyone helping her or even noticing. She pushes away everyone who's ever tried to help her." His gaze returned to his new colleague.

Kirsi's brow had wrinkled again. "That isn't good. It's so important for the elderly to keep in the flow, keep in connection with others." She paused, tracing circles on the table with one forefinger before she looked up. "The community doesn't seem to have a very forgiving attitude. I would have hoped . . ."

Doug leaned forward, wishing he could touch her restless hand. "I'm afraid you would have to see Veda in action to get a full understanding of how she has alienated herself from everyone. She's nasty, loud, and argumentative—all without provocation. It never stops. She's the kind of person who repeatedly shouted curses at Wendy in public when Wendy was only a little girl. I remember that myself." He felt grim, recalling with clarity a few of those scenes.

Kirsi's sober expression told him that his words had finally conveyed the unpleasant truth to her. "That bad?"

Doug exhaled, the stress draining from him. "Sorry, but

yes. And on the other hand, Wendy is pretty much loved by everyone. I don't know if you noticed when she came in to apologize, but it really upset her to leave you alone with Veda."

"I saw." Kirsi traced more circles.

The motion of her slender hand fascinated him. "My advice to you is to go slowly about forming opinions about people. You'll learn where people's attitudes come from and who's related to whom." He hoped she'd take this to heart. *Please, Lord, help this new doctor get started on the right foot. The county needs her. I need her working effectively.* "This is a tight community and you need to spend time observing and saying very little until you have a firm grasp of people and their relationships."

Kirsi made eye contact with him and then nodded. "Sounds like good advice."

The full force of her attention flowed over him—a warm tide. But there was something in her luminous eyes that Doug couldn't identify. As if there were something she wanted or needed. Finding the answer would be up to him. His grandfather's well-being and the county's welfare were on his shoulders.

The door opened and Doug's grandfather—tall and distinguished with his snow-white hair and ramrod-straight spine—walked in. "Ma called me and said our new doctor has arrived." Beaming, he held out his hand.

Kirsi rose and shook hands. "Hello, Dr. Erickson."

"Please call me Old Doc. Everyone else around here does. Seeing you here is wonderful. You were only an idea a decade ago. We've worked a lot of years for this moment."

※ ※ ※

Kirsi squirmed inside at this glowing welcome. "Dr. Erick—"

"That's Old Doc. And I see you've already met my grandson, Dr. Doug."

Doug rose. "We had quite a rush going, Granddad. Three emergencies within a half hour."

"And I missed it." Old Doc shook his head. "I'm here now though. Why don't you run Dr. Royston out to where she'll be living so she can get settled? I'll cover the ER until you get back, Doug."

Doug looked to Kirsi, the honesty in his face cutting up her peace.

She knew she should sit them both down and tell them . . . "Great. I am a bit tired." *And all of a sudden, I seem to be something of a coward.*

As Kirsi followed Doug Erickson down the country highway to where she was to live, she tried to come up with a way to introduce the topic she needed to discuss with him, *should* discuss with him *now. "Oh, by the way . . . did I mention . . . I'm really sorry, but . . ."*

But the scenery kept interrupting her concentration. Miles of evergreens, broken up by small lakes, and here and there a farm with a red barn and black-and-white cows. Did one call them cows or cattle? Anyway, this was America's Dairyland. All the license plates said so.

Doug turned down another road and then another, confusing her. She wondered if she would be able to find her way back to the clinic. The forest grew thicker and thicker. She started to feel a bit suffocated, closed in. The road narrowed and then turned into dirt and gravel. Where was she living—next door to Grizzly Adams?

Doug slowed as he negotiated a rise and turned right. He pulled up in front of a small log cabin. A real log cabin.

Kirsi parked next to him and got out. "Dr. Erick—"

A deer and two speckled fawns made her forget to finish her sentence. A mother and her babies. It was a doe then.

The doe and her fawns strolled past Kirsi as though she weren't there. The trio sauntered into the towering pines on the other side of her cabin. Kirsi realized she'd forgotten to breathe. "Oh, my."

Doug was beside her, reaching into her backseat to grab her duffel and large suitcase. "You travel light."

She glanced at him, wanting to share her excitement. "Didn't you see them?"

He paused and looked where she was pointing. "You mean the deer?"

His matter-of-fact tone only heightened her exhilaration. "Yes, are they so common that you just ignore them?" It had been like watching a wildlife feature—only they had been close enough to touch.

He shrugged. "You'll see them almost daily, especially around here. You have a small lake through those trees."

"I do?" Fawns, a log cabin, a lake! "Show me." It was like waking up in a fairy tale. A wonderful one.

He gave her a lazy grin, one that illuminated his face, feature by feature. "Come on." He carried her duffel and case, left them at the door of the cabin, and then led her around the side. About seventy-five feet through the thinned trees sparkled a small jewel of a lake. "We have a lot of glacial lakes. This one isn't deep or large enough for powered watercraft, but you can fish and swim in it."

The glinting blue water drew her. She couldn't stop herself. She ran toward it and bent over at the grassy shore lined by rocks, trailing her fingers in the cool water. "Wow."

"I take it this is a bit different than you expected."

"Try a bit amazing." She straightened up and grinned at him. He'd shed his white lab coat along with the intensity that had marked him in the ER. In a plaid shirt and khakis, Doug Erickson looked right at home in this wilderness setting. She ignored how aware she was of his lean, athletic build. She almost asked if he was a runner.

She straightened. "For the past four years I've lived in a crowded apartment with two other medical students in the proverbial asphalt jungle." She lifted her arms over her head in a wide sweeping gesture which announced—I'm free and happy. "I never expected anything like this." This was a place where she could have put the past behind her, but no . . .

He beamed at her, glowing with shared pleasure she could see. "We hoped you'd like it. You're renting it from Bruno Havlecek. You met his wife, Ma, today volunteering at the reception desk."

His radiant smile made her grin broaden. "Ma?"

"Everyone calls her Ma. Her name's Lou, if you prefer."

"They lived here?" Had she cheated someone out of this idyllic setting?

"Bruno did. When he married Ma, he moved into her house."

"I see." Reassured, she sucked in a breath of clean air, forcing it down into her lungs as though she were tired and trying to wake up. She looked away from him to the sparkling water. But she still sensed Doug's presence—it was unpretentious, completely natural, lowering her defenses. It made her prickle with guilt. *I'm so sorry. I love this place, but . . . my mother . . .*

"I suppose all these names are a jumble to you right now," he said.

Suddenly she felt very tired. She didn't have the energy to use any of her lead-ins for the news. It could wait till tomorrow. "Show me the cabin."

"Right this way."

She walked beside him, his long legs loping ahead of hers. Her eyes kept straying back to the lake's edge, where the doe and her fawns were calmly sipping water. The tranquility did something to her insides, somehow relaxed her. The hectic clinic activity of just an hour ago seemed to belong to someone else's life, not hers.

And the forest glen—she supposed that was what she was in—was open, even with the tall maples and pines surrounding it. That appealed to her. She didn't like tight places, being closed in. And the cabin had windows, a lot of them. She wouldn't feel shut in there either. She breathed easier. This would be an experience to remember. Her gaze slid again to the solid man beside her. She couldn't help herself. She liked this doctor.

He unlocked the door and insisted on carrying her bags inside. He ushered her into the cabin, which smelled of pine, and opened the door to the small bedroom, where the bed looked freshly made up for her. He set down the suitcase and duffle bag. "I think I'll check the kitchen."

She wrapped her arms around herself, already dreading standing here alone in this strange place and knowing she would love it, never want to leave it. She followed him to the tiny eating-cooking area to one side of the large main room.

"Oh, good. Ma already shopped for you." Doug showed her food staples—milk, bread, butter, and more—already in the refrigerator.

"That is so kind," she gasped. Her every need had been provided for. Even as she warmed at this thoughtfulness, she felt another pinch of guilt.

He closed the door. "It's a little chilly in here."

"That's all right." She unfolded her arms. "I'm tired. I'm just going to lie down—"

"I'll make a little fire for you. Then you can be cozy." Before she could object, Doug headed for the fireplace and removed the fire screen. "I'll make a small one, and you won't have to do anything. It'll burn out on its own."

"Really—" She tried to stop him.

"My pleasure." He selected newspaper, kindling, and a few short logs from a stack to the side of hearth, arranged the crumpled paper, then the kindling, under the logs. He stood to pick a long match from a holder on top of the log mantel, struck it, and set the paper afire.

A fire. Just like at her grandparents' home. Kirsi watched the orange flames catch the small slivers of wood. She sank down on the comfy sofa, curling one leg under her.

Doug replaced the screen with care and then turned to her. "Mind if I join you?"

*No, you should go now.* Instead, she patted the sofa cushion beside her in silent invitation.

"I won't stay long." He settled himself next to her.

She became filled with an overwhelming awareness of him. The rock-hard weight of him beside her rocked her senses. She tried to keep her focus on the intensifying fire—in vain.

Her marked reaction to Doug surprised her. Usually, she wasn't so susceptible to men. She didn't have time for relationships, not with her . . . she closed her eyes, stopping this line of thought. She didn't want to start her mind down the path of recriminations and resentment. Already she knew she'd hate to . . . she stopped that train of thought again.

Doug stretched out his legs, again piquing her notice. No doubt she'd get this awareness of the young Dr. Erickson under control after they'd worked together for a few days. She attributed it to all the changes; it had been her year of the unexpected.

"Have you lived here all your life?" she asked Doug, trying to find an explanation for the "settled or solid" impression he projected. She searched for better words to define it.

"Yes, born and raised here. I was only away for school and residency."

"And you came right back?"

He shrugged. "My dad died early. An unexpected heart attack. He worked too hard and didn't follow the advice he gave to his patients."

"And your mother? Is she still living?"

His jaw tightened. "My mother lives in Minneapolis."

She tried to read the odd note in his voice. Didn't he get along with his mother? "So you came back to work at the clinic."

"Yes, it *is* the Erickson Clinic."

She nodded, trying to analyze his mixed expression and tone—part proud, part . . . tense. Perhaps Doug Erickson wasn't as uncomplicated as she'd thought at first.

"Tell me what your goals are," he said.

"My goals?" Had he somehow sensed that hers had changed?

"I didn't say that right." He rubbed his forehead. "I meant, what made you want to specialize in being an ER doc?"

*Good question, Doug.* "It's never boring."

He laughed. "What else?"

"I think the main thing I love about it is having to think on my feet, the variety of cases." She brushed her palm over the upholstered sofa arm, not wanting to reveal more of herself to this man. She mustn't mislead him with false hope. "I'm tired." A sudden yawn forced itself on her, proving her point.

"I'll leave."

"No." She put out a hand to forestall him. *Why did I do that?* "Sit with me awhile until . . . this feels . . . more . . ."

"Like home?" he suggested.

Feeling counterfeit, Kirsi nodded. "Yes, please." A pause. "Why did you choose the ER?"

He shrugged. "It's what my grandfather needed at the

clinic. It's the kind of medicine I watched him and my dad practice. I wanted to be like them."

"I know what you mean. We both come from medical families. In addition to their private family practice, my grandparents worked together providing free medical care to new immigrants in the LA area."

"Mission work right at home?" He smiled in approval.

The mention of mission work sobered her. For just a few moments, she forgot what she would soon be forced to reveal.

She knew she had to call her mother to let her know that she'd arrived safely, but she resisted this obligation. She wanted to enjoy this pleasant moment now—before the truth had to be told and everything would be turned upside down.

Moments flickered by as the logs burned low and steady, like her heightened but unfortunate awareness of Doug. He settled back against the cushions and seemed at ease with her need for quiet. She closed her eyes. Maybe she should say something. Maybe this was the time. The chill left the room. He was right; it was cozy here. Too cozy. She couldn't speak. She swallowed another telltale yawn.

"I should be leaving." He moved forward off the couch. "How about we meet for breakfast at the Black Bear Café tomorrow morning at seven?" he asked at the door.

His sudden withdrawal hit her like a harsh wind. And a twinge of apprehension trickled through her, giving tomorrow an edge of dread. She hadn't expected this kind of personal welcome. She also hadn't expected the way this man had seized her attention. Everything felt out of control, her control. Too many crosscurrents. "Okay." She didn't have the energy to say much more. "I'll see you there."

*And I'll tell you then. No more delays.*

�֎ ✶ ✵

The next morning, Kirsi hurried into the busy truck stop/gas station to pay the cashier. Another customer was ahead of her in line, paying for many items—cold pills, engine starter, matches, batteries, and a propane tank for a grill—all stacked in tipping-over piles on the counter.

As she idly stared at the purchases and watched the transaction. her mind suddenly came alive.

She looked to the cashier to see if he was aware of what might be going on. The cashier unfortunately looked bored and completely unsuspecting. *I can't say anything here and now.* She tried to look unconcerned also. *Maybe the cashier will call the police when he's gone.*

The customer whom she saw in profile—a scruffy-looking young man wearing a baseball cap and with a small tattoo on his neck—stuffed his change into his pocket. Accepting a large paper bag filled with his items in one arm, he grabbed the propane tank with the other. He turned away, not toward her, so Kirsi didn't get a full look at his face.

She handed the cashier her cash and, angling her body so she could see out the large front windows, tried to see which vehicle the man got into.

"Dr. Royston!" a voice hailed her from behind.

She turned to see the large woman who'd been at the clinic the day before coming toward her.

"It's me, Ma Havlecek. Are you going to the clinic?"

Kirsi accepted her change from the cashier, while trying to keep tabs on the suspicious young man already out the front entrance and nod at Mrs. Havlecek at the same time.

Outside, the suspect customer got into the passenger side of an old, very dirty sedan. She strained to make out the driver—

Ma stepped in Kirsi's line of vision. "I want you to meet my husband, Bruno."

Suppressing a slight irritation, Kirsi went through the motions of meeting her landlord, a dapper silver-haired older gentleman, and thanking Ma for stocking her refrigerator and making her feel so welcome.

Several more customers crowded around the counter to pay. Kirsi was nearer the door than the cashier by now. She conceded defeat. "It's been nice meeting you, Mr. Havlecek." She shook his hand again. "I've got to run. I'm late for a breakfast meeting."

Outside, she got into her car, trying to push away her thoughts. *It's just because of that kid in the ER yesterday. It's made me wary. I need to mind my own business and not jump to conclusions.*

A few minutes later, she hesitated in front of the Black Bear Café on Main Street in Steadfast. Before her interesting stop at the gas station, she'd awakened rested and ready to set things straight with the compelling Dr. Erickson. She'd explain. Assure him that all would be well. At least, for him. An early morning call from her mother had only reminded her of the urgency of telling Dr. Erickson the truth ASAP.

Ready to face him, she opened the door and stepped inside. As if on cue, every head in the busy café pivoted to look at her. Kirsi froze.

Doug Erickson stood up at the rear. "Back here, Dr. Royston."

Voices buzzed to life at his words. Kirsi ignored them and strode back to the booth. She sat down across from him, facing the rear of the restaurant. His thick, brown hair looked scrambled as though he'd just run his fingers through it.

Before his lazy smile could undo her resolve, she started. "There's something I have to tell you—"

"Hi, Dr. Royston. I'm Ginger." A young red-haired waitress handed her a menu and placed a glass of water in front of her. "Coffee?"

"Yes, thank you—" she looked at her name tag—"Ginger."

When Ginger left them, Kirsi faced Doug again, her pulse beginning to thrum. "Doug, I should have told you yesterday but with all the emergencies—"

Ginger arrived with a mug of hot coffee. "Are you ready to order, or do you need some time?"

Kirsi stifled her irritation. "I'll have a mushroom-cheese omelet with hash browns and whole wheat toast," she said without glancing at the menu. After years of medical school, she'd learned to eat hearty whenever a meal was offered.

Ginger jotted it down and left again.

"What is it?" Doug asked, picking up his coffee mug with his long tanned fingers.

Kirsi steadied herself, focusing on the wall beside his right ear. *This won't be difficult. This is a professional decision. That's all.* Or all she would let him know. "This year I unexpectedly received—"

"Dr. Doug?"

Kirsi glanced up to see a deputy sheriff and a tall blonde woman standing beside their booth. Good grief! Couldn't they have two minutes alone?

"Sorry to interrupt—," the woman began.

Doug stood and motioned for the couple to sit down with them. Trying not to appear disgruntled, Kirsi moved over to make room for the woman, while Doug made room for the deputy.

"Dr. Royston, this is Keely Turner, our local principal, who is soon to become Mrs. Burke Sloan." Doug gestured toward the deputy.

"Nice to meet you," Kirsi murmured, keeping a lid on

her impatience—now that the moment for speaking truth had come.

"I can't stay long," Keely said. "I'm due at school, but I want to know if the rumor's true that Weston Blake suffered a meth overdose yesterday."

Doug frowned. "I can't really discuss a patient with you even if you are the principal. But I can say that his symptoms could lead someone to that conclusion."

"How is he?" Kirsi asked. She'd prayed for the young patient last night just before falling asleep. "Did he regain consciousness?"

"Yes," Doug said. "Thanks to God, we were able to keep him here in Steadfast. But he's still critical."

Even after seeing so many of these types of cases, Kirsi felt a downturn in her emotions. The kid was so young that he probably didn't have a clue of the risk he'd taken smoking that joint.

"I hate to see this happen anywhere, let alone here," Deputy Sloan spoke up. "I told Rodd—" he paused—"our sheriff's Rodd Durand. I told him something new and dangerous is beginning to shake up the drug trade here."

"How would you find that out?" Kirsi asked, curious.

The deputy shrugged. "Drug traffic is nationwide, but here we haven't had that much—just local suppliers, small-time stuff. But someone tried to steal anhydrous ammonia from a farm a few weeks ago, and that could mean someone is trying to manufacture crystal meth here."

"Nasty stuff," Kirsi said, running her forefinger around the rim of her mug. "I think I might have witnessed someone buying ingredients for meth this morning."

"What?" Burke stared at her.

"I was paying for gas at the truck stop out on the highway. And the kid in front of me was buying—" she ticked the items off finger by finger—"cold pills, batteries, a propane tank—"

"Could you describe the kid?" The deputy took out a notepad.

Kirsi shrugged. "He was scruffy. I didn't get a good look at his face. He wore a ball cap and had a small tattoo on his neck."

"Sorry to break in, but I've got to go." Keely interrupted, looking at her wristwatch. "And, Burke, you need to drop me off at school."

Burke rose, obviously hesitant to leave Kirsi. "Thanks for noticing this. May I call you later this morning for more specifics?"

Kirsi nodded.

"The sheriff and I have been discussing an unpleasant possibility. I'll share that with you also." The deputy shut his notepad.

"Dr. Doug, Dr. Royston, I will be contacting you." The principal rose also. "Burke and I have talked it over and before summer break, we need to make a concerted effort to give our teens the facts about meth and crack. This is the first time I've seen it on school grounds. And I want it to be the last." Then Keely echoed Kirsi's thought. "I wonder if Weston even knew someone could soak marijuana in meth."

Kirsi shook hands with the deputy and his fiancée before they left. The pall that this subject inevitably brought with it fell over their booth. Kirsi wished the deputy had finished what he was saying. Not knowing gave her an uneasy sensation. She made herself lift her coffee mug to her lips and sip the hot, bracing brew.

"What is it that you wanted to tell me?" Dr. Doug asked her.

She swallowed and made herself smile. Now or never.

33

"I received an unexpected inheritance this year, and I can pay the clinic back the money I owe."

He looked startled, his golden brown eyes widening.

"I also have been offered a chance to go with my grandparents to India this fall on a . . . on a short-term medical mission there. My grandfather is a doctor and my grandmother, a nurse. It will also be kind of a family reunion." Kirsi felt herself rushing her words together as she glossed over the real importance of this reunion.

"This will be the first time my grandmother has been home to India since the early fifties, when she came to the University of Southern California as a premed student. She has one sister left, my great-aunt Uma, who is in poor health. That's why the trip must be soon." She wanted him to realize how crucial this trip was to her and her family—without revealing too much.

"I don't get it." Doug's square jaw tightened.

She rushed on, "I wouldn't leave you, of course, until I find a replacement—"

"You can't mean you're leaving?"

"Yes." She lifted her chin. "After the trip, a family situation makes it necessary for me to return to California."

She'd wanted to serve the people in Wisconsin who had helped her get through medical school. But some things had changed. And others, like with her mother, had regrettably stayed the same. She could pay back the clinic their money and . . . maybe save her mother and Nani more grief.

She looked to Doug. "This trip with my grandparents is very important to me as you can guess—"

"You just got here and you plan to leave?" His tone was incredulous. He didn't seem to be getting all she was saying.

*Lord, don't let him misunderstand me. I'm not a quitter. I wouldn't do this unless I had to. My mother needs this trip. My grandmother longs for it. I need to be with them. I should have known how my leaving would affect my mother.*

"I wouldn't leave you in the lurch. I won't go until I find a replacement—"

"And just how long do you think that will take you?" he cut in with an unmistakable sarcastic edge to his voice.

She stiffened. "It won't be that difficult." She waved her hand. "I've already started looking. I'll have someone by summer's end."

"Ha." Doug looked at her, grim-faced.

Kirsi felt her stomach clench. What more could she say?

"What?" another voice asked.

A heavy plate clattered down in front of Kirsi. "I can't have heard you right," the waitress said. "You didn't say you were leaving at the end of summer, did you?"

Disgruntled at the woman's eavesdropping, Kirsi glared up at her. "Please." *This is hard enough.* "This is a private conversation."

Heedless, the waitress turned to the rest of the café. "Our new doc says she's leaving by the end of summer!"

A cacophony of exclamations exploded in the small café.

Doug reached for Kirsi. His strong hands tugged her to her feet. "Did you have to tell me here? It will be all over the county by noon." He threw a ten-dollar bill onto the table. "Come on."

Kirsi objected, pulling away from him. "My breakfast—"

"Let's get out of here before someone decides to get a rope." He gripped her more firmly by the hand and pushed her ahead of him.

"What!" Kirsi tried to grasp why he was pushing her out. But the murmur of voices behind them had turned unfriendly even to her ears. His body shielding her, Kirsi let Doug nudge her out the back door into an alley and down it. "Where are we going? My car—"

"I'm taking you right to my grandfather. He's the one you should have told yesterday." Doug ushered her into a red SUV at the end of the alley.

She got in, feeling reproached. She'd expected surprise and some negative response to her news, but nothing like this!

Doug got in beside her and slammed his door. "What were you thinking?"

❊ ❊ ❊

He saw her ride past in a red SUV. Just a glimpse, but with that long black hair, she stood out around here.

Who was she? And had she seen them? More importantly—seen him?

He'd watched her from the car while he'd waited for Nail—the bottom-feeder he'd been saddled with—to buy some stuff. He'd told Nail not to buy more than two of the ingredients, but did the no-brain listen—no! *I can't let Nail mess everything up. Too much is at stake.*

He'd bet anything she'd guessed something was up. He could tell by the way she kept glancing around. Then she'd looked out right at his car. Right at him.

Who was she? Did he have to worry about her? Would he have to take care of her?

Not that that would be a problem. He knew just how to take care of people who got in his way. But he wouldn't be in a hurry. He liked watching "problems" dance on the end of his string for a while. No need to rush.

# CHAPTER THREE

HIS SPEEDING CAR rocked to a halt. Doug parked in front of his grandfather's large Victorian house and opened his car door. Before he could reach Dr. Royston's door, she was out. They hadn't exchanged a word since they'd left town.

"This way," Doug said in a curt tone, unable to hide his indignation. "I want my grandfather to hear this first-hand."

If Doug could have kept this from his granddad and solved it by himself, he would have. "I don't know why you had to let the cat out of the bag in public," he muttered. "I thought we discussed that aspect yesterday." There was no going back now. "When I think about all the fine people you're letting down . . ." His voice faltered, seething with frustration. If he said all he was thinking, he didn't trust himself to stay cool.

He led her to the back door, opened it, and summarily waved her inside. He watched her long ponytail swing as she marched up the three steps. Today he wasn't charmed. Her long, lovely hair annoyed him. "I should have known nothing ever runs smoothly around here," he mumbled to himself.

Kirsi didn't even glance his way. Her spine was stiff and her nose pointed skyward. Did she have a clue?

In the kitchen, his grandfather sat at the long trestle table, where he and Doug had eaten breakfast together for years. His grandfather looked up when they entered.

"We've got a problem." Doug pressed his hands down on the top of the wooden chair in front of him, trying to keep a grip on his temper, to keep from shaking Dr. Kirsi Royston's pretty shoulders. *This cannot be happening.*

Then he turned to the mockingly attractive woman beside him. "Go ahead. Tell him."

His grandfather rose and motioned for her to sit down. "Dr. Royston?" he invited.

She shook her head. "Please sit down and eat your breakfast. *Someone* should get breakfast this morning." She cast Doug a dark look.

*Someone who deserves breakfast.* Doug scowled at her. Didn't she have an inkling? Didn't she guess how her words would affect the clinic, his grandfather, everyone in the county who'd worked so hard?

Granddad sat down, looking concerned. "Douglas, please pour our guest a cup of coffee."

Doug recognized the reprimand in the older man's voice. He straightened, snagged two mugs hanging on hooks over the counter, and poured steaming coffee into them from the pot on the stove. Then he set them down on the table in front of the chairs where Kirsi and he had stopped.

She stood there, her proud head cocked to one side and her arms folded. Her combative stance aggravated him more. Why was she acting like the injured party? "Sit," he growled at her. "I'll make toast."

Kirsi obeyed, watching Doug—her movements like those of some displeased, exotic queen.

Even though he had no appetite, Doug dropped four slices of bread in the large toaster near him on the counter, clicked it down, and sat. His treacherous gaze zeroed back on her. Her face, now disgruntled, was no less attractive. Maybe she counted on that; maybe as a lovely woman she was used to tying men around her little finger.

"Now tell me what's happened," Granddad said.

When Kirsi only sipped her coffee, Doug started, frustration coursing through him. After their quiet time together at her cabin yesterday, he'd felt so good this morning as he anticipated having breakfast with her. "We met at the Black Bear for breakfast. And there, in front of the whole county, she dropped her bombshell."

His grandfather raised both eyebrows.

"Tell him," Doug barked. "Tell him what you told the entire county."

Kirsi straightened herself. "First of all, I fail to understand what all the emotional fuss is about. This isn't personal. It's merely that my circumstances have changed. That happens all the time in life."

Her glib words burned inside Doug. "Don't give excuses. Just tell him."

Not looking glib, she pursed her lips. "I received an unexpected inheritance earlier this year, and I can pay back the money given to me for my education."

Granddad nodded and took a bite of buttered toast. "Go on."

*Money isn't the issue here. People are.* Doug took a swig of the strong coffee, forcing his focus from her.

"Also my grandparents want me to go with them, along with my mother—" she paused, letting her eyes flicker around the room—"to India in the fall on a monthlong medical mission." Kirsi continued earnestly, "It would also be a kind of family reunion since my grandmother, who comes from New Delhi, hasn't been home in almost fifty years. And then I have to return to California . . . for family concerns."

Doug tried to understand why this reunion sounded so important to her. He wondered what she wasn't telling them.

"So you're planning on giving us our money and leaving?" Granddad asked very, very quietly.

Doug stilled at his grandfather's tone. He'd heard it a few times. His grandfather, as he'd expected, was not happy.

"Of course not," she said, her black eyes snapping. "I resent—" she glared at Doug—"the implication that I'd shirk responsibility like that." She inhaled deeply. "I plan on finding a replacement. I told you that. I've already started contacting residents who are nearing the end of their studies." She cast Doug a smoldering glance. "I should have someone for you by summer's end."

The glance sparked Doug's temper. "See! She thinks she can just snap her fingers and a replacement will appear." Doug couldn't keep the sarcasm out of his voice, his righteous fury blazing now. How could she disappoint the people he loved, the people who'd worked so hard to bring her here?

The toast popped up. The sound was striking in the tense room. Doug stood up and dropped the bread onto two small dishes and plunked them on the table. The browned bread sat, untouched.

Only yesterday, the next six years—brighter now because of this doctor's arrival—had stretched out in front of Doug. Grandfather could retire and there'd be another doctor here to shoulder the burden of the clinic, of the patients.

Dr. Royston's words at the Black Bear had muted that hope. He felt himself prickling with anger. He should have guessed that a woman like this—like his mother—wouldn't be interested in staying here. But this woman had signed a contract. Now what would happen?

"Dr. Royston," his grandfather started in his deliberate way, "I can see how your circumstances have changed, but our contract hasn't. You signed a binding legal document. We paid you thousands of dollars, hard-earned cash, which the residents of this county worked hard to raise over seven years, in return for your practicing medicine here for six years—at a substantial income—in addition to what we've already paid you. Did you read the contract before you signed it?"

"Of course I did," she replied, hunching up one shoulder. "I even had a law-student friend read it."

"Then you know it has no clause that allows you to pay off the money and leave." He looked her straight in the eyes. "We don't want the money. We want you."

Doug clenched the mug with both hands.

"No," Kirsi countered, "you want a doctor, a competent doctor, not me personally."

Granddad put his cup down on its saucer with care. "Dr. Royston, I'm eighty-one years old. I should have retired over ten years ago. That's why, when I saw that I wouldn't be able to retire unless another doctor came to take my place, I started praying. I knew that only God could find my replacement—"

"I believe in prayer too," Kirsi cut in. "God can supply a replacement and in time."

"Please let me finish so you understand where we are coming from." His granddad met her gaze.

She began tracing circles on the tabletop.

Doug recognized the nervous habit and watched as her slender fingers rotated again and again.

"I started contacting medical schools and going to their campuses to talk to med students, trying to interest them in

Steadfast." Granddad paused. "No one was interested in a rural practice. They said, 'I'd be on call all the time. I wouldn't make as much money. It's out in the middle of nowhere. I like to be near a city with all its cultural advantages. Too much snow in the north. I want to practice where the living is easy.' "

"All those things occurred to me too," she said, her voice rising. "But at the time, things that had happened . . . it felt like this was where I was supposed to be."

*You* are *supposed to be here!* Doug swallowed more hot coffee, wondering how a mission trip could compare to her commitment to the clinic. *We need you.*

Granddad nodded. "But I kept praying, and the idea of paying for a student's education in return for his or her practicing medicine in Steadfast for as many years as he or she received support came to me. I started advertising in medical-school newspapers."

"I know. That's where I saw your ad."

Granddad looked at her from under his bushy white eyebrows. "But did you know I advertised for over two years before you answered my ad?"

Doug's mouth twisted.

"You mean," she said slowly, "that I was the only one who replied?"

"No." Granddad took a swallow of coffee. "Others applied, but some I discouraged, and some bowed out before the contract was signed. You were the only one who decided you wanted our deal. And you were the only one I decided would work out."

Silence.

Doug stared at the coffee mug and toast in front of him as if they were ashes. *I should have expected this—why would a doctor from Los Angeles want to settle in a small town in Wisconsin? Where do we go from here, Lord?*

"But this is a family matter. I feel that if I don't go back to California, it will negatively affect . . ." She paused. "My grandparents, my mother, and I have been praying for a family recon . . . a family reunion for years," Kirsi insisted.

Doug could sympathize with her on family obligations, but he didn't know why she had signed the contract if it would adversely affect her family.

"I believe those prayers have been answered too," Kirsi finished.

"That's one of the reasons I decided you were our candidate," Granddad said. "You mentioned your faith in your application. I wanted a doctor who was also a person of faith working with my grandson and for the people of this community."

"Then if we've both had our prayers granted by God, which of us is right?" she asked with a lift of her chin.

"Good question," Doug muttered.

"I think God will have to work the details out." The older man drew in a long breath. "Any replacement you find would have to meet the same standards that I used to accept you. We won't take just anyone. That's one thing I'm sure of."

Kirsi frowned.

"I'm sure of one thing too," Doug spoke up, feeling the gaping hole inside him. "It will take a flat-out miracle to bring the right replacement here by summer's end."

✻ ✻ ✻

Doug held the door open for Kirsi. She slid past him onto the seat of his SUV. He tried to overlook the subtle cinnamon fragrance that suffused the air around her. He'd liked her so much yesterday . . . the way she'd behaved at her cabin near the lake—like a child opening a gift. *I thought there was a chance she could love this place. I should have known better . . . from experience.*

His eyes straight ahead, he drove back down the drive. Neither of them spoke. There was nothing left to say.

As the miles into town zipped past, Doug thought of all the excitement this past spring as the community had anticipated the arrival of the new doctor, this subdued woman sitting beside him.

Now he admitted in his heart that he had been the one with the highest expectations. Dr. Royston had been the light at the end of a very long tunnel to relieving the burden of the clinic.

After nearly fifty years of practicing medicine in Steadfast, his grandfather deserved a few healthy, easy years before he went to be with the Lord. Doug wanted to give that to him for all he'd done for others. They'd been so close to that goal! And just yesterday, working with Kirsi those few minutes had given him a feeling he'd never known, such complete harmony. . . .

"I won't leave, you know, until God provides a replacement for me," Dr. Royston offered, sounding defensive.

He'd stopped thinking of her as Kirsi. Why become friends when she was leaving? Sadness, a sense of loss leaked though him. "I think that has already been discussed to death."

"You don't have to take it personally."

"Doctor, this *is* personal," Doug bit out. Her words had cut him like razors. "I can't shoulder the clinic all by myself." There the truth was out.

"There are other doctors in the county—"

"A few." He pulled himself together. "But they're all nearing retirement, and my grandfather started the clinic here." *My grandfather* was *the clinic. Now I am the clinic.* The weight of this bore down on him.

"I can't believe that I will have any difficulty in finding—"

"Without the clinic," he cut her off, "in an emergency, people would have to drive to Eau Claire for treatment— well over an hour's drive." *Not to mention how long it takes in winter weather. I won't let that happen.*

"I didn't sign a contract for the rest of my life." She waved a hand in the air. "I would have been leaving anyway in six years."

He didn't bother to respond. Dr. Royston's presence for six years would have allowed enough time for God to act again, bring another doctor here. Doug didn't like to limit God, but it had taken nearly a decade to get Dr. Royston to Steadfast.

❈ ❈ ❈

Back on Main Street, Kirsi let herself out of Dr. Erickson's car, glad to get away from his reproach. His intensity was what had impressed her yesterday. But then it hadn't been aimed right at her. Now it was. "I'll see you at the clinic."

"You're not on duty till Monday."

His gruff tone rasped her raw nerves. "I want to check on my patient." *You may think I'm a shirker, Doctor, but I'm not.*

"Fine." He drove away without a backward glance.

"Good-bye," she said to the rear of his SUV, feeling herself bristle. *This isn't as personal to you, Dr. Erickson, as it is to me. If you knew the pressure I'm under. If you knew about my mother . . .* Fleetingly, she recalled him yesterday—his lazy smile, his strong back to her when he knelt to build the fire.

*Don't you have any faith, Doctor?*

Very alone now, she stood on the street beside her Jeep and glanced around. She thought about going back into the café and ordering another breakfast, nixed that crazy idea, and climbed into her car.

She drove through town to the sign for the clinic and turned. From her rearview mirror, she glimpsed a gray sedan on her tail. In her preoccupation, had she cut someone off without realizing it? she wondered. Did they have road rage in Steadfast?

A cascade of images and sounds flowed through her mind. A few years ago, she'd driven up to an accident scene on California Highway 101. A man had shot a woman who'd cut him off by changing lanes. The woman had died in Kirsi's arms. Her two small children watching it all, sobbing.

Kirsi took hold of her pulsing panic and tightened her grip on the wheel. She looked in the rearview mirror again. She pushed away worse memories, ones she suppressed and would not let surface.

Was the car the one she'd seen at the gas station earlier? It might be or it might not. Maybe the driver had noticed her watching him.

The driver behind her had the sun visor pulled down so she couldn't see if it was a man or woman. *Lord, take away this dread.* Under the weight of courage and faith, her fear ebbed.

After a few more tense moments, the sedan eased back, giving her a sense of relief. She drove on and turned into the clinic lot to a spot designated as physician parking. She glanced back and saw that the car had vanished.

The incident had given her a surge of adrenaline. Probably due to all the brouhaha over her announcement this morning. She shook herself mentally. *I'm in a small town in Wisconsin. Nothing is going to happen to me here.* Momentarily, she recalled the irate buzz in the café. Would people really be angry with her? Douglas Erickson, M.D., was.

She shook off her unease and walked through the double doors of the ER. One involuntary backward glance and she entered.

After slipping on her white lab coat in the doctors' lounge and stopping at the nurses' station to pick up the patient records, she walked down the corridor of rooms. Outside the first room, she studied the chart before entering.

Though hooked up to an IV, Veda McCracken still looked pale and drawn. As Kirsi approached the bed, Veda's eyes opened. Kirsi put the chart in one hand and grasped Veda's large rough hand as she had in the ER yesterday. "Hi."

Veda stared at her. "You're holding my hand," she said in a thin, gravelly, slightly slurred voice.

Kirsi squeezed it. "Yes."

"I thought you was a dream."

Kirsi grinned. "No, I'm real. I'm glad you're calmer today. It will take us a while to get you rehydrated. What happened? Did you take a fall?"

Kirsi diagnosed that Veda must have had a stroke. The slurred speech pointed to that, and her records noted some paralysis and weakness on the woman's right side. The mental disorientation along with weakness would explain Veda's lying on the floor for a couple of days. And that still upset Kirsi. She'd seen it all too often—the elderly living alone and at risk to die alone.

"I want to get out of here," Veda mumbled thickly.

"As soon as you are well enough—"

"Now."

Kirsi shook her head. "You can't even walk steadily yet."

Veda let loose a string of obscenities.

Kirsi only raised her eyebrows. It was common in her experience for older people, especially stroke victims, to curse. They often lost the mental "brake" or inhibition that kept such language suppressed.

Then Kirsi thought of the character sketch Dr. Erickson had given of this woman yesterday. She flipped through the chart and found no record that any antidepressant had ever been prescribed. None. Kirsi frowned.

If what she'd been told was true, Veda obviously needed a psychological evaluation. Why hadn't one been done before now? That was a question she would enjoy putting to the self-righteous Dr. Douglas Erickson. And one more reason not to tell him everything about her change of plans. *Why did I ever think I could make this move work in the first place? I gave in to fear and . . .* She halted her thoughts there.

"I'll see you tomorrow," Kirsi said soothingly and squeezed the woman's hand once more.

Then she headed to Weston's room. She walked down the hall quietly to match the hushed tones of the patient wing. She stepped inside. What she saw there brought her up short. A young man with his back to the door was fiddling with the teen's IV. "Hey!" she shouted. "Stop that!"

The intruder lunged at her, knocking the clipboard from her hands. It hit her face. Then he yanked her lab coat up over her face and shoved.

She went down hard. The white cloth smothered her. She clawed at it—screaming.

Footsteps pounded.

She wrenched the suffocating fabric off. She yelled, "Security!"

❖ ❖ ❖

Doug leaned close to Kirsi, trying to comfort her with his nearness. Her face was somber and pale. He fought the urge to gather her close to him.

"Did you see his face?" Deputy Burke Sloan sat across from them at the table in the doctors' lounge. A pot of fresh coffee perked on the counter behind them.

Obviously trying to hide her agitation, Kirsi pressed her hands together in her lap. "N-no," she stammered.

Doug made himself keep his own hands folded on the table. He knew by the way Kirsi held herself—stiff and self-contained—that she wouldn't welcome any overt reassurance.

"No," she began again, her voice gathering strength. "He wore a dark baseball cap pulled low on his forehead and a ragged T-shirt. It . . . it happened so fast." She took in a calming breath. "All I got was an impression of a young man, medium height and build, in denim."

"Caucasian, black, or Hispanic?"

"Not black. That's all I can say."

Unable to stop himself, Doug squeezed her slender shoulder, letting his grip communicate his concern. Their differences, which had loomed large just an hour ago, had withered in the face of this attack. *Dear God, could I have foreseen this? How can I keep this woman, my patients, my staff safe?*

"This sounds like the same description that you gave me earlier today." Burke eyed her.

"Yes, I realized that too. But it happened so fast that I can't be sure. It might be the same person. I had my head down looking at the patient chart as I walked in. I was so shocked to see someone unexpected in the room and doing something to harm my patient . . . I didn't get a chance to do more than react, and then he was right on top of me."

She looked over at Doug with a wry expression. "I called for security, but we don't have any, do we?"

Her words hit him. *I should have been ready for this.*

"You do now," Burke put in before Doug had a chance to speak. "I'm staying at the door of Weston's room for the rest of my shift today. Then another deputy will take over. The nurse at the station didn't see the assailant enter so he must have come in—"

"We had a short time when there was no one at the

reception desk and one nurse was on break." Doug shook his head. "We cut costs by having volunteers man the reception desk. We will be hiring a security guard now—ASAP." Kirsi hadn't moved away. He squeezed her shoulder again.

"Sounds like you're way ahead of us. The sheriff and I would have advised you to do just that." Burke stood. "I'll get to my post then."

Kirsi rose, pulling stubbornly from Doug's grip. "If you don't need me, I'm going to head home."

Doug got to his feet, close beside her, all his protective instincts blaring. He couldn't stop himself from asking, "Do you think you should be alone?"

"I'll be fine," she snapped, her black eyes flashing. "This isn't the first time I've been assaulted by a patient or . . . someone trying to hurt a patient." She gave him a confident expression. And though her lower lip quivered, she lifted that chin of hers. "I'm from LA, remember?"

Doug had to give her credit for sheer nerve. "What do you think, Burke?" he asked.

Kirsi visibly bristled at his overruling her, assuming her angry-queen look.

Doug ignored it, waiting for Burke's reply.

"I don't think she's in any danger," the deputy replied. "Weston was the target. She just surprised the perp."

"But the perp may think she can identify him now," Doug pointed out. He wanted to keep an eye on Kirsi.

"No, I think he'll realize she didn't have time to get a good enough look to ID him—"

"Pardon me." Kirsi folded her arms and glared at both of them. "I don't like being talked about as though I'm not here."

Doug smiled in spite of himself. *She's got nerve. I'll give her that.*

"Sorry, Dr. Royston," Burke said with an apologetic grin. "Just be sure to lock your car doors as you drive home and then lock yourself inside."

"I always do. Remember," she emphasized, "I'm not from around here. I grew up in the big city."

"I still think—," Doug began.

"I'll be fine!" she insisted with—was it bravado? "I can take care of myself! I faced down a knife-wielding mugger once. Someone knocking me down isn't going to make me paranoid."

Doug shoved his hands into his pockets. What could he do? He couldn't hover over her. He'd looked forward to this day for years, but nothing had gone as expected. First her revelation this morning and now the sudden appearance of danger in his own clinic! *Lord, what's going on? Help me protect my patients and staff . . . and Dr. Royston in spite of her stubborn self.*

❖ ❖ ❖

Later that day near evening, the phone rang in Kirsi's new kitchen. "Kirsi, is that you?"

Kirsi recognized the voice, her nani, her grandmother, who spoke with the lilting rhythm that came from her native language, Hindi. Kirsi wanted to pour out what had happened to her today, but she tightened her control. Nani had enough to contend with. "Hi. How are you and everyone doing?"

"Fine. Fine. Your mother misses you, of course, but I keep telling her it won't be long till you're back with us." A pause. "Have you told them?"

"Yes." Kirsi didn't want to discuss their reaction to her news. Or the feeling of falling to the clinic floor with fabric smothering her.

"They weren't happy, were they?" Nani asked.

"No." *No, no one is happy, including me.*

"I feel badly about this, dear child. Maybe you could stay . . ."

Kirsi let her nani's words flow through her. Both of them knew Kirsi was needed in California. And why.

"I hate the pressure this puts on you, Kirsi."

"Just pray that I find a replacement soon. I've promised I'd find one before I leave. I don't want to be forced to break my word. And I signed a contract." *I hate this.*

"I pray that God will work it all out. You'll be leaving on such short notice. . . . We must depend on Him." Nani paused. "Will you be calling your mother later? She's been anxious to hear from you."

Guilt clumped in Kirsi's middle. "Yes, I will."

"Thank you, dear. Good-bye."

Kirsi hung up and gazed out the window of her cabin to the lake beyond. She picked up the phone to call her mother as she had promised. The phone rang several times before she got her mother's answering machine. "Ammu, Mom, not to worry. I'm fine. Hope you are too. I'll call you tomorrow after you're home from church. Bye."

*Should I call Nani and tell her that Ammu didn't answer? Should I be worried?* Kirsi pressed her thumbs against her throbbing temples. *I don't want to go home, Lord, but what choice do I have?*

※ ※ ※

After her first week at the clinic on this spring Saturday evening filled with the scent of lilacs, Kirsi got out of her Jeep. She was careful not to catch the skirt of her silk sari in the door as she closed it behind her.

Tonight she'd decided to give Steadfast, Wisconsin, the full effect of who she was. And after being knocked down last week and facing Doug Erickson's smoldering anger, she'd had an added incentive. Dressing with care for her first public appearance in Steadfast had helped her pull herself together for the ordeal of the hostile reception she would surely be receiving.

She'd put up her hair the way her grandmother had taught her—swept back and confined in a low chignon at the back of her head. Then she'd chosen to wear the one sari she'd brought to Wisconsin for dress occasions, royal blue with gold thread woven through it.

Each piece of jewelry she'd chosen with care and each one had reminded her of her link to her family. On her arms, she wore the heavy gold bangles her grandmother had given her upon graduation from high school. The large gold loop earrings her mother had given her on her sixteenth birthday swayed against the sensitive skin of her neck as she looked around. Wearing leather sandals, she walked around the other parked cars, hearing the gentle jingle of the bells on the golden anklet that had been her great-grandmother's, a present that had been sent along with the inheritance from her Indian great-grandfather.

The undulating tide of voices swelled as she neared the small, white-framed VFW hall. Recalling Doug Erickson's overprotectiveness after her being attacked and his subsequent coolness throughout the week, she wondered how he would behave tonight.

She said a prayer for God to give her the courage to face all the strangers inside. Would people be angry with her? Or would they want to hash over what had happened to her at the clinic a week ago? Neither possibility was attractive. But the jingling of her anklet bells added to her aplomb. *I am who I am. I have my responsibilities, and I won't let anyone here or in California down.*

She took in a deep breath and reached to open the door. *Here I come, Steadfast, ready or not.*

The door opened for her. Doug Erickson, in a well-cut dark suit, crisp white shirt, and amber silk tie, held out his hand to her. "Wow! Or should I say, 'Good evening, Dr. Royston'?"

# CHAPTER FOUR

KIRSI'S BREATH CAUGHT in her throat. Doug's warm welcome threw her off stride. They'd been cool to one another all week—very formal. Why was he so . . . so welcoming tonight? Did he think she needed his support? Or was she overreacting? She stared at him, impressed against her will by the way he deceptively exuded charm.

She didn't know what she had anticipated from him tonight. But whatever she'd expected, it hadn't been his waiting for her at the door with that smile of his!

She stepped inside, loosely holding Doug's hand, trying to ignore the electric shiver it sent up her arm. Immediately, she was sucked into the sights and sounds of the crowded room filled with voices, laughter, bright colors, and the smell of coffee. Then a general chorus of "She's here! The new doc's here!" fell and rose around her. It was dizzying. She'd never before been the center of attention.

Now she was. It made her nervous.

"How are you doing?" Doug whispered close to her ear. "Are you up to this?"

His words snapped like a whip. Did he think she was still upset about being knocked down a week ago? Or did he think she couldn't face en masse hostility about her plan to leave before her contract barely started?

Crackling with sudden indignation, Kirsi sent him a tart look. "I can handle this. I'm not a cream puff. I've worked in the ER on gunshot wounds while gangbangers fought around me, still trying to kill each other—"

"Okay! Okay!" Doug held up a hand in surrender.

*I suppose he can't help himself from giving me the you-poor-little-thing treatment.* That kind of behavior could drown a person in helpless fear, but maybe he didn't know that. "I didn't mean to bite your head off."

"You did a pretty good job without trying." He flashed her a sheepish grin.

Interrupting their exchange, the senior Dr. Erickson beckoned her up to a podium at the end of the long room. With Doug walking tall at her side like a color guard, she made her way around crowded party tables, over a vast stretch of aged, gray-speckled linoleum.

"Isn't she pretty?" an anonymous voice pronounced as she passed.

"What's that she's wearin'?" someone else commented. "It looks foreign."

"She's American, isn't she?" another asked.

Her ear caught a gruff voice saying, "I expected a blonde."

"A blonde?"

"Yeah, I thought Kirsi was short for Kirsten. I thought she was Norwegian or—"

That made her chuckle silently. Well, she'd come dressed in this fashion to let everyone know who she was, and it had created a stir. Fortunately, a positive one. But what was all the excitement about here? Surely not her. She'd come expecting perhaps a polite reception to welcome her, or hostility even, but certainly not a public celebration. Why were they making her arrival such a big deal? She wasn't Mother Teresa!

"Wonder what Dr. Doug thinks of her?" another voice asked.

She wondered that herself. What *did* he think and more important—why did she care? Why did he have the power to get under her skin so?

She kept her gracious smile in place and wished she could hear the jingling of her anklet instead of the beating of her heart. Finally, she stood between the two Ericksons at the podium. Doug's presence seemed to add tension, a heightening of her senses. The blue and white streamers overhead were vibrant, and the faces around her glowed with excitement. She couldn't explain why this was so.

The white-haired doctor leaned to the microphone and rumbled into it, "Good evening."

The crowd responded with a jubilant, almost unison, "Good evening!"

"It is with great pleasure that I welcome Dr. Kirsi Royston to our county and to Erickson Clinic."

Applause drowned out his next sentence. Kirsi realized that he didn't sound like he was going to mention that she was planning on leaving Wisconsin early. Was that wise or unwise? Surely many were aware of it already.

Old Doc waited, beaming at the gathering until everyone fell silent again. "I don't need to go over how and why Dr. Royston is here. You all know that and had a part in bringing her. For over seven years, you held bake sales, craft bazaars, rummage sales, carnivals, walkathons, and more to help pay for Dr. Royston's education. You need to give yourselves a round of applause. Without your hard work, today would not have come!"

Thunderous applause and whistling.

As Kirsi considered Dr. Erickson's words, she began to understand what all the fuss was about. *They are all a part of this. This is their night to celebrate—not mine.*

When the noisy crowd subsided, Old Doc turned to Kirsi and offered her his hand. "Welcome, Dr. Royston." They shook hands to another round of raucous applause. Doug shook her hand also, giving her an encouraging smile. She forced herself to look away from Doug. Then both men dropped back, leaving her alone in the limelight. The clapping and noise died down.

The impact of all that had just been said sank in, and Kirsi finally had the full picture. Now she understood why her announcement to Doug a week ago had gotten such a big reaction at the café. Everyone here had played a part in bringing her to Steadfast.

She had never given much thought to how the money she'd received in timely checks over the past six years had been raised. But the people in this room had given of themselves, working hard to bring her here. She recalled Doug's explanation this morning of why she was crucial to his plans. *A lot of hope rests on me.*

She looked out over the faces before her with a new appreciation. *Lord, I can't lie to them. But what do I say?*

She cleared her throat. "Thank you for this . . . stirring welcome. I hope to do a good job at the clinic. . . ." *For as long as I am here.* "It is a pleasure to be here. . . ." She thought of the cabin in the clearing and the excitement that had hummed in the café that morning when she entered. Even after the confrontation with Doug and her assault later that morning, she had felt welcome in this town.

She took a deep breath, ready for the plunge past politeness to plain truth. "Some of you have heard that I won't be staying." Some faces registered surprise, some concern, others disapproval. "But I would never leave the clinic before a replacement who is acceptable to both the Ericksons has come to take my place by summer's end—when I need to leave you. I ask for your prayers in this. God brought me here, and He can surely bring another doctor or even more doctors. Until then, I will give one hundred percent to the clinic, to you."

The audience listened in silence.

*They need to know why I'm leaving. But I can't tell them everything. How much will be enough?* She swallowed, moistening her dry mouth. "You may be wondering about my sari." She lifted her arms to display it. "My grandmother arrived at UCLA in the early 1950s as a premed student. She became a Christian and fell in love with an American student. They married. This caused a rift with her family, who had already arranged a marriage for her in India."

No one in the audience moved or even whispered. She found she couldn't explain further. That family rift had borne consequences that had lasted for more than two generations. She saw her mother's pinched face in her mind. When had her mother ever looked happy? That's why the India trip was so important to her mother, to her. *How can I make Doug and his grandfather—everyone—understand this without telling them everything?*

"I am very proud of my heritage," she continued, "and that's why I often wear the traditional East Indian costume. My family is also very important to me. Your support lightened the financial load on my grandparents.

"We are a very close family and I am the first to leave California." *Too close.* "That was hard on all of us." She couldn't say more. Facing everyone tonight and talking about her family had exacted a steep toll on her emotions. "Thank you again for your warm welcome. I'm happy to be in Steadfast. And I promise I will give you my best."

Applause burst out around her as if she'd just given the pithiest speech since the Gettysburg Address. Indeed, she'd probably gotten a bigger audience reaction than Abraham Lincoln had.

"Come on," Dr. Doug said at her elbow, his touch once again sensitizing her to him. "You need to cut your cake." He guided her through the press of well-wishers over to a table where there was a large white sheet cake which declared, "Welcome, Dr. Royston!" in gold and blue frosting.

"You match your cake," Doug murmured into her ear.

What kind of man was Doug Erickson? First, he'd welcomed her on Friday. Saturday he'd been fuming at her. Then he was distant all week. But now all was peachy keen? And why did his presence have to carry such an unexpected and unwelcome punch? *I have to leave! This is no time or place for me to become infatuated with a handsome doctor.*

"Lighten up," he whispered close to her ear lobe. "Don't ruin everyone's fun."

This she understood. She forced a smile and took the proffered cake server and cut a piece of cake. Again, her slightest action was cheered.

Her self-appointed escort, Doug followed her as she went down the buffet table, spooning up a few mixed nuts on her plate and giving her a glass of bright red punch. He led her to a white-paper-covered table.

"I didn't expect such a big deal being made over me," she said as he seated her in a metal folding chair.

"I guess this is your fifteen minutes of fame," he teased.

Uncomfortable with his gallantry, she munched a bite of the gooey sugar-sweet cake. "You're not having any?" she asked him.

"I don't eat cake; clogs the arteries."

"I eat cake."

"You would."

She looked him directly in the eye, ready to contend with him.

"That's a joke," he said with a grin so authentic she couldn't take it any other way—he was teasing her.

Her tension eased and she decided to get real. Maybe that would tame her reaction to him. "So, Dr. Doug, have you adjusted to my stay being only temporary?"

". . . they make a cute couple, don't they?" a feminine voice from behind intruded.

"Yes, they're made for each other."

Catching the last of these comments, Kirsi looked around to see whom the women passing behind her were talking about. They beamed at her and Doug.

Dr. Doug nodded and then looked away.

The women had been talking about *them*. Had it embarrassed him? Had she somehow betrayed the way he affected her? Surely not. She took another sweet mouthful of cake. Why make a big deal out of the idle speculation of strangers? She supposed that matchmaking was big in small towns.

"Well?" she prompted him, again focusing on their conflict. "Did I convince you that God will provide—"

"Douglas, mind if Nick and I join you?" A thin elderly man stood beside Doug.

Kirsi closed her mouth. She'd have to wait until she and Doug were alone. They could discuss nothing in this crush. *I don't want to be alone with you, Doug.* But she knew tonight this was just bravado. A part of her *did* want to be alone with Doug so she could confess everything that was pushing her to leave. So he wouldn't continue to distance himself from her. *No! I don't need any more complications!*

"Of course, Harlan." Doug motioned toward the chair next to him. "Please sit down."

The older man sat down, then offered Kirsi his hand from across the table. "Dr. Royston, I'm Harlan Carey. We are so happy you are here."

She shook his gnarled hand and murmured a polite reply, grateful to the man for breaking up her twosome with Doug.

"This is my friend and boarder Nick." Harlan gestured toward a handsome teenager who had sat down beside her.

"Pleased to meet you, Dr. Royston," Nick said with a nod, and then he dug his white plastic fork into the huge square of cake on his plate.

Harlan chuckled. "I told them to give him extra." He looked to Kirsi again. "We're so sorry that you were hurt last Saturday."

Kirsi looked askance at Doug. Had he and the deputy broadcast the assault?

Harlan answered her unspoken question. "I know about it because my grandson-in-law is the sheriff. I hear most of what's going on around here." Then the older man looked toward the door. "Nick, Jayleen just came in with her grandmother."

Nick shot out of his chair and headed for the door.

Thankful for the distraction that took the attention away from her, Kirsi had to smile. "I take it that Nick is interested in Jayleen?"

Harlan nodded. "They are enjoying getting to know one another. It's good to see them happy again. He and his uncle live with me."

"Oh, is his uncle his guardian?" she asked.

Harlan nodded again. "Yes, but his mother will be visiting this summer."

Another fractured family. With her fork tines, Kirsi made circles in the frosting.

Dr. Doug nodded toward Harlan. "Kirsi, Harlan is Wendy Durand's grandfather. He's Veda McCracken's brother-in-law."

Kirsi gave the man a speculative look. "I've been treating Veda this week."

"Yes. I've been to the clinic to visit her. I hope you'll call

me when she's ready to be released. I'll give her a ride home
and see that she gets settled in."

Kirsi analyzed his tone. He sounded sincere. No trace of
acrimony in his face or voice. "I will, Mr. Carey."

"Call me Harlan. Everyone does."

Kirsi would have to get used to this small-town infor-
mality—Dr. Doug, Old Doc, Harlan, Ma. But she didn't
think she'd be comfortable calling this man by his first
name or the senior Dr. Erickson, Old Doc, though she
would call Doug by his first name. She didn't care for the
name Dr. Doug. It sounded . . . she couldn't find the right
word, and *unprofessional* wasn't quite right.

"I wanted to talk to you about Weston's drug overdose,"
Harlan spoke up. "I think we need to do more than educate
kids about drugs. We need prayer. Nick and I talked it over,
and I'm going to invite a few people to an early morning
prayer meeting over the summer. I was thinking that Tuesday mornings might be good."

"I'd come." Doug surprised her by offering.

"I don't know where you live," Kirsi began, interested
but hesitant. Getting settled in at the clinic would take most
of her time and energy.

"I'm only a few miles from Bruno's cabin," Harlan
replied.

"I'll show you," Doug invited.

Doug was definitely starting to hover. She gave him a
tight smile and concentrated on Harlan. *Don't, Doug.*

The evening passed. In singles and couples, people
came over to introduce themselves and welcome her.
Finally a young DJ began playing requests. A few couples
danced at one end of the room. Little girls gathered at the
edge of the dance floor, spinning to the music, amusing
themselves by watching their full party skirts flare.

The senior Dr. Erickson stopped by with Wendy and

a tall, handsome man in a brown-and-khaki uniform. Kirsi hadn't noticed the policeman come in. "Dr. Royston," the doctor said, "you've already met Wendy. This is her husband, Sheriff Rodd Durand."

Hoping the sheriff wouldn't make a big deal about what had happened to her in Weston Blake's room, Kirsi offered her hand, and the sheriff shook it thoroughly.

"Glad to meet you, Doctor," Sheriff Durand said in a rumbling deep voice; then he leaned closer. "And I'm sorry but I have to bother you."

The seriousness in his tone alerting her, Kirsi sat still. What now?

The sheriff looked around. "Would you step outside with me, Dr. Royston?"

Cool apprehension seeped down her spine. She stood up. "Of course."

Doug got up too.

She was going to tell him to stay, but she doubted he would listen to her. The three of them trooped to the door and stepped out into the cool night. Her bare midriff instantly prickled into gooseflesh.

A few steps away from the doorway, the sheriff halted. "I hate to ask you tonight, but I need you to identify a body."

Doug gasped.

The request sent a shiver through her. At first, she didn't feel as if she comprehended what the sheriff was saying. His words confused her. "But I don't know anyone around here," Kirsi said.

"There was a fight at Flanagan's tonight," the sheriff said.

"That's the worst bar in the county," Doug explained. "They send us a lot of business. Brawling is common there."

Kirsi tried to make sense of the information they were bombarding her with.

"When the dust had cleared," the sheriff went on, "someone staggered out back to be sick and stumbled over a dead body in the parking lot."

"But I don't know—," Kirsi started again.

"The body had been there awhile. The man had been shot. A dark baseball cap lay beside him, and sunglasses were in his pocket."

Then she understood. It was like being punched in the stomach.

"I think it might be—"

"The man who assaulted me," Kirsi finished for Sheriff Durand, her cool apprehension turning to icy dread.

Doug took her elbow.

With her stomach sinking, she knew she should pull away but couldn't.

❖ ❖ ❖

Kirsi stood between Doug and the sheriff in a very clinical, very white, very cramped room at the LaFollette Funeral Parlor. It had that hospital-mortuary smell of disinfectant. She tried to breathe through her mouth instead of her nose. Why did the room have to be so small? There was barely enough space for them to maneuver around the body.

"The county saves money by renting a separate room here for our morgue," Rodd explained. "We don't have that many dead bodies, rarely more than one at a time."

Kirsi appreciated the sheriff's attempt to ease the mood, but identifying a dead body in a morgue was not routine, not even for a doctor.

The stainless-steel slab with the white-sheet-covered corpse looked like something out of a fifties movie, not one of the modern forensic TV shows that were so popular now. The three of them made an almost ludicrous party in the setting—a woman in a blue sari, a man in a suit and tie, and a formidable-looking sheriff in brown and khaki.

Rodd edged around to the head of the table and folded back the sheet to reveal the face of a young man with a bruised eye.

"It looks like he's been in a fight," she said, focusing on the body as a clinical study.

Rodd nodded. "I think he might have been killed in someone's fit of rage."

"Where did the bullet enter?" she asked, still playing her role as medico.

Rodd lifted the sheet to expose the man's bare chest, revealing a small entrance wound in the region of the heart.

"There's tattooing," she said, referring to the tiny pin-point hemorrhages around the wound.

Doug nodded but said nothing.

"You know what that means?" Rodd asked, looking into her eyes.

"His killer must have shot him at point-blank range and deposited unburned powder into his skin. Which means it must have been someone he knew or someone who surprised him in the dark." Kirsi brought this up from memories of her conversations with policemen in the Los Angeles ER.

"Not a bad analysis," Rodd agreed.

She stared at the pale, bruised face, trying to decide if it was the one that had swooped at her in Weston's room. "I can't tell you. I don't remember his face. Just the hat and sunglasses."

"Burke's notes of your description mentioned a tattoo on the neck—"

"You're right! I'd forgotten that."

"That's understandable. You've had a lot on your mind." Rodd nodded toward the corpse.

Kirsi looked at both sides of his neck. A small insignia-type tattoo was on the right side. She nodded. "That's it, all right. This definitely could be the man who was buying meth ingredients at the gas station that day."

Looking grimly satisfied, the sheriff laid the sheet carefully back in place and then pulled a stainless-steel tray from the counter behind him. "Do these look familiar?"

She stared at the dirty, worn baseball cap and sunglasses. Memory of the suffocating feeling when the lab coat had covered her face swooshed over her. She clenched her hands at her sides. "Yes, those I recognize."

The sheriff sighed and set the tray back on the counter. "So now we know this guy was mixed up in drugs and he might be the one who knocked Dr. Royston down, but we still don't know who he is."

"Maybe you can trace his fingerprints?" Doug suggested, standing so close to Kirsi, his warm breath tickled her right ear.

She hadn't noticed him edging closer. Involuntarily, she felt herself leaning toward his solid weight.

The sheriff shook his head. "Whoever shot this man messed up his hands, too."

"Messed them up?" Kirsi echoed, making herself focus on the facts.

"You know Flanagan's has a gravel lot?" Rodd asked.

"Yes," Doug replied.

"Well, after he shot his victim, the murderer must have ground both of the victim's hands into the gravel, I think, using his boot heel. He did a good job too. The palms and finger pads are unidentifiable. His boots and belt were wiped clean, so there are no fingerprints either."

The act seemed an unnecessary desecration. "Why?" Kirsi asked, her mouth dry.

"My guess—" the sheriff leaned back against the counter, folding his arms across his chest—"the victim must have a record, and his murderer didn't want us to trace him that easily."

❋ ❋ ❋

Kirsi eased herself more deeply into the booth at the truck-stop restaurant. Doug had brought her here when she'd told him she couldn't go back to the reception. The thought of making polite conversation had been overwhelming. And going home alone to her cabin hadn't appealed to her either. In her sari, she felt very much out of place. In his suit Doug looked attractive, but he was definitely out of place too.

The visit to the county morgue had left her numb like she'd felt in medical school on the first day she'd worked on a cadaver.

In front of her sat a bowl of deliciously fragrant vegetable-barley soup. She breathed in the aroma and picked up her spoon. "I feel like it's been a week since this morning."

Doug looked up from squeezing a lemon wedge over the cod he'd talked the waitress into having broiled not fried. "Make that two weeks."

She held her spoon but couldn't make herself eat. Her susceptibility to the man across from her swept over her in a wave. She gazed at him.

He chewed a bite of fish. "You've had a rough first week here."

"An understatement." She made herself dip the spoon into the broth. If she could get one spoonful into her mouth, she'd be able to swallow. Someone near the cashier laughed; the sound grated on her.

"I'm sorry. It wasn't supposed to be like this. . . ."

Doug's statement hit her sense of the absurd. "You

mean personal assault and a dead body weren't part of your welcome plan?" She felt like laughing but recognized it must be just a flash of hysteria. Taking a deep breath, she clamped her self-control back into place.

She grimaced. "Sorry. Gallows humor, I guess." She made herself take a sip of soup. For a fraction of a second, her throat squeezed shut; then it opened and the broth coursed down, warming her.

"Well, you are allowed whatever humor you can find in this." Doug rested his back against the booth, looking at her. "I've never seen anything like it. No one's ever been attacked like you were in our clinic. And then the man turns up dead days later."

She zeroed in on his words, not the way his golden brown eyes conveyed how concerned he was about her, about this. "It worries me. What does Weston know or what does someone think Weston knows?" She drew in another swallow. She wasn't overreacting. This all added up to one dangerous situation.

"That's the sheriff's problem," Doug said. "My problem is making sure our patients and staff are safe. We've never had to employ a security team before. But I do now. I'll put the word out—"

"Usually, security is retired or off-duty police officers moonlighting," she suggested.

"Right. I don't know if we have any retired policemen here. Our deputies are pretty young. But I'll talk to the sheriff first, in any case. He'll know whom to recommend."

"I still can't figure out why the murderer messed up the victim's hands," she said, looking into her bowl, avoiding his caring brown eyes. "Can't they identify him by his face?"

"I don't know if it's true to life, but on TV when police want someone to identify a person's face, the poor victim has to sit and look through books of mug shots. And they may find someone or not."

"You're right." She frowned. "But why would someone kill him?" As soon as the words were out, she knew how pointless her question was. Had the dead man made a fatal mistake or argued with a cohort? Had that cohort shot him in a rage? They could only guess at a motive for the killing or about who the killer might be.

Doug shook his head. "I don't know. I'm a doctor."

Unable to settle her nerves so she could eat, she dragged her spoon through the chunks of vegetables in the soup. "I'm still worried about Weston. How can he go back to his regular life if this is hanging over him?"

"It's hanging over all of us." Doug's voice was sober. "It seems like a million years ago, but it was just that first morning at the café when Burke was warning us that the drug trade around the county was becoming stirred up."

"But maybe that's it." She lifted her spoon as though punctuating her point, wanting to lift his mood. "Maybe Weston could identify someone in the drug trade, so the attacker came to the clinic to try to hurt Weston. But he failed, so he in turn was killed by some third person who didn't want the trail to lead back to him."

"Maybe," Doug commented.

"I'm so tired." Kirsi sighed. "I may not be making very much sense. But my point is—if Weston could only ID the murder victim and now he's dead, Weston shouldn't be in any more danger. I mean if he couldn't identify anyone else. Should he?"

"That might be true if Weston could identify only that one person, the one we saw at the morgue. But how do we know that's true?"

She didn't have a response for him.

Doug put his fork down. "We need some answers."

"Who has them?" she asked, trying again to eat.

Doug went on without answering her question. "The clinic has already been affected by this . . . whatever it is. Something tells me it's only the beginning."

# CHAPTER FIVE

ON THE NEXT Thursday evening after the VFW reception, Doug leaned back against the counter and scanned his grandfather's kitchen. Since his granddad hated bright lights at home, just the light over the stove and a small lamp on the counter glowed.

On one side of the trestle table sat Granddad. To Doug's left, Sheriff Rodd Durand slouched against the counter, holding a mug of coffee. Outside, a June storm flung tree branches skyward and earthward. Rain poured down the darkened windowpanes at the end of the room.

The unidentified dead body in the morgue had alarmed Doug. He'd called Rodd and Burke to arrange this powwow to learn what was happening and what he and Granddad should be doing now. Tight with tension, Doug waited with an ear cocked for Burke's arrival. Then they could start.

The back door swung open with a bang. Rain pelting against the house suddenly sounded louder. The door banged shut. After some noises and footsteps on the back stairs, Burke appeared in the kitchen doorway. "Sorry I'm late." The deputy crossed to the far side of the table as he sat across from Doug's grandfather.

In one smooth action, Rodd straddled a chair backward at the head of the table as he sat and faced them. "Okay, let's get started. First, if Doug hadn't arranged this meeting tonight, I would have."

"You couldn't keep me out of it if you tried," Doug insisted. Distant thunder grumbled.

Rodd tightened his lips. "Burke and I have been discussing what happened last weekend, and we've decided that we don't have the manpower to handle this alone.

"In the past few weeks, informants have been giving us tips that a new drug ring is trying to take over the local drug territory. Weston's drug overdose, the attack on Dr. Royston, and then Saturday night's murder cinched it."

Doug leaned forward. "What I want to know is how we get the new element out of here—"

A wave of heavier rain beating the windowpanes competed with the sound of pounding on the back door. *Who could that be?* Doug straightened and hurried to the small, back stairwell. He swung open the door and felt cool rain swish up into his face.

"Hi!" Kirsi stepped inside, making him move back up on the stair.

The sight and nearness of her notched his tension higher. *I don't want you here.* "What—"

"Sorry I'm late," she said with a mocking edge to her voice as she unzipped her saturated rain jacket.

"Late?" Doug echoed. *You weren't invited!*

"Yes—" she gave him a steady look—"you wouldn't hold a meeting to discuss what happened last weekend and how it affects the clinic without the new doctor on staff, would you?"

Her insistence annoyed him, especially because her point was valid. *I just don't want you here.*

"Your grandfather invited me." She had the nerve to

give him a saucy grin. "Besides, I have ears. There are no secrets at the clinic."

*Why would Granddad invite her and not tell me?* He wanted to say to Kirsi, 'But you're leaving. Why should you be involved?' Instead, he masked his irritation at her showing up, falling back on his role as host. He motioned toward the jacket that had become a second skin to her. "Let me help you with that."

When she about-faced, he peeled the sodden fabric from her back. The scents of fresh rain and her cinnamon fragrance mingled in the air above her. He resented her elemental effect on him, making him more aware of her presence and scent. It was as if a part of him had been sleeping and she had awakened it. Determined to keep this reaction hidden, he hung her jacket on a hook in the back hall to drip onto the frayed beach towel on the floor.

Before he could direct her up the three steps to the kitchen, she leaned forward, her hair flowing over one shoulder. She grasped the dark mane in a bunch between her hands and wrung it out like laundry. Straightening, she swung her head, flaring the wet tresses around her like a raven fanning its wings.

Watching this act—so natural, so feminine—riveted Doug to the top step. *I can't let myself go any further with this. She wants to leave at the end of the summer. She* will *leave. And I will stay. Accept it.*

On the step below him, she looked up with a grimace. "Is the ark ready for passengers yet?" Her wry humor caught him off guard.

What was with this woman—fiercely independent one moment and funny the next? "It's in the garage," he finally deadpanned.

One brow arched, she looked up at him. "What's the price of admission?"

"What?" he asked from a dry throat.

"Can I come in, or do I need to buy a ticket?" She cocked her head to one side. "You're blocking me."

His face blazed. "Well, since you're here, you might as well come in." He couldn't conceal his lack of welcome. Moving into the kitchen, he gestured her toward the table. Again, he would merely act the host. *I'll let the sheriff deal with you.* "Coffee?"

"Yes, if it's decaf." Greeting the others with a smile, she took the open seat nearest the foot of the table. With a flip of her hand, she flung her wet hair over the back of her wooden chair, a cascade of black silk.

Turning away from this captivating sight, Doug poured coffee and then set the steaming mug in front of her. Kirsi had a way of affecting him. He didn't have an easy answer. *Is it because she intends to leave? I should be glad she's come tonight. But how can I be? She'll be concerned—until she leaves us.* He slid onto the chair at the foot of the table, kitty-corner from Kirsi.

Keeping his chin low, he camouflaged his marked reaction to the woman. She'd blown into town and disrupted all his plans. *And she's at it again tonight. Maybe that's it, or is it that everyone wants us to become a couple?* He looked to his grandfather and tried to read his face. Doug couldn't believe that Granddad had thrown them together away from work, matchmaking like the rest of the county.

"Dr. Royston—" Rodd nodded his greeting—"we were just beginning. I think you're already all too aware that a new drug gang is trying to shove its way into our county."

As Kirsi smoothed damp tendrils back from her forehead, Doug made himself focus on the sheriff, not on her—or at least he tried.

Doug cleared his throat. "What do we do to get rid of this new drug gang? If the past week is any indicator, the clinic can't help getting involved. And after Weston's over-dose, I want meth out of here." Involuntarily, Doug glanced at Kirsi.

She had both hands wrapped around her mug. Was she cold from the rain? She looked damp around her shoulders and neck. Otherwise, she appeared dry. Perhaps all that wet hair was chilling her. He forced his gaze away from her.

"We do everything we can to harass the drug dealers here." Rodd's voice pulled Doug back to the discussion.

"And when we have enough evidence to make a charge stick," Burke spoke up, "we make arrests. That keeps the dealers from getting too sure of themselves."

Doug tried to concentrate on Rodd's voice, but glimpses of Kirsi in the low-lit room, even the subtle sounds she made, shifting in her chair and setting down her mug, distracted him. *I have to stop this. I can't make the same mistake my father did.*

"Right," Rodd agreed. "But we need to stop the new gang from getting a firm foothold in the county; otherwise this could go on for years. . . ."

"What exactly do you plan to do to stop meth?" Kirsi's voice overrode Rodd's.

Silence. Doug realized that this was the question he'd wanted to ask. But Kirsi's presence had distracted him, made him lose focus. It made him remember how he'd felt when he'd lost his father. He'd been in a fog for weeks.

"Or maybe you don't think I should ask because I'm an outsider?" she asked, looking toward Rodd.

"We're going to collect enough evidence to put some of them away," Rodd said, returning Kirsi's gaze. "And make the rest scatter."

"And then we'll harass their retreat," Burke added.

Lightning flickered in the windows. Doug watched it, turning over in his mind how to attack this problem.

"Dr. Royston, we'd like to stamp out the drug trade completely." Rodd frowned, his face drawn into grim lines. "But that's not feasible. As long as there is a demand, there will be a supply."

"I was asked to speak at the high school," Kirsi offered. "I don't know how much that will help—"

"Yes, at the Black Bear you met my fiancée, our high school principal," Burke said to Kirsi. "She thinks her students will listen more closely to you since you're a new face."

"You need to tell kids what to do if approached by a dealer," Doug inserted, finding his way back into the exchange. "I'm thinking of Weston in the hospital. He may still suffer aftereffects of his overdose—"

"Am I missing something?" Kirsi cut in on Doug. "If you're dealing with a new element, wouldn't it be fairly easy for you to pick them out? I mean, this is a sparsely populated county. Wouldn't strangers stand out here? Couldn't you just put them under surveillance and then arrest them in the middle of a drug deal?"

Sobered and completely invested in the discussion now, Doug let himself look at her—along with everyone else.

"You'd be right," Granddad said, competing with a rumble of thunder overhead. "But it's nearly summer, camping season. Lot of fishermen coming in for different tournaments—fishing for walleyes, bass, muskies."

"And we can't make the mistake of thinking of the stereotypical appearance of the drug dealer that we see in movies and on TV," Rodd added.

"There are yuppie dealers," Burke said, "and they could come up here and rent a resort cabin on a lake and look no different than anyone else."

Kirsi turned to look at Doug. "I've worked in this kind of drug war before," she said in a gruff tone. "This can get real ugly real fast. Innocent people can get in the way and get killed or . . ." She made a face. "I hate this."

Doug's stomach tightened at the harsh tone she used. She sounded fierce, ready to fight. He felt the same emotions clawing him. "We all hate it," he said, his voice grating low in his throat.

"But that's not all!" she continued. "New suppliers will offer great deals to get users to switch to them." Her voice gained an edge of sarcasm. "They'll give free samples to entice more people into becoming customers. I think that may be what happened to our young patient. And it nearly killed him."

Kirsi's words sickened Doug. *Lord, we've got to stop this from happening here.*

"Do you think Saturday night's killing was just the first?" Doug raised his voice to compete with the storm. The sight of Kirsi's somber face that night in the cramped morgue came to mind again. He gripped his mug, trying to get control of his own self-reproach. *I didn't protect her.*

Rodd shrugged. "That case is still under investigation. But since Dr. Royston connected some of the articles found with the corpse to Weston, there will probably be some link."

"But I couldn't ID the deceased positively," she objected, sounding uncertain.

Doug resisted the urge to touch her hand that must be resting on her knee under the table, only inches from his.

Lightning glimmered in the shadowy room. Doug felt Kirsi's shoe graze his calf as she crossed her legs. His focusing on her made him jumpy. *Is the fact that she's leaving causing me to be attracted to her? The forbidden-fruit factor?*

"Maybe we should have asked Fletcher Cram to this meeting," Doug muttered, resenting his own thoughts.

Kirsi leaned toward Doug, a question on her face.

Doug bent and whispered in her ear, "Cram's the local

newspaperman." Her black hair fell forward, cascading over her small shell-like ear. Doug gritted his teeth. *I will not give in to this foolish attraction.*

Pushing her hair back, she murmured, "Thanks."

"I want to control what information I give Cram," Rodd said. "He can be pretty independent at times, and I don't want to give the new gang anything they can use for their purposes. But I will be talking to Cram tomorrow about public awareness and how to report anything suspicious, like someone buying a lot of cold pills with ephedrine or large amounts of drain cleaner and batteries, alcohol, etc. If that truck-stop cashier had been on the ball, he would have been a second witness, along with Dr. Royston."

A damp lock of black hair flew past Doug's face. Kirsi finished passing a hand under her hair at the back of her neck, flipping her hair up to spread it out more.

Was she trying to snare his attention on purpose? Was she the kind of woman who had to be noticed no matter what?

"Then what can we do?" Doug asked, letting his frustration with Kirsi come out in his tone.

Nearing thunder boomed louder.

"I want you, Dr. Royston, and Old Doc to help Doug prepare your staff for whatever comes," Rodd said. "Overdoses, victims of violence, burn victims if a meth lab explodes . . . anything and everything. We are literally under attack and we must expect casualties."

Though it was only what he'd expected, this statement of fact chilled Doug. *Lord, help us be vigilant.*

❊ ❊ ❊

The two lawmen said good night and bolted through the back door, splashing the few yards to their vehicles. Thunder exploded overhead.

Kirsi lingered at the table with the senior Dr. Erickson. She nervously gripped her empty coffee mug between her icy hands. Listening for Doug to come back into the kitchen, she gave the doctor sitting across from her an apologetic grin. "Sorry, but I'm not used to thunderstorms like this."

And she dreaded having to call her mother back tonight. Their last call had ended with Ammu in tears. Kirsi had called her twice since, but she had not left a message on her machine. *Please, Lord, help her calm down before I speak to her. I'm carrying about all I can right now. Help me, please. I don't want to upset her more. But I can't drop everything and go home because Ammu wants me with her. And don't let me slip and give her an idea of what's going on here. Or my grandparents—*

Dr. Erickson called to his grandson, who'd just closed the back door. "Doug, pour our guest another cup of coffee."

"I don't want to be a bother," she said, glancing around, glimpsing only Doug's back. *Why am I still here? I should have left. It's late and I'm scheduled in the ER at 7 A.M.* But she had some unfinished business to discuss with the younger Dr. Erickson.

"No problem." Taking her mug and his, Doug walked over to the stove and filled them both. "Just enough for two."

Rain lashed the windows. Kirsi accepted the warm mug with both hands. It seemed that Doug made sure his fingers didn't touch hers. Why? Was he still angry because she had come tonight? Or because she was leaving without honoring her full contract?

Doug seemed stiff, not like himself at all. Or at least not like the man whom she'd spent last Saturday evening with. Maybe he was simply preoccupied with all this drug business.

Doug's grandfather rose. "Past time for me to be in bed. Good night, Dr. Royston." With an endearing smile, he bowed.

"Good night, sir," she replied as a shiver shook her.

As he departed, he waved a hand over his head. "Doug, take her into the den. I left the heater on in there. She needs to take off those wet socks and shoes and warm up before she leaves."

"No—" Kirsi looked up, uncomfortable to be caught between crosscurrents inside her—"if I'm chilled, I should just go home. I don't want to keep you up—"

A crash of thunder blotted out her voice. She jumped in her chair. "Oh!"

"That was a close one. Maybe you should stay." Doug seemed to study her. "Granddad goes to bed early. I don't, so you won't be putting me out." He motioned for her to precede him—his mood or opinion of the evening, of her—still cloaked.

*Does he want me to stay? go? What does he think of me? Has he accepted my leaving before my contract terms, or does he have some plan he's considering? Is that why he didn't want me here tonight?*

Rising with her mug still in hand, she studied his face in the low light. He needed a haircut. The wind from his standing at the back door had tossed his brown wavy hair into an enticing disarray. She wanted to finger it into order.

"Okay . . ." She shrugged and proceeded down the hall. *I'll only find out what you're thinking by asking. But do I really want to know?*

He caught up with her and slid open a pocket door to her right. Then he reached in and switched on the lamps.

She entered a room that had a comfy, lived-in look. An old, oak, rolltop desk with a clutter of paper contrasted with the modern black laptop upon it. The monitor flickered blue and green.

Jammed bookcases lined two walls. Faded leather bindings with gold lettering glowed here and there in the subtle lighting. A worn rocking chair and an adjacent love seat in dark green cotton duck occupied one corner. It was definitely a masculine den. The warmth of the room and her damp clothing triggered another shiver.

"You should warm up fast in here." Doug pointed toward a closed oil heater in the corner. "This is an old house, and it can get drafty even in early summer, so we keep that in here to take off the chill."

Lightning gleamed outside, making the room feel doubly snug. A hand-knit ivory afghan lay across one arm of the love seat. She crossed to it, sat, and put her mug down on the coffee table.

"Take off those wet socks," he suggested.

She made a face but went ahead and peeled off her shoes and saturated socks. She got up to drape and arrange them around the heater.

When Kirsi returned to her seat, she slid both legs under her and tugged the afghan over herself. Her damp toes were cold to the bone. She burrowed them deep into the twisted yarn. Relinquishing her socks made the setting feel even more intimate. *I should go home.* But guilty reluctance to place another call to her mother kept her where she was.

Harsh thunder boomed, rattling the window glass. Involuntarily, she glanced out the window and used the weather as a stall. "We don't have thunderstorms very often in California. Are these common here?"

"In the spring and summer, yes." Doug sat in the rocker adjacent to her.

She sensed that he was still holding himself detached from her. Why was her leaving galling him so? A gust of wind clattered the shutters outside ominously.

"And you get tornadoes?" she asked, pulling the afghan higher around her shoulders. *Yes, let's talk about the weather—always a safe subject.*

"Yes, but no earthquakes." He gave her an impersonal grin. "Don't worry about tornadoes. This house is nearly one hundred years old and it's still standing. We've lost a few shingles, but that's all. Are you settling in okay in the cabin?"

"Yes." Then, tired of polite topics, she switched to the one that mattered now. "What do you think of the sheriff's plans? I thought they were too general." She'd start here and work up to the personal issue that stood between them.

"I'm glad we have people like Rodd and Burke in our sheriff's department," he said without hesitation. "Both of them have years of experience in law enforcement, and both have solved a couple of very nasty cases over the past year."

"I'm not the newspaper editor," she said wryly. "I won't quote you. Are they equal to this crisis?" She stared out the dark windows behind him—lightning gleaming brighter.

He frowned at her. "Yes."

"Just yes?"

He nodded. "I don't see why you are so concerned."

*So that's it! I don't care because I'm not permanent.* "I'm concerned because I'm a decent person," she snapped. "I'm concerned because I'm here."

"You're here now, but summer's end is only three months away," he retorted.

She stared at him. Now they were getting to the heart of what was going on between them. *So I was right.* "I thought I made myself clear. I'm here until someone qualified, someone that you and your grandfather will approve of, comes to take my place. God will provide. And while I'm here I'm a part of what's happening. Why is that unacceptable to you?"

He snorted. "Because I don't foresee that happening."

"Which?" she demanded. "Finding a replacement or being a part of what's happening?"

"You're not going to find someone. And I don't want to start counting on you—"

"God will provide," she interrupted. "He *has* to! Why won't you believe that?" Her heart pounded with her desperation.

He frowned at her, the bridge between his brows creasing deeply. "If you're going, I wish you would just go," he replied slowly. "You irritate me because I don't want you here against your will."

"I don't want to rehash our disagreement," she murmured. "I'm not here against my will. My will is to be here doing my job until God frees me from my obligation here."

She met his rich brown eyes, and an unbidden warmth blossomed inside her. She stiffened, resisting it. "Now do we both know where we stand?" She tried to make herself relax.

He stared at her.

"Is that why you didn't clue me in about tonight's meeting? Because I'll be leaving?"

"No."

Another thought swooped into her mind. "You weren't trying to protect me, were you?"

He grimaced.

A hit! This motive she understood. All her life, her grandparents had done all they could to protect her from the effects of her mother's illness. All to no avail.

As though protecting herself, she snuggled deeper into the comforting afghan. "Don't try that again, Dr. Erickson. I'm not delicate bone china. Bad news won't break me or make me run," she said to disabuse him of his false notions. "And I needed to be here tonight. I'm on the front line too."

"Sorry." He offered her his hand. "It won't happen again."

"I hope not." She shook his man-size, strong hand, analyzing the feel of it in her own palm. A capable hand. A kind hand.

She sighed. "Doug, I'm here—one hundred percent for now. Things are better at the clinic, aren't they? Your granddad is only coming in one day a week and is on call one night a week. That must feel like retirement to him."

"You're right," he conceded. "And I'm glad you're here—one hundred percent."

This time his words sounded sincere to her. She watched the way a sudden smile crinkled his face. It was genuine Doug. It made her want to smile back. From forbidding to welcoming just like that. No wonder he had a power—no one else had—to distract her.

"I'm glad too." She forced herself to concentrate on their topic, not on Doug's killer smile. How could he change moods like that? "I didn't expect to face the influx of meth we may be confronting. I *thought* I'd left gang wars behind me."

"We live in a wicked, fallen world wherever we call home."

His words, followed by another string of thunder, lowered her spirits. *Lord, this isn't what I wanted, what I expected.*

Now Doug switched topics. "Weston was up walking today. Did you see him?" He leaned forward.

Only inches separated their faces. Her focus zeroed in on his lips. No man should have such a perfect cupid's bow.

"No, he was sleeping again when I looked in on him." Unable to stop herself, she studied Doug. They'd only known each other for barely two weeks. Just days, really. How could so much happen in such a short time? Maybe that was why she felt as if she'd known him longer.

She scrambled for something to talk about, something

that would take her mind from her perplexing fascination with him. "I'm worried about Veda McCracken. She won't do anything the physical therapist tells her to do."

"That's what I'd expect from Veda." He gave her a slight grin. "I warned you that she's a very destructive person, and evidently she's turning that in on herself now." He used the tone of one colleague talking to another.

Kirsi relaxed. He was being himself now. *How do I know that? We're barely more than strangers.* "The kind of behavior you described her exhibiting before—" she made herself continue their discussion—"is self-destructive, don't you think?"

His quizzical expression held her as he said, "How is Veda's previous behavior self-destructive?" At least he was taking her words seriously.

"Well . . ." She worried her lower lip. "Hasn't her anger alienated her from everyone? That's pretty self-destructive."

"I hadn't thought of it that way," he said in a way which let her know that her input was sinking into his mind.

She liked the way he didn't let his ego insert itself into their exchanges. He may not be happy with her and he had years more medical experience than she did, but he dealt with her as an equal. It was hard not to like him.

"Anyway, I've prescribed an antidepressant for her," she continued, "and I'd like to get one of the county social workers to set up a psychologist to come in and assess her." Kirsi listened for more thunder. It came but sounded more distant.

"A psychologist?"

"Yes. I was wondering why that hasn't been done before—"

"It hasn't been done before because Veda has never been sick enough to be hospitalized," Doug retorted. "She's been hale and hearty until this slight stroke. It's not like she

physically attacked people so she could have been arrested."
He looked out the window, obviously scanning the darkness for lightning.

"I had some success." Kirsi grinned. "I said she had to
work with the physical therapist or she wouldn't be able to
walk out of the clinic. That seemed to get her attention, but
I still think she has serious psychological problems—
depression for sure." She wondered if it was just her imagination, but had the storm quieted?

"I applaud your efforts." Doug grimaced. "But Veda
McCracken has consistently nullified any attempts to reach
her for the past fifty years. So don't feel bad if you strike out."

Doug's words made Kirsi wonder what it felt like to live
in one place with one set of people for a lifetime. How many
times in her childhood had her mother's losing another job
sent her back to her grandparents' home? For a moment,
she envied Doug Erickson.

※ ※ ※

The storm had broken—finally. Only the unrelenting wind
chased her home. By the porch light, Kirsi unlocked her
cabin, her loosened hair flying around her.

Inside, she locked the door behind her and switched on
the light. A lamp glowed in the snug cabin, which already
felt like home.

She slipped off her shoes and headed for her bedroom.
As she reached for her pajamas, a wave of exhaustion
swamped her. It wasn't just trying to find her way around
town and learning new names and faces at the clinic. It was
all the celebration, the shock and worry about what had
happened last weekend, and all the conflict with Doug.
Now tonight's conversations—the questions, the answers,
and the questions that couldn't be answered . . .

Doug's smile came to her. She turned back her

comforter and sat down on the cool sheets. Her relationship with Doug had gone through so many phases so quickly. He'd been an eager new colleague and then a disgruntled one. Now their conflict over whether she'd be here for six years or for only the summer had been overshadowed by the discovery of the corpse last Saturday night.

A glance at the clock told her that her anytime cell-phone minutes were in force now. She slid her phone out of her slacks pocket and punched in her mother's number.

Her mother picked up immediately. "Kirsi! I've been waiting!"

"Sorry, Ammu, but I was at a meeting and couldn't get away."

"No, I'm sorry—" tears sounded in her mother's voice—"to be such a burden to—"

"Mom, you're not a burden." How many times had Kirsi been forced to say that? "I've just been so busy."

"And I'm glad. You'll be happy to know that I'm taking up crocheting." Forced cheerfulness now in her mother's tone. "Dr. Ansgar said I should have a hobby."

"So how's that going?"

"Okay."

"Great." Kirsi made herself sound positive. Crocheting wasn't the answer to her mother's illness.

Hearing the wall phone in the kitchen ringing, Kirsi promised to call her mother tomorrow and said good-bye. She hurried out of her bedroom and reached for the phone near the kitchen table. As always a late-night call sparked anxiety in her. "Hello?"

No answer.

"Hello?"

Just breathing.

She frowned. *A breather phone call? Here in small-town Wisconsin?*

Not likely.

Maybe a telemarketer dialing several numbers at a time and she'd answered last. No, too late for that. It was nearly eleven.

It wasn't breathing; it must be only a muted buzz on the line. Caused by the storm?

She hung up, but her hand stayed on the receiver. Her mind brought back those few moments on that first Saturday morning when she'd thought someone was following her to the clinic. The visor had covered the person's face . . . but could it be . . . ?

She felt again the lab coat being pulled over her face . . . falling. . . .

Then a far worse fear, one cold and undiluted by time, gushed through Kirsi, weakening her knees. She slid down on the kitchen chair, trying to reel in the sick dread. *It's been years, Lord.* She closed her eyes as if that would take away the images, the memories, the demoralizing panic coursing through her veins.

Kirsi pressed her hands together in front of her face and rocked slightly, trying not to remember the horror she'd lived through for nearly a year.

*Lord, take these feelings from me. I'm not in danger here. Don't let the past threaten my peace of mind. I don't want to end up like my mother. Please, Lord.*

"This is crazy," she said aloud, trying to convince herself. "It's all this stuff we talked about tonight. And the storm! I'm just jumpy." She stood up, taking her thoughts captive. "Time for bed." She looked at the door to check the lock and then made herself walk to her bedroom—without a backward glance.

# CHAPTER SIX

Over a week later, Kirsi was sipping strong, hot coffee in the rear booth at the Black Bear Café. She glanced at her watch. She had a few more peaceful minutes until she had to leave. She had allowed time for a stop at the clinic before reaching her appointment at the high school.

⁂

He sat at the counter, his back to the front window. From there, he could keep track of her. He held the local paper with one hand and acted like he was reading it. But he could see her plainly. And that's what he'd come to do.

So far she didn't have a clue about him, not really. What were a few late-night phone calls? He hid his grin behind his coffee cup.

⁂

Hearing the bell on the front door of the café jingle, Kirsi looked up. An older man, very tall and painfully thin, entered. With a newspaper rolled up under one arm, he looked around and headed straight for her, ignoring all greetings and people who reached out a hand to stop him.

"You're Dr. Royston." He glared at her from under bushy white eyebrows.

She gave him a quizzical glance. He looked like he could play the scarecrow in *The Wizard of Oz*. "And you are . . . ?"

"Fletcher Cram." He sat down without an invitation. "Ginger!" he growled loudly over his shoulder. "Coffee and a sweet roll!"

"When I get there!" the waitress called back.

The older man turned back to Kirsi. "I'm the newspaper editor. What's going on with you trying to leave? Find anybody to replace you yet?"

Kirsi sipped her coffee. "What have you heard?"

"What I hear isn't worth printing." He took out a frayed and grimy spiral notebook. "Have you got anybody lined up yet?" he insisted.

After yesterday's mail, this was the last question she wanted to be asked. "No, but I have put out feelers and I'm hoping to get a few nibbles soon." Avoiding the editor's piercing glare, she carefully spread rose-colored fruit jelly onto a triangle of whole wheat toast.

"Why don't you just stay?" he barked.

She grinned. "Not a very original question." She wished she had a dollar for every time she'd been asked that in the past three weeks. "I think Veda McCracken is the only one I've met who hasn't asked me that."

"That old biddy." He humphed. "When you leave, why don't you take her with you? Do us all a favor."

Kirsi frowned at him. Veda was evidently skilled at making enemies. Old Doc had visited Veda yesterday and bullied her back to the clinic. This time her blood pressure had been off the chart. It had given Kirsi a chance to contact the psychologist.

⬚ ⬚ ⬚

Head lowered, he watched the way her hands moved, buttering her toast—so sure of herself. He liked a woman, a victim, with confidence. It was so satisfying to watch it crumble—bit by bit—as he dangled her over the edge and panic set in.

His grin broadened.

⬚ ⬚ ⬚

The waitress plopped down a mug of coffee and a sweet roll in front of the newspaperman and turned away.

"You didn't bring me any butter," Cram complained.

"You didn't ask for any," Ginger replied over her shoulder, "and you never tip so you get what you ask for the first time."

"If I ever got any real service, I might leave a tip," Cram retorted.

"In your dreams," Ginger chortled.

Hiding her amusement, Kirsi flipped a foil-wrapped cube of butter onto Cram's plate. Steadfast didn't lack for colorful characters. *I should be keeping a journal:* My First Practice.

Without thanks, Cram picked up the butter pat and opened it. With the back of his coffee spoon, he spread it over the top of his cinnamon roll. "What about that kid that overdosed? How's he doing?"

"You'll have to ask him or his parents." She chewed a bite of toast. Weston still had memory loss and some motor problems. Doug was worried about him.

Cram tossed a rolled newspaper on the tabletop. "Hot off the presses. Read the front page."

She picked it up with one hand. "Police Ask for Help" was the headline. The article started: "A new menace threatens our county—methedrine. New doctor to address high school students on dangers of drug abuse." *So I made the front page twice in a row—the story about the reception and now my talk.* She sipped more coffee.

"I'm going to cover your talk at the school today," Cram said between chewing his roll and swallowing coffee. "Do you think your little speech will help?"

Kirsi took her time answering. She touched the paper napkin to her lips. "If it puts teens on their guard, that can only help."

He humphed again. "I think drug education is a farce, along with sex education. Kids don't have the sense—"

"I don't agree," Kirsi interrupted him. "Teens *can* make good choices. Not all teens and not all the time, but giving them the facts is my . . . our job. What they do with them is their choice."

Cram glared at her. "Got an answer for everything, huh?"

She shook her head, the letter in her purse weighing on her mind. "No. Unfortunately, I don't."

※ ※ ※

He glanced at the paper's headline and laughed to himself. So the county was feeling threatened? And she was going to give the kids the word. How could he miss that?

Putting money by his plate, he laid down just enough of a tip so he wouldn't be remembered by giving too much or too little. *Later, Doc. Thanks for making my day.*

※ ※ ※

After Cram had eaten his roll and drunk his coffee, he departed, saying he'd see her at the high school. Kirsi set the amount of her bill, plus the tip, beside her breakfast plate and slipped out the back door of the noisy Black Bear Café.

She walked down the deserted alley to the end of the block. She halted. A gray sedan was parked behind her Jeep. Her mind flashed back to the gray sedan that had tailgated her when she first came to town.

An older woman walking briskly up the side street passed Kirsi to the sedan. "Good morning, Dr. Royston. I'm Emily Benser." Turning, the woman offered Kirsi her hand.

Jarred, Kirsi shook it. "Hello. I—"

"You don't have to remember my name," the silver-haired, neatly dressed woman said. "I clean house for Old Doc and Douglas. I'll introduce myself again the next time we meet."

"I'll appreciate that." Kirsi smiled, brushing away the last wisps of her overreaction. "I'm headed for the clinic."

"And I'm off to scrub floors and dust." The woman beamed. "That house needs more than cleaning. Since his mother went off to Minneapolis, it could use a woman's touch full time. It's past time Douglas found a wife."

"Oh?" was all Kirsi could think to say. It wasn't the first time someone had commented to her that Douglas needed a wife. What would they say if she told them the truth—that she didn't plan on marrying? And what was this about Doug's mother?

"Yes, you'll probably meet her this summer. She usually manages to spend a few weeks here in August. Have a nice day!" The woman waved as she got into her gray sedan.

Shaking her head at the woman's matchmaking attempts, Kirsi slid into her Jeep and started the ignition.

She sighed at her own irrational response to seeing a gray sedan. *Paranoia isn't attractive. Get a grip. A few hang-up calls and a car tailgating once and you jump to the worst-case scenario. Drop it. You left that all behind you, remember? Leave the past in the past. Carrying it into the future only causes untold pain.*

Turning onto Main Street, she headed toward the clinic. The envelope in her purse had discouraged her. She hadn't told Cram that she'd already gotten her first official refusal from a medical resident she'd known in California.

*So? I didn't expect to find someone the first time out.* But it still bothered her. *Lord, I've prayed for You to find someone to replace me. I know that You'll bring the right person here. Lord, help my unbelief.*

She turned into the clinic parking lot and headed inside.

"Mornin', Dr. Royston!" The robust Ma Havlecek in her pink volunteer smock greeted her from the reception desk. "You need to head right down to Veda's room—"

"No! She don't have to come to me!" Veda roared down the hall. The telltale slurring was still in the woman's voice.

"Ma, hand me her chart!" Kirsi hurried toward her patient, who was standing in the hall in her faded hospital gown. "Veda! You're walking so much better. That's great!"

Ma chased after Kirsi and handed her the clipboard.

Kirsi thanked her, speeding up to intercept Veda.

"Don't give me that!" Veda replied with an attempt at a sneer. "You said I had to do what that physic . . . al ther . . . pist told me and take my medicine. I did and now I want out."

"Come in the room." Kirsi urged the woman back toward her room. "We'll talk—"

"I don't want to talk. I want out." Veda halted.

"If we don't talk, you don't leave." Kirsi gave her a beatific smile.

Veda shouted obscenities.

Kirsi took her arm and turned her gently. "Oh, I bet you say that to all the doctors."

Veda gaped at her.

But Kirsi succeeded in getting her back into the room and seated on the side of her bed. After she'd taken Veda's blood pressure, she noted it on the chart and then looked up. "Now before I release you, I want to see your improvement. Please stand and walk to the door and back . . . and don't make me get after you or you're stuck here for the rest of the week."

"I'll leave if I want—"

"I'll have you put into restraints," Kirsi warned. "Walk to the door and back so I can see how well you do. *Now.*"

Veda grumbled, but she rose, and Kirsi observed her as she shuffled to the door and back to face Kirsi.

Kirsi offered her hand. "Please grip my hand with your right hand."

Veda raised her arm slowly as though it pained her and took Kirsi's hand. The grip was slight.

Not reassured, Kirsi released Veda's hand and jotted a note on the chart. "Please sit down while I read the notes from the social worker and the night nurse."

Veda cursed again.

Kirsi gave her the same serene smile, and Veda muttered her way over to the bed and sat again. The social worker's notes were extensive and agreed with Kirsi's assessment: Veda needed counseling and was probably suffering from chronic depression.

Kirsi was all too familiar with how that affected a life. "Veda, do you have trouble sleeping?"

"I do all right."

With pursed lips, Kirsi stared at her. "Answer me." She waited.

"All old people sleep less," Veda admitted finally.

Kirsi nodded. "Has it gotten worse over the past year?"

"No," Veda growled, "I've always been a poor sleeper."

Kirsi noted this on the chart. The reply didn't surprise her. It was consistent with her emerging diagnosis. "I'm worried about your high blood pressure. You realize that you had a stroke and that if you don't take care of yourself, you'll have another, perhaps a worse one?"

"Yeah, so what?"

Kirsi gazed at the old woman with sympathy. *Lord, how she fights any attempt to turn her toward health!* She thought of Saul on the road to Damascus. What had the Lord said, "Saul . . . it is hard for thee to kick against the pricks."

Kirsi leaned forward and searched Veda's eyes. "Do you want to be rendered helpless, bedridden?"

"No! I want to die!" Veda railed. "And I'm going to stop my mail. It's all junk anyway! That way—next time I'll be left to die in peace! They had no business bringing me here! I'd have died there on the floor in another day!"

Veda's words sliced through Kirsi. How often had she heard her own mother utter these words? *Oh, Lord, such despair, such anger turned inward. What can I do to turn this around?* A feeling of helplessness racked Kirsi, but she made herself go on. "It's not up to you to decide when you die. That's up to God."

"God and me don't mix," Veda snarled. "I've gone to church every Sunday of my life just so I could stare down the hypocrites. They've told you about me, haven't they? I hate everybody and they hate me. That's the way I want it."

Everyone had failed this troubled woman. "I don't believe that for a minute." Kirsi rose. *Lord, in the brief time that I have here, please help me not to fail this woman too.* "Veda, you can curse me and be as rude as you want, but you're my patient and I'll take care of you with or without your cooperation. Now you're going to work with the physical therapist again today—"

Veda tried to interrupt.

Kirsi forged on, "And the county psychologist will come to evaluate you this afternoon—"

"Psych . . ." Veda couldn't form the word. Her puffy face

turned red. "You're not sending me to any insti . . . nuthouse!" She stood up and tried to charge at Kirsi.

Kirsi sidestepped and neatly propelled Veda safely back onto her bed. She gripped Veda by her upper arms. "No one is sending you anywhere but home." She waggled Veda's arms slightly. "Listen to me."

Veda looked up with a resentful expression and her mouth tightly closed.

"No one is sending you anywhere but home," Kirsi promised again. "But I need to have you evaluated by a psychologist. I think your problem is chronic depression, but it might be more. It's obvious to me that you should have been treated for depression—"

"I'm not depressed!" Veda shouted.

"Anyone who speaks of dying alone and likes the idea is depressed. Period. End of discussion." Kirsi released her arms. "Now if you cooperate with the physical therapist today, take your blood-pressure meds, and cooperate with the psychologist, then I'll let you go home tomorrow. In fact, I'll drive you myself."

Veda glared at her.

"Do we have a deal?" Kirsi took her hand.

Veda let Kirsi hold her hand for a moment before she yanked it away. "Do I have a choice?"

"Not if you want out of here." Kirsi stood her ground.

"All right." Veda turned away.

Kirsi thought the woman was near tears. Unwilling to embarrass her, Kirsi stepped back. "I'll check back in later to see how everything went. Now cooperate one more day, and then I'll prescribe the medications you need and take you home. Deal?"

"Deal," Veda muttered without looking at her.

Kirsi touched her shoulder and marched out of the room, not giving Veda a chance to fire up again.

Ma waited in the hallway near the reception desk. She looked as though she'd been prepared to come to Kirsi's aid if necessary.

Kirsi gave her a smile and handed her back the chart. "I'm on duty at three today."

"You gotta go to the high school now, right?" Ma asked.

Stepping out of the doctors' lounge, Doug appeared in bloodstained and rumpled scrubs. "Good morning, Dr. Royston."

Assessing his obvious fatigue, she replied, "Long night?"

"Brawl at Flanagan's. Lots of stitching and bandaging."

"The joys of night duty in the ER." She started putting distance between them. Doug's smiling face had begun popping up in her mind whenever she wasn't busy. If she weren't very careful, she might convince herself that she had a crush on her colleague. And how unprofessional and foolish was that? And impossible. *I better keep busy*.

"Will I see you later?" he asked her.

"Don't know. I've got the high school thing first, and then I need groceries and there's laundry. Wish me luck!" She walked out into the morning sunshine, not waiting to hear his reply. Doug's effect on her was beginning to be an intriguing enigma—one she couldn't afford to unravel. That comment about Doug's mother only added to the mystery.

She headed for her Jeep. Behind the steering wheel, she glanced at the sheet of directions to the high school that Keely Turner had dictated to her over the phone. Going back through town, she turned onto the highway. She noticed that an older silver blue pickup turned after her.

Involuntarily, she eyed it in her rearview mirror. "Doctor, stop imagining things! You are starting to irritate me," she said to herself in a firm tone. How many years was she going to have to fight the fear? *I will fight it as long as it takes*.

She forced herself to admire the scenery along the highway. She'd never seen leaves in the vivid, fresh shade of green found here. Was this spring green? she wondered.

She glanced again at the map and into her rearview mirror. The pickup was still behind her, but not too close. "Can't anyone drive down the same road as you?" she demanded of herself. *Don't give in!*

Again, she focused on the road ahead and the striking scenery along the highway. The pastoral scene of pines, maples, and pastures dotted with black-and-white cows soothed her. A sign on the right announced the turn to the high school.

She made the turn and then allowed herself one more glance in the mirror. The pickup was still with her, but now at the slower speed, she could make out the driver—a woman. Kirsi sighed, scolding herself silently. *You're letting the attack at the clinic and a few phone calls stir up old memories and get the best of you. Stop it.*

Pulling into the high school parking lot and the visitor's spot she'd been directed to, she saw Keely Turner, her tall, graceful, blonde form advancing toward her with a welcome on her face. The woman's obvious confidence made Kirsi put her own back into place.

Keely escorted Kirsi down locker-lined halls to the gymnasium for the planned assembly. The thought of speaking about drugs and their abuse hadn't held any misgivings for Kirsi. But now as she stood on the speaker's platform and looked over the empty auditorium—while speaking into the microphone so the AV teacher could regulate the sound level—it hit her. She realized she'd be speaking to . . . teenagers. Memories of her own adolescent school assemblies played in her mind. Her stomach sank.

"The kids are all eager to get a look at you and hear you," the principal said. "You're big news around here. And they are really ready to get out for the summer. We are making up the last few snow days." She touched Kirsi's elbow. "You'll do fine."

Had her emotions been that transparent? Kirsi smiled but said nothing. Her heart was beating too hard for her to speak. She recalled a survey she'd read that said a majority of people were more afraid of speaking in public—than of dying! What had she gotten herself into?

Keely showed her to a seat on the platform. A bell rang and noise burst in from the hallway—voices, lockers slamming, footsteps pounding the linoleum, laughter, playful shrieks.

*And they're all coming to gawk at me!*

In a stunned and frozen silence, Kirsi observed the bleachers filling up—kids pushing each other, yelling, tossing books around, and a few earsplitting whistles. . . .

The bell rang again. Kids left standing rushed to seats. The noise quieted, yet voices filled the gym with a kind of restless hum.

Staring out over the assemblage, Ms. Turner tapped the microphone. Silence fell.

Kirsi looked up at the principal in awe. This was a woman who had presence.

"Good morning, students," Ms. Turner spoke in a genial but commanding tone. "You all know why you are here. Our new physician, Dr. Kirsi Royston, is going to give us a brief talk on narcotics and the dangers of using them. Please give her a warm welcome." Ms. Turner clapped her hands and turned to Kirsi.

Kirsi rose as though on puppet strings and shook the principal's hand. Then she stood alone at the podium, the black mike in her face and her gaze on the faces focused on her. She glimpsed the newspaper editor standing beside the bleachers at the far left and scowling at her. Great. Looking at his grumpy face would boost any woman's confidence. *Yeah, right.*

She cleared her throat. "Good morning, students. Thank you for your welcome." The words came as though on autopilot, words she'd heard so many speakers use during her life as a student.

From her pocket, she slipped out a few three-by-five-inch note cards she'd prepared. "Methamphetamine (commonly known as methedrine, or meth) is a very dangerous drug, and its use is on the rise. I'd like to read you a list of substances used in the production of methamphetamine, and I'd like you to think of what they all have in common." She cleared her throat. "Acetone, ether, sulfuric acid, methanol alcohol, battery acid, lye, muriatic acid, and red phosphorus." As she read the chemical names, she fought to keep a quaver out of her voice that threatened to reveal her stage fright.

When she finished reading the list, she scanned the faces before her. "If we were in a small group, I'd spend time pulling the answer from you. Since that's not possible, take a moment and think." She paused. "Now I'll give you the answer. What all these chemicals have in common is that they are all poisons."

Her nerves began to calm as she realized more and more that this was a message she'd longed to give. And the students' absolute attention bolstered her poise. She would persuade some—as many as possible—to heed her.

"Would any of you think of drinking a bottle of poison? Of course not. If anyone tried to make you, you'd fight them. So why do people—not just teens, because I've treated men in thousand-dollar, three-piece suits for taking meth or coke— take drugs? I have no answer. Since it isn't anything I have ever wanted to do, I can't supply it. Maybe you can." She gazed out over the audience, surprised at their continued concentration on her.

"You are all aware by now that one of your fellow students nearly died recently because he made the wrong decision. He said yes to poison when he should have said no. Meth not only can kill; it can be addictive. It can change your brain so that your brain and body crave it, need it, and always in greater amounts. I'm not here to preach to you. But I'd like to give you an image of what I think of when I picture narcotic abuse."

Absolute silence continued.

Her voice filled it. "You've all, I'm sure, studied the Civil War and slavery. Now historians can and do debate about whether slavery caused the Civil War. And what has that got to do with drugs? you ask."

She pinned the faces in front of her with her stare. "Sometime in the future, someone may offer you drugs—meth, crack, heroin. It doesn't matter which. Before you accept, I want you to take a moment and imagine yourself holding out your wrists for handcuffs and offering your ankles for leg shackles. Would any of you do that willingly? I don't think so. But if you buy the drugs or accept them, that's in effect what you are doing. You are giving control of your life to the drug dealer and to the substance he is offering you—"

"There's nothing wrong with a little weed!" an anonymous voice challenged her.

Kirsi fell silent. Should she respond to this or ignore it?

The principal rose and stood beside Kirsi, scanning the audience. Kirsi said nothing, but no one offered another challenge to her. Ms. Turner retook her seat.

The principal's example showed her the way. Full speed ahead. "Unfortunately, some people have that opinion." Kirsi grimaced. "But since marijuana cigarettes, joints, can be soaked in meth, can you be sure you are getting marijuana or something much worse than you expected?"

No reply.

She gathered up her nerve and pressed on. "There are so many types of drugs. The point I want you to get is that poison is poison and slavery is slavery. Don't let someone— a disgusting greedy criminal, someone you wouldn't even allow in your home—take control of your life! Did your friend think he was just smoking a joint and found out the hard way he was getting more than he'd bargained for?" She shrugged. "He can't remember. But he nearly died because of it."

Kirsi slid the note cards back into her pocket. "That's all. I hope if you have specific questions that you will ask your parents, your teachers, your pastor, or come to the clinic and ask one of the doctors. We would be eager to give you any information you want. Thank you for your kind attention." She eased down, feeling like a snapped rubber band.

Ms. Turner stood and joined the audience in its applause. She spoke into the mike. "Students, you have four minutes passing time. Go to your second-period class. You are dismissed."

The gym erupted with shouting, calling, shoving, running.

Kirsi sat in her chair, drained. "How do you do that?" she asked the principal. "I'm exhausted."

Keely smiled. "How do you stick needles into people? I couldn't do that in a million years!"

Chuckling, Kirsi shook her head. "Needles are easy."

Keely laughed. "I think I should walk the halls now, encourage the lagging to get to class. Why don't you sit here until the coast is clear?"

"Gladly." Kirsi remained sitting on the platform and watched the students exit. Cram didn't come up for a quote, and after the first rush he left. Finally, the gym had cleared, and the noise had receded to muted pandemonium. A bell rang.

Recalling the time-honored prohibition against walking on the gym floor with street shoes, Kirsi rose and walked around the perimeter of the polished hardwood floor to the nearest exit between the bleachers.

It was shadowy there, out of the direct lighting of the gym. She sighed with relief. It was over.

Suddenly hands seized her from behind. An arm around her throat. A dirty palm over her mouth. She tried to scream and fight. The arm tightened. She was thrust forward through a door into darkness. The door slammed behind her. She heard the door click.

In the blackness, she whirled around and fumbled for the doorknob. She gripped it and tried to turn it. It wouldn't give.

She screamed.

# CHAPTER SEVEN

*KIRSI? UNCONSCIOUS! HOW?*

His nerves stretched as tight as tendons, Doug pushed his way through the crowd. Teens clogged the corridor outside the high school nurse's office. Concern for Kirsi goaded him. "Let me through," he barked.

The students pulled back and separated, creating a narrow slit for him to squeeze through. He shouldered his way inside and shut the door.

Kirsi lay on a seventies vinyl medical lounger. Keely Turner was offering her a paper cup, probably water. But Kirsi's eyes didn't even flicker.

Concern tightened into worry. *I should have foreseen this.* Doug fell back on his role as doctor. He reached for Kirsi's wrist and felt for a pulse. "Where's the school nurse?" he asked Keely, his tone sharper than he'd intended.

"She's only here in the afternoons." Keely stood by, still holding out the paper cup. "That's why I called the clinic."

"Tell me what happened." It was time to let go of Kirsi's wrist, so he laid it gently beside her. Her pulse was nearly normal. This reassured his mind, but did nothing to bring his own racing pulse back to normal. He hadn't gotten many details—just the message that Kirsi had lost consciousness and to come right away. It was broad daylight and during school hours. What could have happened here? Well, Weston had gotten his almost-fatal overdose here. Not a good thought.

Kirsi's eyes flickered open. "I'm sorry to make such a fuss." She tried to sit up.

"Stay down for a few more minutes. Let your color get back to normal," Doug warned. He shifted on his feet, irritated that he could do nothing more to help her.

Keely offered the cup again. Kirsi took it this time, leaning on one elbow to take a sip.

He couldn't wait any longer. "What happened?"

Kirsi didn't even look at him.

"I left Dr. Royston in the gym after her talk," Keely started. "I thought she'd headed out after the kids cleared the hallways. I thought she was gone over an hour ago."

Deputy Burke Sloan, successfully scattering the crowd outside, entered the office and shut the door behind him. He walked directly to the principal and touched her shoulder. "What's happened?"

Doug wished he could do the same to Kirsi, but he doubted she would notice it. *And I shouldn't want to.* But worry made him care.

"I'm fine." Keely gave Burke a weak smile. "But Dr. Royston was attacked in the gym."

"Attacked? How?" The deputy gaped at Kirsi. "I got your message thirdhand with few details. Did anyone witness the attack?"

Clenching his fists at his sides, Doug moved closer to Kirsi. "I can't believe it." *This is Steadfast!* Had they entered the twilight zone?

Kirsi took another cautious sip of water.

"I don't think anyone saw what happened, but I don't

know. I haven't had time to ask if anyone was there." Keely pressed her clenched hands to her mouth. "I feel awful. Nothing like this has ever happened here. And especially to the new doctor—everyone will be so upset!" She gazed down at Kirsi. "I'm so sorry you were attacked at my school!" She gave Burke a pained look.

"How did it happen?" Burke asked.

Keely continued, "When the PE teacher went to get volleyballs out for third period, he found Dr. Royston lying unconscious—locked in the gym closet. She must have been in there nearly an hour."

Kirsi pushed herself up, swung her legs down, and sat up. "I'll be fine," she mumbled. "I'm fine."

That's what Doug had expected. Kirsi had already begun to rally. Even in the short time she'd been in Steadfast, he'd seen her determination not to depend on anyone before.

"Don't stand up yet," Doug cautioned. "Your color still isn't good." He pressed his hand on her shoulder to keep her from rising and to feel with his own fingertips that she was warm and whole.

Kirsi didn't resist his touch. Maybe she didn't even feel it.

Burke sank down, sitting on his heels, so he was eye level with Kirsi. "Can you tell me what happened? Try not to leave out any detail."

Doug moved behind Kirsi, both hands on her shoulders now. He felt her lean back onto him. Touch helped more than words. He gripped the soft cotton of her blouse. Her slender shoulders felt frail to him and very tense.

"I waited until the students had left; then I started out of the gymnasium." Kirsi paused to take another sip of water. "I was just walking out between two banks of bleachers when I was grabbed from behind."

Doug tightened his grip on Kirsi, anger igniting, flaring inside him.

"I started to scream." Kirsi trembled in one sharp motion. "He . . . he put his hand over my mouth. His arm was around my neck. I felt like . . . he was choking me. I tried to fight, but he was too strong."

Rage boiled inside Doug. He wanted to break something. Instead, he clamped his mouth tight. *Someone's going to pay for this.*

"He shoved me through a door and slammed it shut . . . behind me." Kirsi's voice broke. "I tried to open it . . . the door . . . it was locked. I pounded on it and screamed." She erupted into full-scale shaking.

Doug slid around the end of the chaise and sat beside her, still holding himself in check. Recounting what had happened was working against her, not for her.

"I'm claustrophobic," Kirsi admitted, her voice quavering and thin.

Doug cursed himself silently. "I should have come with you," he muttered.

Kirsi turned toward him. "How could you have known? It was broad daylight and in a public—"

"She's my responsibility," Keely broke in. "This happened on my school grounds."

"Neither of you is to blame," Burke said.

Doug assented that Burke was right, but with his mind only. His gut said he was to blame. He squeezed Kirsi's shoulder.

She tried to smile up at him.

"Did you see anything of your assailant, Doctor?" Burke asked.

Kirsi shook her head. "It happened so quickly. He came from behind. His hand was . . . dirty."

When Doug inched closer to Kirsi, she didn't move away. *I should have come with her. God, why didn't You protect her?*

Burke nodded glumly and rose. "I'll dust the door and

knob for fingerprints. I probably won't find anything but smears. But I'll do it anyway." He turned to his fiancée. "Do you have any suspects in mind, Keely?"

Keely frowned. "No. I have some students who are capable of doing something like this, but which one?"

"Are you sure a teenager is capable of overpowering Kirsi?" Doug asked. They couldn't assume that this was just a nasty prank. But he didn't want to say this in front of Kirsi.

Keely cocked her head to one side. "Have you seen some of our football players? Unfortunately, most of my male students, sophomore and up, are capable of overpowering Dr. Royston."

Then Doug realized that God *had* protected Kirsi. Anything could have happened to her today. She could have been raped, murdered. . . . Then he realized what he'd just thought. No wonder he felt drawn to Kirsi now. *She's my responsibility!*

"Did any student give Dr. Royston flak during her speech?" Burke asked, going on with his questioning.

Doug wondered what the deputy was thinking. Did he know more than he was saying?

Kirsi shook her head.

"Someone yelled, 'There's nothing wrong with a little weed,' " Keely recalled, "but I don't know who. How could we connect the two occurrences?"

Burke frowned.

Doug gritted his teeth, holding back words. He drew another inch closer to Kirsi.

"Can either of you give me any more information?" Burke asked. "Anything that might relate to this?"

"No," Keely said.

Kirsi shook her head, her eyes downcast. She leaned her head against Doug's shoulder.

Doug held his breath.

"Okay, I'll get busy lifting prints then." Burke kissed his fiancée on the cheek. "Don't worry. We'll clear this up ASAP." He strode out.

"Dr. Royston—" Keely bent down to be at eye level with Kirsi—"I'll leave you in Doug's care."

"I'm fine." Kirsi rose, shifting away from Doug in one swift move. "It just shook me up. That's all."

Doug stood up, bereft. Yet relieved. Being so close to Kirsi had made him feel things he didn't want to feel about her. *Don't play with fire.*

"Your reaction is completely appropriate." The principal touched Kirsi's arm. "You'd be abnormal if you hadn't been shaken up. Again, I sincerely regret this happening. I hope this won't give you the wrong impression of our young people. Most of them are good kids—just a little immature."

Kirsi nodded.

Keely left, closing the door quietly behind her.

Doug gazed at Kirsi, trying to think of any further comfort she'd accept from him.

"I'll be all right," she said with some of her usual grit.

Doug wanted to offer sympathy but hesitated. She was back to her independent self, and he didn't want to irritate her. Or for once, did she need reassurance? He groped for something to say, something that would get her talking and let her release some of the stress. "You said you were claustrophobic?"

"Yes, my mother . . . I . . . one of my earliest memories is riding in an elevator with my mother. She was gripping the railing and looked so . . . in pain. It scared me. I remember clutching her skirt and watching her, hoping nothing would happen to us."

He nodded, hearing how deep this went by her intense tone. "The strongest of our fears," he quoted, "are those passed on by our mothers."

She gave him the ghost of a smile. "Child Psych 101?"

"I read it somewhere." He studied her, imagining what nearly an hour in a dark closet did to someone who feared tight places.

"Well, it's true. My mother had . . . had suffered a horrible experience when she was a child, and she was claustrophobic afterward. Still is. I am too."

Doug refrained from asking about her mother's horrible experience. Kirsi had been through enough for one day—whether she'd admit it or not. Dredging up the past could only deepen her distress.

"What time is it?" she asked, appearing to pull herself together.

He glanced at the wall clock behind her. "Nearly noon."

She pressed a hand to her forehead. "I had things to do today before my shift starts at three."

"Are you sure?" Doug asked and then paused.

"I'll be fine," she declared. "I need to go grocery shopping before I get ready for my shift. I'll be fine," she repeated.

Doug knew better than to contradict her. "Mind if I tag along to the grocery store?"

She pinned him with a look.

He held up both hands while thinking fast. He came up with, "I'm out of my favorite snack."

"You may go to the store. It's a free country." She stood up and walked past him and out the door.

Impressed by her, worried for her, he followed. Would this independent woman be safe later at the clinic?

※ ※ ※

Kirsi felt the last of her quivering ebb as soon as she stepped inside the clinic for her shift. Merely donning her scrubs and braiding her hair before leaving her cabin had bolstered her. But all day she'd had flashbacks to the feeling of the arm clenched around her neck, the sensation of choking . . . the darkness swallowing her. . . . She stiffened her self-control. *I will not think about that. It's over. I will not let fear rule my life.*

In her mind, her grandmother's soft voice murmured, " *'But in my distress I cried out to the Lord; yes, I prayed to my God for help. He heard me from His sanctuary; my cry reached His ears.' Don't be afraid, dear child,"* Nani's voice added.

*Lord, why would anyone do that to me? What have I done to incite that kind of attack?*

Kirsi had been tempted to call home to California but had vetoed that. Even if she hadn't told her family what had happened, her grandmother would have sensed her troubled heart. She'd called her mother's apartment when she knew she would be at work and had left a falsely cheery message.

Her weary and treacherous mind reached into the past, bringing back cruel images—those of women who'd come to the ER after being raped or others who'd been beaten by husbands or boyfriends. She forced herself to blot these memories out. *I was only locked in a closet. Just locked in a closet—nothing more. Nothing like what happened to . . .*

She stopped at the nurses' station. Being here made her think of Doug. His nearness—so reassuring—came to mind. How had he known when to offer his touch and when to let her go?

*Don't come so near me again, Doug. I'm leaving. You're staying.* Her mind took her back to her cabin, her refuge. How safe she felt there—how isolated from pain and sin.

Wendy Durand, the sheriff's wife and Veda's great-niece, waited at the nurses' desk. "Good afternoon, Doctor."

Kirsi read the concern for her in the nurse's eyes, but she chose to ignore it. "Who do we have?"

"Weston and Veda are our only overnight patients." Wendy handed Kirsi their charts.

Kirsi noted hesitation in Wendy's expression and guessed its cause. "Don't worry. I'll take care of your aunt if necessary."

"I'm sorry—"

"No problem. As Veda's physician, I don't want anything upsetting her. I hope to release her again tomorrow."

"I'm glad. She hates it here," Wendy said. "Then both of them should be leaving tomorrow. Weston's finally well enough to get around by himself. Except for some weakness in his hands, he's doing fine. When he goes home, it will feel like things are getting back to normal around here."

"Let's hope so." Kirsi repressed a flashback of the blackness of the gym closet closing in around her. "I'll just look in on Weston Blake and then have some coffee in the lounge."

Wendy nodded, then answered the phone.

Glancing at his chart, Kirsi walked into Weston's room. "Hi, Weston. How does it feel to be finally getting out of here?"

The thin teenager smiled briefly. "Great. Can't wait."

Why didn't he sound more excited? Was he still not feeling strong enough to go home? "Is your mom fixing your favorite meal tomorrow?"

"Yeah, I guess."

Kirsi studied the young man. She'd heard about his being the father of a child due to be born in early summer and the fact that the mother, a girl named Carrie, was refusing to let him help her. Was he concerned about that? Or was he still worried about what had happened in his room that Saturday morning when he'd been asleep?

Now though, she only smiled at Weston. As soon as the emergency exit doors had been installed, police protection for Weston had ended. And the sheriff, as well as Old Doc, had decided that Weston could go home safely.

Who was she to argue?

❈ ❈ ❈

The shift had gone smoothly. Just a couple of minor burns and a bad sprain had come to the ER. Kirsi looked up at the clock near the ER entrance: 9:12 P.M. Her shift was nearly over, and she felt completely back to normal. The familiar routine had done the trick. If she could stay busy—

The ER doors burst open. "Where's the doctor?" the local pastor's wife, carrying her infant daughter, called out.

Standing at the nurses' station talking to Wendy and the receptionist, Kirsi hurried forward. "Into the first examining area!"

Kirsi, followed by Wendy, met over the table as Penny Weaver lay Rachel down. "She fell from her crib," Penny exclaimed. "She doesn't usually wake up at night and if she does, she calls me. This is the first time she's ever tried to climb out by herself."

Wendy began taking Rachel's vitals as the child cried, "Mama, Mama."

Kirsi questioned Penny, "She hasn't had any convulsions since the last episode?"

"No, she's been fine! I shouldn't panic, but I think she hit her head." Penny wrung her hands.

"Is the bedroom carpeted?" Kirsi asked, trying to assess how dangerous the fall had been.

Penny nodded.

A fall onto a carpeted floor? Unless the crib side had been unusually high or the floor wood or cement, why had Penny brought the child in? Why didn't she call for advice first? There wasn't even any bleeding, only a patch of pink on the child's forehead.

When Wendy supplied the child's temp and pulse rate, Kirsi began soothing the toddler. "Hi, there, Rachel. Did you take a fall?"

Rachel hiccupped and stopped crying. Kirsi repeated her question. The little girl nodded.

"Oh, that's too bad. Does it hurt?"

Another nod.

"Where?"

A chubby little hand touched her forehead where it had reddened.

"There?" Kirsi touched the little girl's hand. "Did you hurt your head there?"

Another nod.

Kirsi looked into the child's eyes. They were clear and alert though red-rimmed from crying. "Does it hurt anywhere else?"

Rachel shook her head.

"I'm going to touch you, Rachel, to see if everything else is fine, okay?"

Rachel just looked at her.

Kirsi gently examined the child's arms and legs, then turned her on her side and looked at her back. She smiled. "I think I have exactly what you need to feel better." She reached into a drawer of brightly colored Band-Aids, chose one, and applied it to the bump on the baby's forehead. "There. Now you're going to be all better."

Kirsi looked over at Penny. "Just watch her. If she seems abnormally sleepy, bring her back tomorrow. Otherwise, she should be fine."

Penny sagged with relief. "After those convulsions . . . I just worry so. The adoption isn't final yet! I don't want anything to disrupt the process."

Kirsi nodded, though she didn't know exactly what the woman was worried about. She'd met the pastor, his wife, and little son her first Sunday at church and had heard that the Weavers were in the process of adopting Rachel.

"What's all the commotion?" Veda McCracken's voice boomed through the quiet hallway.

Kirsi stepped out of the examining area. "Just a child who took a fall. You can go back to bed, Veda."

Veda voiced several obscenities and ended with, "I'll be glad to get out of this joint tomorrow. I'm never coming here again."

With a wry smile to show Veda that she was amused instead of annoyed, Kirsi waved her toward her room.

The old woman stalked back to her room, grumbling.

Coming out of the examining area, both Wendy and Penny gave Kirsi understanding glances. Did they think Veda's shenanigans upset her? Kirsi shrugged. "I'm going to get a cup of coffee in the doctors' lounge; buzz me if we get another patient." Kirsi wished Penny and Rachel farewell and headed to the doctors' room door behind the reception area.

She poured herself a cup of decaf coffee and switched on the radio to catch the local weather forecast. She listened to a golden oldie, "Wake Up Little Susie," and then local news. Finally, she heard, "The high today was sixty-eight. Tomorrow's high—"

"Dr. Royston!" Wendy's voice came through the intercom into the lounge. "Come to Weston's room. Stat."

Kirsi jumped to her feet, ran out the door and down the short hallway. She looked to Wendy first, who was standing beside Weston's bed. Her frantic expression turned Kirsi cold. "What is it?" Then she realized the bed was empty. "Where is he?"

"I've looked everywhere!" Wendy said, holding her voice down in spite of the urgency in it. "I stopped in to check his vitals. I've searched everywhere he might be—"

Unable to credit Wendy's words, Kirsi stooped and

looked under the bed and at the same time the other bed in the room. Nothing. She whirled to the bathroom.

"I've checked everywhere!" Wendy repeated right behind her.

"Then we'll check again!" Kirsi ran from the room, Wendy at her heels.

They rushed from room to room together, searching closets, bathrooms. They left Veda's room with her yelling after them and hurried on. Finally, they stopped at the nurses' station—both breathless.

The unexpected, the improbable had happened! Weston was gone. Why? Where? How? Kirsi tried to speak but couldn't. She cleared her throat and finally managed, "I'll call the younger Dr. Erickson and you call your husband."

Wendy stared at her. "What next?"

What next indeed? Kirsi headed for the lounge and reached for the phone there.

※ ※ ※

Doug bolted into the ER. He found Wendy at the reception area. As he ran by her, she told him the sheriff had already arrived and hurried after him. When Doug entered Weston's room, Kirsi stood opposite the sheriff—one on either side of Weston's empty bed. "What happened?"

"He disappeared sometime between Wendy's last two rounds." Kirsi spoke in a professional tone. "The patient was here at 8 P.M. Wendy checked him again at nearly ten and he'd vanished. She called home just in case he'd gone there—"

"Why would he go home—" Doug interrupted her.

"He wasn't there," Kirsi said. "Wendy behaved as if she'd simply called out of politeness to discuss some details about the insurance claim. She didn't want to alarm his parents . . . till we had to."

Doug went to stand beside Kirsi. "And no one saw him leave?" A feeling of unreality gripped him.

Kirsi shook her head. "He ate his evening meal and was watching TV—just the usual. . . . We think it might have happened when Wendy and I were busy with Rachel Weaver. Penny brought her in after a fall. Afterwards I went to the lounge, and Wendy went to check on our two patients. He must have slipped out—"

"And no one saw him?" Sheriff Rodd Durand asked.

Doug echoed the sheriff silently.

"I told you, no," Kirsi reiterated. "Your wife is the floor nurse tonight—you know that. But the ER nurse called in sick so we're shorthanded. I've been here since three this afternoon for my scheduled shift. During the time in question, the receptionist ducked into the rest room. Weston must have been watching, waiting. . . . He was supposed to go home tomorrow," Kirsi finished, her professional facade dissolving before Doug's eyes. She shook her head as though not believing her own words.

Doug moved closer to her but held back. Her stance bristled with "Don't touch me. I can handle this."

"That may have been the problem," Rodd said.

Doug tried to figure out what that meant and couldn't. "What?"

"I mean he may have felt safer here. It's been only three weeks since . . ." Rodd didn't have to finish his sentence.

Doug nodded.

"But why didn't he say something?" Kirsi insisted. "Ask for protection?"

Rodd hunched up his shoulder. "I . . . Weston convinced me that this had been the first time he'd used drugs. He wouldn't tell me who had given him the meth. I showed him a photo of our unidentified body. He said he'd never seen the guy. I believed him."

"He may have been telling you the truth," Doug said.

"Or now it seems more likely that he was lying through his teeth." Rodd grimaced. "Well, we can surmise that Weston went out through the ER entrance. The emergency exit doors didn't sound an alarm and are still secure."

"He'll be a sitting duck," Kirsi murmured.

Doug didn't know whether to respond to her or not. The doors had merely given Weston only one choice of an exit. "The security guard starts soon. He had to give notice and couldn't start immediately."

"I will have to treat this like a crime scene." Rodd looked at Doug as though he hadn't heard him. "Do you want me to notify the parents?"

Doug found his voice. "No, I'll call my grandfather. Granddad delivered Weston. I think the parents would take the news better from him than from anyone else. I hate to ask him, but I think he'd prefer to do it, too."

Doug fought his own frustration. He'd treated Weston's childhood illnesses himself. What had the kid gotten himself into? Was this tied up with the new drug gang? Who had the answers?

"I'm going to fingerprint everything in this room and the hallway outside his door," Rodd said, "in case someone helped Weston leave. I'll get to work right away. Will you call your—"

"But," Kirsi interrupted. "I . . . is that possible? I can imagine Weston dressing quickly and slipping out. But no one could come in—"

"Anything's possible in light of what happened to you earlier today." Rodd's crisp tone snapped in the quiet room.

Kirsi fell silent, her expression deeply troubled.

Doug stepped closer to her and touched her shoulder. This time she didn't draw away.

"Sorry," Rodd apologized. He looked like he wanted to

say more, but he just shook his head. "I better get started here."

"I'll make that call." Doug took Kirsi's elbow. Without demur, she turned with him and walked by his side out into the hall. Wendy was standing by the nurses' station.

"Wendy, your shift's over," Kirsi said in a strained voice when they reached her.

"I'm going to stay a little longer. I don't know how long Rodd will be here, and I don't want to go home to an empty house." Wendy's voice vibrated with her distress, giving voice to the helplessness Doug felt.

He had to talk to Kirsi alone. He headed into the doctors' lounge. Kirsi followed him. They faced each other but said nothing. Doug took the receiver from the wall phone and dialed home. His grandfather hadn't gone to bed yet. Granddad said he'd call Weston's family and go right over to break the news in person. Doug hung up.

Silence throbbed in the small room.

"I should be the one to tell the parents," Kirsi objected, a delayed reaction.

"You heard my reasoning." He folded his arms to keep from reaching for her.

She bit her lower lip. "This has been an awful day." She moved toward him.

Reading the look in her eyes, he opened his arms and she walked into them. They stood like a sculpture of a couple embracing. She was in his arms but did not rest against him. It was as if she craved human touch, but she wouldn't give in to the need completely.

He didn't try to coax her closer. He wanted to. He wanted to comfort her, hold her, but . . . she was not meant to stay here. And he didn't want her to resent him like . . .

Minutes ticked by audibly. The battery-operated clock was loud in the silence.

Finally, she let her forehead rest against his cheek.

The softness of her skin against his snared him, tied him in knots.

"I can't think what possessed Weston to run away the day before he'd go home—"

"Things are happening that we don't know about," he whispered, "and can't see."

She nodded.

He tensed.

"We need that evening security guard—," she murmured.

"I'll see he starts tomorrow night. I know it's like locking the barn door after the horses escaped, but . . ."

"You had to take your time to find the right person."

He sensed her drawing away. He wanted to hold on to her. Instead, he loosened his hold.

She pulled away. "Thank you for coming so quickly." She led him from the lounge.

His heartbeat thrummed at his temples. But she showed no evidence that being close to him had affected her. Just as well.

Doug stood by Kirsi and Wendy, and watched another deputy arrive. Doug forced himself to show nothing of his inner turmoil. When one of the other doctors in the county who took turns helping cover the clinic ER arrived to relieve her, Kirsi's shift officially ended.

She went and got her purse.

Doug was waiting for her at the door. "I'm going to follow you home." Ready for an argument, he waited for her to refuse his escort.

"Okay." She walked out through the automatic doors.

Was her acquiescence a good sign or not?

He hurried to catch up with her. She jumped into her Jeep before he reached her. He drove behind her, following her through the summer night. His windows were down, and he listened to the croaking frogs as he neared a wetland area.

He wished he could come up with some reason to go in with her and make sure she was all right. Bruno's cabin had seemed the ideal place for the new doctor. But now it hit him how isolated it was. Where would all this craziness lead? Was it almost over or just getting started?

Finally, they turned up the dark lane to her cabin. Would she want him to come in? let him come in?

She parked by her door. She got out, unlocked the cabin door, and stepped inside. She turned on lights and waved to him from the doorway. Then she closed her door.

Doug still waited, quelling the urge to get out and ask her if she wanted him to stay until she fell asleep. At last, he turned his car around and headed home. Evidently, those few moments in the doctors' lounge were all the commiseration the independent Dr. Royston would accept. He liked that. He didn't like that at all.

※ ※ ※

He watched the other car pull away. So she'd asked the doctor to follow her home. She must be worried. Sweet. In the silent, black night, he waited to see her lights go out, one by one.

It was starting now. She was getting it that someone wanted to hurt her. This was the fun part. He'd drag it out step by step, enjoying each twist and turn he'd invent. He chuckled. *I'm good at this.*

And then one night . . .

He liked to think about the time he'd finally go inside and turn the lights out himself.

And then he'd finish the game, finish her.

# CHAPTER EIGHT

ON A LATE-JUNE morning, Doug clenched his hands on top of the maple table, holding in all the images and sensations unleashed at seeing Kirsi here in Harlan Carey's kitchen. Doug had come to the prayer meeting more to gauge how his colleague was dealing with the aftermath of the past week than to pray. *I'm sorry, God, but it's the truth.*

It had been a week since Weston had disappeared. Doug sat beside Nick, Harlan's teenage boarder who was also Burke Sloan's nephew. The scent of bacon from Harlan's just-finished breakfast filled the room.

Across from them sat Kirsi. She wore an open-necked, plaid, short-sleeved shirt and dark slacks. As he observed her, she looped some of her hair over one ear. The morning sunshine from the bank of windows behind her picked up the warm highlights in her dark hair. She shimmered in the light.

Even as he fought his attraction to her, he sensed her disquiet. She'd distanced herself from him ever since Weston had vanished. Why? Did she think he blamed her? Doug tried to focus on Harlan at the head of the table.

" 'Come with great power, O God, and rescue me! Defend

me with Your might. O God, listen to my prayer. Pay attention to my plea!' " After this opening, Harlan looked up from
his worn black leather Bible lying open next to his mug of
coffee. "I'm glad you've all come this morning. After Kirsi was
attacked at our high school and then reading the *Steadfast
Times* Tuesday, the story about Weston running away, I
decided that this prayer group had better get started."

"Yeah," Nick said, setting down his empty glass of
milk. "School's out, but, I mean, everyone's talking about
Weston running away. He wasn't a friend of mine, but . . ."

"I know it's . . . unnerving," Kirsi said. "I feel so bad for
his parents."

Unspoken but very evident in her voice was "I'm
responsible for his parents' pain because I didn't prevent
their son from slipping out." How could he convince Kirsi
that it hadn't been her fault? Doug's nerves tightened
another notch with his frustration. He rubbed his hands
on his thighs, trying to release the tension in them.

Doug wasn't surprised that Kirsi made no mention of
the attack on her. That was like her.

"I talked to the sheriff last night," Kirsi said, her
anxious tone increasing Doug's awareness of the way she
edged forward on the chair, taut with stress. "They're doing
the best they can to find Weston, but there aren't any
witnesses or clues."

"We will pray for Weston and his family," Harlan
handed a small spiral notebook and ballpoint to Nick.
"We'll write down whom and what we pray for, so we can
see how God answers our prayers."

"I'd also like prayers for my mother," Kirsi added, looking downward. "My grandmother called me about her last
night. Mom has a chronic condition and it's flared up again.
We don't want this to interfere with the India trip."

Doug recalled Kirsi's words to his granddad: *"My*

*family's been praying for a family . . . reunion."* He wondered again what had happened to make Kirsi's mother claustro- phobic. What was the horrible experience? Why was that family reunion in India so important to her? Was something more than Weston's disappearance upsetting her?

"I'd also like prayers for Veda McCracken," Kirsi ventured.

Grimacing, Nick noted this on the open page in front of him.

Harlan beamed at her. "Thank you. I think you're the first person in a long time who has looked past Veda's rude- ness to the pain underlying it."

Doug thought of Kirsi's kind treatment of Veda. It took a special woman to see something redeemable in Veda. How did she continue to be unfazed by the old woman's cranki- ness and venomous words? Watching Kirsi handle the most hated woman in the county had given him more to think about. Each day he found himself looking forward to his first glimpse of the new doctor. . . . *But she's leaving. Don't do this to yourself.*

Nick frowned. "My uncle says that things are gonna get a lot worse. That new drug ring . . ." He shrugged.

"Everything I've done hasn't made any progress," Doug muttered, surprising himself. He hadn't meant to speak aloud. He experienced once more the powerlessness he'd felt each time Kirsi had been the target of this evil that threatened them all.

"I tightened security at the clinic." Doug couldn't stop the flow of his frustration. "I met with Rodd and Burke—"

"You aren't responsible for making the county safe," Kirsi reminded him.

Doug recognized the irony of her words. *You aren't either.*

She reached across the table and touched his hand with

hers. For only a moment, their fingers entwined; then he released hers.

"The answer is here." Harlan pushed the Bible in front of the teen. "Read the next two verses of Psalm 54 and see what God has to say about our situation."

Nick bent over the Bible. " 'For strangers are attacking me; violent men are trying to kill me. They care nothing for God. But God is my helper. The Lord is the one who keeps me alive!' " He looked up. "Cool."

Harlan grinned. "Cool."

This morning, Doug had come up with another strategy to put an end to all of this turmoil. He'd talk to his granddad and the sheriff about it today.

Kirsi needed a break from all this stress. So trying to shift the focus to a nonhospital and nondrug topic, Doug spoke up, "I'm concerned about the Weavers adopting little Rachel."

Nodding, Harlan folded his hands. "We must remember that prayer isn't only for intercession—asking for God's help—but also to glorify God and to center Him in our lives and our hearts. Prayer brings us back to the throne where we can experience the awe of a God who is able to answer prayers. In Hagar's words, 'the God who sees.' Before we pray, ask yourself if you have truly given God all your burdens."

Doug paused. It was as if Harlan's last words were darts aimed right at him. He hadn't given God his burdens—especially the faceless threat that's endangering us all. *It's impossible for me not to worry about this. I'm no saint.*

"Doug," Harlan interrupted Doug's introspection, "will you read verse five of that psalm?"

Glad for a distraction, Doug read: " 'May my enemies' plans for evil be turned against them. Do as You promised and put an end to them.' "

"Cool." Kirsi grinned at Nick.

Doug again marveled at this woman's ability to use humor even in the midst of a crisis.

Harlan smiled and then his face became solemn again. "I think that is our prayer about what is happening to our community. Let's pray that God uses their own evil against them. Let's go to the throne." Harlan bowed his head. "Dear Father, we need Your guidance. We only see shadows. You see what is really happening and You know the intent of every heart."

Unable to stop himself, Doug opened his eyes and glanced at Kirsi. Even as she bowed in prayer, her brows drew together in worry. Her dark lashes fanned her café au lait cheeks. He shut his eyes. *Lord, I want to lift her burdens. Let me.*

"Center us in Your love and provision," Harlan continued. "Let us go boldly into the arena for those we love and those we fear. Lead us with Your mighty hand. . . ."

※ ※ ※

The time of prayer had just ended when Wendy entered her grandfather's back door. "I'm sorry I'm late."

Relieved, Kirsi stood up. "I was wondering if we were still on for today." She'd been half afraid something might have happened to Wendy. *I have to stop imagining danger behind every corner.* But her last few nights had been marred by repeated breather calls. She rubbed her forehead, willing away a headache that threatened her.

Silently she recited another verse: *"Give all your worries and cares to God, for He cares about what happens to you."* *Lord, too much is happening. Why? I expected peace and a slower pace here, but nothing has gone as I anticipated.*

Doug stood beside her. She tried to ignore his nearness.

"I had a lot to do around the house this morning," Wendy explained, "and couldn't get away early to meet here first."

Harlan hugged his granddaughter. "Are you sure you're feeling all right? You look a little pale."

Wendy grinned. "I'm fine." She turned to Kirsi. "Ready for a day of home-health visits?"

"Can't wait." Kirsi lifted her purse to her shoulder. She turned, carefully putting her jaunty mask in place. She would leave everything behind her. The verses and the prayer had lifted her load of concerns. "Thanks, Harlan. This morning has given me back my perspective."

He squeezed her shoulder and smiled.

"Same time, same place next week?" Kirsi asked.

Harlan nodded. "We'll be here."

She waved to Nick and Doug, avoiding the latter's eyes. Why had he been watching her? She'd felt his attention all through the brief meeting. Perhaps he had picked up on her unease. She felt again his warmth as he'd let her draw close to him the night Weston had disappeared. But she couldn't give in to shock like that again.

"See you later," Doug said.

Nodding, she accompanied Wendy out to her station wagon and set off. Her mission today—to get a taste of Wendy's main job, home-health care, and a feeling for the county and its residents.

After a short ride, Wendy pulled up in front of a large white farmhouse with green shutters. "This is the Olson place. Olie and his son live here." Wendy grabbed her bag and headed toward the back door.

Kirsi hurried to keep up. But a line of tall bushes weighed down with lavender blooms snared her with their fragrance, making her pause to cup a cluster in her palm. "Lilacs! How lovely!" She smiled at Wendy. "They smell delicious!" *I won't worry today. I will have faith.*

Over her shoulder, Wendy smiled.

The back door opened before Wendy and Kirsi reached

it. "Hey, Wendy girl, you brung the new doc with you. I ain't got a close look at her yet."

"Dr. Royston, this is Olie Olson," Wendy introduced them.

A large, dry hand gripped Kirsi's. "Glad to meet you, Mr. Olson."

"Call me Olie!" The tall, thin man with flyaway white hair exclaimed in a bluff voice. "Everybody does!"

Then he waved them inside. "I been takin' my pills, Wendy. So you don't have to scold me!"

Kirsi tried to let the banter distract her thoughts that had strayed to that dawn phone call she had received. Another breather call. It's just some kid . . . but some kid had pushed her into the gym closet. *Stop it!*

Wendy pushed Olie playfully toward a kitchen chair and then set her bag of medical supplies on the table. "The proof's in the pudding, Olie."

"Hey! Let the new doc take my blood pressure. I'm tired of you, Wendy." Olie grinned like a boy.

Wendy chuckled and stepped back, handing Kirsi the blood-pressure cuff and ball.

Pushing away the fact that someone might be delighting in unnerving her, Kirsi stepped closer to the table and proceeded to take Olie's blood pressure. "Not bad—" she grinned—"127 over 84."

"You *have* been taking your meds!" Wendy gave Olie a thumbs-up.

Olie beamed and turned to Kirsi. "I guess you changed your mind and you're stayin'."

Kirsi refolded the cuff and handed it to Wendy. These questions had become standard fare for her. Maybe her announcement that she would be leaving had triggered the hang-up calls?

"I'm still looking around for a replacement," Kirsi gave

her regular reply. "But as I told everyone at the VFW reception, I'll be here as long as I am needed."

"Well, it took us a long time to get you here." Olie shook his head. "Don't think you're going to find anybody to take yer place."

Kirsi let this go. "That's what I hear." She smiled, ready to say good-bye.

Wendy sat down and Kirsi followed suit—though she wondered why they didn't leave. They'd come to check Mr. Olson's blood pressure. They'd done that, so why did Wendy think they needed to stay longer?

"How's your son, Ted?" Wendy asked.

"He's nuts," Olie declared. "He's selling his truck and it's only five years old. I told him, 'You just got it broke in!' I said, 'You don't see me selling my '72 Chevy, do ya?' He's crazy!"

"He probably wants something new."

"New-schmoo!" Olie said in disgust. "He's gonna take out another loan. Just throwin' money away!"

Kirsi tried not to fidget. But they had a lot of calls yet to make.

"That was a bad thing that happened to you, Doc," Olie said.

Kirsi steeled herself against her mind bringing up the terror of those dark minutes in the gym closet. "Just a scare," she passed it off.

"I call it nasty." Olie's voice became gritty. "I'd like to get ahold o' that person and not just me. There are plenty who'd like to get their hands on him," the older man barked, his face twisted.

"I appreciate your concern, but I can take care of myself," Kirsi said in as mild a tone as she could muster.

Olie tightened his jaw. "I hear you been takin' care of that McCracken woman."

Kirsi nodded, bracing herself. No one took Veda lightly.

"You watch out for her." He shook a gnarled finger at her. "If she can do you a mischief, she will. No matter what you done to help her. I knew her all through school from the time we were little, and she was the nastiest kid. Stealing other kids' stuff, sassin' teachers. She spent most of her school days sitting in the corner with her back to the class."

This information didn't have the effect Olie intended. Kirsi's heart ached for Veda. *Lord, I want to help her. I know You love her even if no one else does.*

Wendy gave her a look that she couldn't read.

"Everybody thinks you're gonna fall for Doug and marry him." Olie cackled.

Kirsi tried not to bristle. But this constant matchmaking was getting to her. "Doug's a great guy. But my family is in California. And sooner or later, I'll go home."

"Right! I told all of 'em—they're nuts. Just 'cause you're both doctors, that don't mean you're gonna up and fall for Doug—"

Wendy looked abashed. "Stop it, Olie. Dr. Royston's going to think you're the worst gossip in the county."

"That honor belongs to Mabel Frantz, and you know that!" he shot back with a grin.

Kirsi waved a hand in the air. "I don't let gossip bother me."

"Good! Don't pay them no attention. Buncha people always stickin' their noses where they don't belong."

The older man's assessment tickled her. Kirsi chuckled. "I don't know what you mean," she teased in an exaggerated tone.

Olie laughed out loud. "Old busybodies."

Soon Wendy and Kirsi waved good-bye to Olie and headed on to their next visit. "I could tell you wanted to leave right after you finished the blood-pressure check," Wendy commented.

"I thought you said we had a lot of calls to make."

"We do, but part of each call is to spend a few minutes with each patient. I plan out my route very carefully to be fuel and time efficient. Old Doc likes me to spend time with them because he wants me to keep track of more than just blood pressure. He wants to know if their family situation is okay."

Kirsi began to understand.

"Also this staying for a visit helps us keep our costs down in the long run. It prevents crises from cropping up." Wendy halted at a four-way stop. "If Veda would have let me drop by like this, she wouldn't have gotten to the point of needing critical care." She drove on.

Kirsi digested this. She thought Wendy was kinder than she would have been in these circumstances. *Have I ever forgiven the one who hurt my mother and started all this?*

"It also keeps elder abuse down. At least, Old Doc thinks it does."

Kirsi made herself concentrate on the present. "Because you come right into the home for more than a quick visit?"

Wendy nodded.

More and more, Kirsi was impressed by the senior Dr. Erickson. Not that the younger Erickson had proved any less capable.

❖ ❖ ❖

The day had passed smoothly. With their windows down, Wendy and Kirsi drove away from their final stop with Leo Schulz, who was recovering from a broken ankle. The day was warm and sunny, and it was hard for Kirsi to imagine how upset she'd been over another breather phone call this morning.

"Do you mind if we make a stop before I take you back to Grandfather's and your vehicle?" Wendy asked.

"Where?"

"I want to stop at the Family Closet and drop off a box of clothes. It's on our way."

"Family Closet?" Kirsi asked.

"It's the resale shop here in the county. It funds services for mothers and children in need."

"Sure. I love thrift stores. You never know what you'll find."

Wendy turned right at the next intersection and drove down a road that crossed the highway and then meandered through many different farms. Farmers drove tractors over fields, loosening up the soil between the rows of crops. Cows and their calves grazed in pastures. Daisies bloomed along the road.

Wendy drove up to a new house with a sign saying Family Closet in the window. She pulled in at the rear and jumped out. She opened the back of her station wagon and dragged out a large cardboard box.

Happy for a break, Kirsi followed her up the few steps, where Wendy pushed open the door of the back porch and walked into a kitchen.

A familiar-looking woman was putting price tags on a stack of infant clothing on the kitchen table. "Hey, Wendy! Hi, Dr. Royston! Got some more goodies for me?"

"Hi, Patsy," Wendy replied. "I managed to get Rodd to go through a few closets. He still had a lot of stuff from his great-uncle."

"Men! Pack rats!" Patsy Kainz shook her head.

Wendy put the box down on the counter and turned to Kirsi. "Would you like to browse?"

"Show me the way!" Kirsi grinned.

Wendy led her to the front of the house. In each room racks and tables displayed used clothing for all ages, plus toys and housewares. The place had been decorated in pale yellow, like sunshine on a perfect summer day.

Kirsi began looking through the household gadgets and then moved on to a box of like-new combs and brushes. Her hands paused as a thought struck her. *Did I clean my brush last night or not?* She couldn't remember. But this morning when she'd picked up her brush it had been free of her long tangled hair. . . .

She shook off the funny feeling that was trying to come over her again. *Stop the paranoia. I was tired and simply forgot I'd cleaned it.*

A petite, silver-haired woman whom Wendy—interrupting Kirsi's thoughts—introduced as Mabel Frantz approached Kirsi and asked if she could help.

A very pregnant young girl with dark hair was refolding and arranging items on one of the tables.

"How are you feeling, Carrie?" Wendy asked as the teen picked up a pair of frilly infant shoes.

Kirsi recognized the name and wondered if this was the girl who was carrying Weston's child. She looked at Carrie from the corner of her eye.

"I've had a bad backache all day," Carrie complained. "But I wanted to finish my hours here so I'd be able to pick out a few more clothes for the baby." The girl pursed her lips. "Your husband asked me if I had heard from Weston." She folded her arms, looking grumpy. "We haven't been on speaking terms for a long time."

"This is a hard time for you—"

"I'm okay." The girl turned away.

Kirsi wondered what Carrie thought about Weston's disappearance. Did she really not care?

Kirsi's cell phone rang. She lifted it from her belt. "Dr. Royston here."

"Hello, Doctor, this is Rodd Durand. Can you come to my office? A student has admitted to attacking you."

Icy needles pierced Kirsi's spine.

"Dr. Royston?" Rodd asked when he received no answer.

"I'm still with your wife. We're at the Family Closet. We'll come right over."

# CHAPTER NINE

WITH WENDY AT her side, Kirsi walked into the sheriff's department, one of the last places she wanted to visit. *For years I haven't had to deal with law officers over and over again. What's going on with my life here? Lightning doesn't strike twice—please, Lord!*

Deputy Burke Sloan met them. "Have a seat, please. I'll go tell Rodd you've arrived."

Kirsi sat next to Wendy on a row of metal-and-vinyl chairs near the counter. Wendy turned to Kirsi and murmured in nearly a whisper, "Why did the student come here? Wouldn't this be something that the principal would handle?"

Kirsi pursed her lips. *What's normal in this situation?* "I don't get it either," she replied in the same low tone.

"Dr. Royston?" Burke waited in a nearby doorway. "The sheriff will see you now."

Kirsi stood and her mind went into reverse. The scene where Rodd had interrupted the gaiety at the VFW to take her to the morgue washed over her. She couldn't move.

"Do you want me to come too?" Wendy touched her arm. Taking charge of her emotions, Kirsi shook her head.

"You don't have to wait with me. I'm sure someone will run me out to Harlan's to get my vehicle." *I'll be fine.* You don't have to hover, she wanted to say aloud to convince Wendy, and even more, to convince herself that she meant it.

"Are you sure?" Wendy rose, still hesitating.

With a smile and a shake of her head, Kirsi turned and walked to Burke. Thank heaven, she hadn't lost her ability to hide behind bravado. Through the window in the door, she glimpsed a teen. She passed Burke, entering the small interrogation room.

The room was plainly furnished with a scarred Formica table, gray metal straight-back chairs, and an overhead lamp. When she entered, Rodd rose and motioned her to the seat at the table facing the teen, who sat hunched over, head down. Kirsi stared at this stranger as she lowered herself into the stiff chair. Could he really be her attacker? Burke stationed himself at the foot of the table.

"Dr. Royston, this is Matt Witowski." Rodd stood at the head of the table. "Matt, tell the doctor what you told me."

Matt glanced up at her.

Kirsi studied the young man's face. The look in his eyes captured her notice. He appeared trapped, resentful . . . and afraid.

Lowering his eyes, the teen again stared at the tabletop. "Why do I have to tell her?" he mumbled. "I told you. Isn't that enough?"

"Tell her," Rodd repeated without a change in his voice.

Kirsi shifted, uncomfortable in this strained situation. *Why do I have to be here? I can't identify him as my attacker. I didn't see him.*

"Okay. I did it," Matt said, grudging each word. "I pushed her into the gym closet. I didn't mean to hurt her. I mean I just grabbed her and pushed her in."

"Why would you do that?" Kirsi didn't like the thin sound of her voice. But Matt's words had brought back the hollow feeling she got every time she recalled the attack. Cool panic lapped inside her, threatening to take hold once more.

Matt shrugged. "Don't know."

"Did someone pay you to scare the doctor?" Burke asked.

"No!" Matt raised his voice. "I told you she got on my case—telling me what I could and couldn't do—and I just wanted to scare her." Matt looked up resentfully. "Do I have to prove it to you?"

Kirsi knotted her hands in her lap. The terror of those moments in the blackness swirled inside her, rising higher.

"Yes, prove it to me," Rodd said in a quiet tone filled with menace.

Matt glared at the sheriff. "Why won't you believe me?"

Kirsi stared at the clock on the wall above Matt's unkempt head, hoping to block out the interview or at least trying to. The words of a psalm her grandmother had taught her came into her mind in her grandmother's lilting, East Indian–accented voice: *"In Thee, O Lord, do I put my trust; . . . deliver me in Thy righteousness."*

"Matt, tell us what you did," Rodd ordered. "Only you and the doctor know what happened. Tell her and she will tell us if you're the one."

Matt switched his glare to Kirsi.

She returned it, though unwillingly. Why prolong this? *"Bow down Thine ear to me,"* her grandmother's voice crooned. *"Deliver me speedily: be Thou my strong rock."*

"I hid under the bleachers," Matt said in a gruff tone. "I couldn't be seen there. After the bell rang, it got real quiet. I heard her get down from the platform and walk across the gym. I could see her through the spaces between the bleachers."

The thought of having been watched gave Kirsi goose-flesh. *"For Thou art my rock and my fortress,"* Grandmother murmured.

"I had figured which way she would go out 'cause it was the closest way to get out of the school."

Kirsi's insides tightened. The attack had been premeditated. Her heart pounded. *"Therefore for Thy name's sake lead me, and guide me."*

"Anyway, when she walked past me, I was ready." Matt almost sounded pleased with himself. "I caught up with her. I put my arm around her neck, and I covered her mouth with my other hand. She tried to break my hold, but she couldn't. I was gonna just push her down under the bleachers. There was a folded volleyball net lying there.

"I figured that'd make it hard for her to get up quick. Then I was going to run out the exit and circle around to the athletic field. If no one saw me do it, they couldn't prove anything."

Kirsi closed her eyes, hearing in her mind: *"Pull me out of the net that they have laid privily for me: for Thou art my strength."*

"But then I saw that the gym closet was just barely open, so I pushed her inside and pulled the door shut. I didn't know it would lock if I closed it."

Kirsi recalled the awful click of the door sealing her in. Her stomach quivered. She clenched her hands together and made herself open her eyes. Grandmother's voice whispered, *"[Thou] hast not shut me up into the hand of the enemy: Thou hast set my feet in a large room."*

"Then I took off." Matt shrugged. "I got lucky. I remembered my class was going to the school library. I saw them through the window. So I went inside and got in the library and acted like I was looking up something in the encyclopedia section. When my teacher finally saw me, I told her I'd thought we were supposed to meet at the library so I had gone there first. She bought it."

Kirsi tore herself free from the web of memory, from the dark closet. She insisted her senses deal with the present— the sound of a phone ringing, footsteps passing the door.

"Dr. Royston, what do you think?" Rodd asked.

Kirsi forced herself to look at Matt. She went over in her mind what he'd just said. Had he left anything out? "It sounds right, but why did he come here? Why didn't he just confess to the principal?"

"That's what I'm wondering." Rodd leaned toward the teen. "What's the answer to that?"

Matt's face wore a sullen expression. "I don't like having a woman principal, specially a Turner. I wouldn't confess nothin' to her."

Kirsi wondered what being a Turner meant and why Matt looked at her as though she had wronged him.

"Why confess at all?" Burke asked in a deceptively mild voice. "What are you up to?"

Matt swore and shoved back from the table. "Fine!"

Kirsi jerked back.

"Fine! You don't believe me!" He started for the door.

Burke intercepted him. "Sit down."

Matt tried to go around the deputy.

Burke grabbed his shoulder, whipped him around, and sat him back down in the same chair. "We're not done with you."

"You can't keep me here!" Matt flared.

Kirsi tried to make sense of what was happening. He'd admitted attacking her, but why?

"I can keep you here for twenty-four hours," Rodd said in an implacable tone. "Now I want to know why you have confessed to attacking the doctor."

"I'm not tellin'."

Kirsi was struck by how childish this sounded. Her anxiety ebbed a fraction. This teen had made her a target of a nasty prank—nothing more. But what was he so obviously afraid of?

"Yes you are," Rodd insisted.

Matt stared down at the table.

Kirsi looked to Rodd and Burke. What did they expect from her? She pushed back from the table. *You don't need me for this.*

Rodd stood up straight. "Okay, Matt, we'll let you stew for a while. Think it over. Dr. Royston, do you want to press charges?"

Kirsi wondered why he asked her in front of Matt. Did he want her to say yes so he could use that as a prod to get the truth? Or was she supposed to say no? "Can I think about it for a minute?" she hedged.

"Sure. Let's step outside and leave Matthew alone." Rodd motioned toward the door.

Burke opened the door and let Kirsi walk out. Rodd brought up the rear and shut the door behind them.

"Let's go into my office, Doctor," Rodd suggested. "Burke, make sure he doesn't leave."

Burke nodded and sat down on a chair outside the door.

In his office, the sheriff gestured to an institutional-looking chair in front of his neat desk. "I can't figure this out," he began without preamble. "I don't know why he came to me and confessed."

"I don't know why he would either," Kirsi said, reassured that she and the sheriff had picked up identical vibes. "This doesn't make sense."

"I know," Rodd agreed. "We have no evidence that we can use to prove anyone guilty of shoving you into that closet. I don't see his motive."

"Perhaps he thought someone else was about to squeal on him?" Kirsi suggested.

Rodd shook his head. "In that case, it might have put him on the spot, but all he had to do was deny it. We have no hard evidence against him."

Kirsi stared at Rodd and he stared back. Her mind tried in vain to come up with another motive. She thought of Doug. What would he say to this? "What do you want me to do, Sheriff?" she finally asked.

"I don't think there's anything you can do for me. I'll go back and question the kid again and try to rattle him enough to get at the reason behind his confession. I might be able to do it. If not, I'll send him home." He looked up at her. "Unless you want to press charges."

She lifted both palms. "Should I?"

"I wish I had an answer for you. Matt could very well have done it. But why the confession? And why come to me? Until we have those answers, I'd like to wait on pressing formal charges. I don't like to do that unless I'm clear on what's going on."

"I don't blame you." Kirsi rose. *Should I tell him what's been happening?* But she couldn't bring herself to voice the cause of her sleepless nights over the past week.

Rodd followed her out the office door. "I'll have one of my deputies drive you home."

"Thanks. But I need to go to Harlan's to pick up my Jeep." She walked past the small room where Matt was still sitting.

As they reached the entry area, behind them they heard Burke demand, "Matt, what do you think you're doing?"

Kirsi and Rodd swung around.

"Hey!" Matt called after Kirsi and Rodd, starting after them. "Hey! Where you goin'?"

Burke had caught Matt by the arm.

Matt's fear—very real and very obvious—colored his voice and lit his eyes.

Kirsi stared at him.

"Where Dr. Royston is going is none of your business," Rodd barked.

"Has she pressed charges against me yet?" Matt whined.

"No!" Rodd nearly shouted. "We haven't decided what to do with you yet."

"She's gotta press charges!" Matt wailed in real panic. "She's gotta!"

✴ ✴ ✴

Later, in the Erickson kitchen, Kirsi leaned past Doug to pick up the creamer on the counter. Doug had met her at Harlan's and insisted she come home with him for supper. She'd accepted, dreading going home . . . alone. She realized that she liked—and didn't like—Doug worrying over her. He was showing more concern than if she were just his colleague. Did he realize this?

She turned to the open refrigerator and filled the creamer from the pint carton of half-and-half. The shared meal had done much to relieve her inner commotion. Before, question had chased question through her mind. Now she concentrated on the cool feel of the china creamer in her hand and the buttery scent of cake. Shutting the door, she set the creamer on the table.

"You're telling me that Matt *wanted* you to press charges against him?" Doug repeated as he cut squares from Mrs. Benser's luscious-looking, golden pineapple upside-down cake.

"His exact words were 'she's gotta press charges.'" Kirsi rested her back against the counter beside Doug.

The senior Dr. Erickson sat at the head of the table. "Matt comes from a troubled family. His dad left his mother to raise three sons by herself. She has to work too many hours and isn't really strong enough to keep three teens in line. Matt's been in trouble before—vandalism, petty theft, that type of thing."

Another beleaguered single mom. "I don't know if he even did it or not, and if he did, why confess . . ." Kirsi let her words trail off. As Doug cut the cake, she stole a pinch of the brown-sugar topping that had fallen on the counter. Popping it into her mouth, she savored the rich sweetness on her tongue. *This will all blow over. Please, Lord!*

The phone jangled.

Kirsi flinched at the sound.

Doug's grandfather reached for the receiver. He gave one-syllable replies and then said, "I'll come right away." He pushed away from the table. "I have to go in."

Involuntarily, Kirsi held out her hand as though to stop him.

Doug looked over his shoulder and frowned.

Kirsi guessed that he didn't want his grandfather to leave them either.

"Just put my dessert plate in the fridge, and I'll eat it when I get home." Dr. Erickson walked toward the back stairwell.

"Okay," Doug said, sounding disgruntled.

*Now I'll have to leave,* Kirsi thought—even though it would have sounded ridiculous if spoken aloud.

Dr. Erickson chuckled as he lifted his keys from the rack by the door. "I'm happy to be needed on my one night on call. I'll be back before you know it. Just a rush at the ER." With a wave to Kirsi, he ambled out the door, heading for his car.

Kirsi stared after him.

The confrontation at the sheriff's office had shredded

her peace. Being here eating and making conversation with both Doug and Dr. Erickson had made her feel like the whole world hadn't gone crazy.

Dr. Erickson had been there, as a buffer between Doug and herself. His sudden departure altered the atmosphere in the kitchen. Now Doug and she were alone together. She felt even more defenseless, exposed. Why?

Kirsi pulled away from the counter, distancing herself from Doug. She couldn't hold back her complaint any longer. "Is it just me or does it seem to you—over the past month . . . that everything that can go wrong has gone wrong?"

His hands stilled. "Yes, that's exactly how it seems to me."

Raising her arms overhead, Kirsi arched her back, stretching her spine, trying to work out her tension. Suddenly aware of Doug watching her, she righted herself and folded her arms. "I know it's a coincidence that the incursion of the new drug gang started right before I arrived. But it feels personal. Like someone's out to get me." Her voice lowered in her throat, thickening with pent-up emotion as she spoke these words for the first time.

Doug handed her a gold-rimmed china plate with her piece of cake on it. "Let's try to get some perspective." He motioned for her to sit and then he followed suit.

She faced him across the table. His calm voice irked her. What perspective?

"Someone's not out to get you," he began. "If I'd gone to give the talk at the high school, you wouldn't have been attacked."

"And if I hadn't gone to check on Weston," she mimicked his soothing tone, "I wouldn't have been knocked down and that . . . that man might not have been killed. I can't become invisible so nothing happens to me. It's impossible!" She put down her fork and cupped her forehead in both hands. Her temples throbbed with a budding headache.

Doug put down his fork and put both his hands around her arms propped on the table.

The strength in his long fingers reassured her, yet keyed her up more. Her nerves tingled.

"This isn't productive," he continued in a steady pace. "No one's out to get you—"

"Then who keeps calling!" She let her hands fall from her face. "Who keeps calling me and then hanging up?"

* * *

Doug's hands froze around Kirsi's arms, her words shooting shock waves through him. "Calls? What do you mean?"

"Someone keeps calling and hanging up without saying anything." She gazed at him, her valiant chin lowering. "In LA, we called them breather calls. I try to ignore—"

"How long has this been going on?" His voice grated low in his throat. He tightened his grip on her bare arms, her skin warm and silken under his touch.

She turned her face away from him as though ashamed. "Since the night we met here with the sheriff and his deputy."

His breath caught. Didn't she trust him? "What? Why haven't you said anything?"

"Because it might not be anything!" Kirsi tugged away from him and stood up. She began pacing. "How do I know that it isn't just kids doing it for a prank?"

"Because someone—" Doug pushed back from the table—"knocked you down at the clinic—"

"And that someone is probably still lying unidentified

at the county morgue." She turned her back to him. "And the kid who says he pushed me into the closet is just that—a kid! I thought you just told me *not* to take this personally—"

"That's before you told me about the phone calls."

"Why does that make a difference? If this isn't personal, then the phone calls aren't personal. But that's how they feel." Her lower lip quivered.

"You should have told me." He reached her side.

"Why?"

"Because . . . because you're my responsibility!" The words felt ripped out of him.

She swung around to face him. "No I'm not! I'm your colleague. You take too much on yourself. You think you're responsible for everyone. You're not! You're only responsible for your patients, your grandfather, and you. It isn't your job to protect me! I can handle this."

He gripped her slender shoulders. "We brought you here."

"I came of my own free will." She half turned from him. "And I've taken care of myself for years. . . ."

"Sometimes you're too independent, Doctor." He had to make sense of this. "I don't want to smother you," he entreated her understanding. "I just don't want you to take risks. Now tell me what's been happening." He tugged her to him.

She gave way in one swift movement, letting herself rest against him.

He folded her into his arms. He felt her tremble. *Lord, help me protect her.*

"I get calls. I pick up. No one answers. I hang up." Her voice sounded muffled as she let him draw her closer. "I keep telling myself that this wouldn't worry me if all the rest of what is going on hadn't worked its way into my mind. I don't like this feeling . . . the feeling that I'm in danger, that someone is watching me."

Doug held her to him, pressing his cheek to her soft hair. "I don't think anyone is watching you—unless you've seen someone—"

"No," she cut him off.

"Okay. Then your worries are on target even if it's only phone calls. You should be concerned. This county may have a low crime rate, but that doesn't mean that bad things can't happen here." *They already have!* "Now tell me how often you get these calls."

She turned her face toward him, imploring him without words. "At first, just one every few days, but now I'm getting at least one a day, sometimes two or three." Her troubled expression hit him hard.

"Then you're not making a big deal over nothing." His voice roughened. "We need to tell this to the sheriff—"

A single tear rolled from her eye down her tan cheek. "But maybe the caller was the kid who has confessed to pushing me into the closet. Maybe they'll stop now."

"We have no way of knowing that." He gently wiped away the tear with his finger, the tip gliding over her smooth skin. "And we should tell the sheriff. I don't know how easily they can trace calls, but this might help him in his investigation."

"I . . . I . . ." She buried her face into the cleft between his neck and shoulder. "I just want them to . . . stop."

Doug pressed his cheek against the top of her silken head and rocked her gently. *Lord, what's going on? What do I do?*

"I'm sorry to fall apart like this." Kirsi turned her face up toward his. Only an inch separated their lips.

He felt her warm breath against his mouth.

"I had a . . . a roommate in college who was stalked by

a former boyfriend." Her voice shook. "That makes it worse. It makes me remember what I . . . we—" she took a deep breath—"all we went through until he was finally prosecuted."

The naked anguish in her expression caught around Doug's heart.

Her black luminous eyes looked up into his. Her lips parted.

He kissed her.

# CHAPTER TEN

KIRSI'S LIPS WERE soft under Doug's. So soft. So willing. His mind tried to intrude—*this is a mistake.* He blocked it out and concentrated on drawing in more and more of the excitement that kissing Kirsi brought him. He tightened his embrace, her softness a wonder. He couldn't draw her close enough. He longed to blur their separation.

"Kirsi," he whispered, or did he just imagine speaking her name? Her name cascaded through his mind and with it, images of her—in her bright saris at church, in her scrubs examining a patient, in her cabin doorway, looking out with that wistful expression. *Don't leave,* he urged silently.

This thought shocked him. *I've fallen in love with this woman.* He loosened his hold on her. *She doesn't even want to be here. I'm making the same mistake my father made.* But he couldn't stop kissing her warm lips. *Kirsi, change your mind. Stay here with me.*

She pulled away.

Doug reached for her but then let his arms drop. *Kirsi, I need you. But I can't hold you here. I won't try.*

❈ ❈ ❈

Kirsi stumbled backward from Doug. *What was I thinking?* Her conscience replied, *You were thinking that kissing Douglas Erickson was more exciting than you had imagined. You were enjoying the feel of his arms*—Kirsi cut off her inner voice.

"I'm sorry," she mumbled and took another step away from him while he stood there—exuding temptation, beckoning her to return to the warm nest of his arms.

"I'm the one who should apologize." He didn't meet her eyes. "I started it—"

"No, I shouldn't have turned to you like that. It isn't like me." *It's my fault.* She rubbed the back of her tight neck. "It must be everything that happened today . . . ," she alibied, "everything that's happened since I arrived here." She folded her arms in front of her, presenting a physical barrier between them. She wasn't afraid he would try to breach her tenuous defenses; she was afraid she would take a fatal step forward and . . .

"I've gotten a nibble," she blurted her news from out of nowhere. *Why didn't I tell him earlier?* "A resident I knew in LA. He wants to get out of the city and live in a more natural environment. I e-mailed him photos of my cabin, and he went berserk!" She could hear herself babbling. *Stop it!*

"That's good to hear," Doug said, his arms now folded too. But he didn't sound happy. He still appeared to be focusing on a point over her right shoulder.

*Why did I kiss him back? Why did I let this happen? I'm leaving soon. I have to! I'm an idiot for starting . . .* "I think it's time I went home—"

"Wait." Doug stopped her. "We're going to phone the sheriff about your phone calls."

"It's late," she quibbled. *I should have called the sheriff myself and not involved Doug.*

"I'm calling him now." Doug walked over to the phone and lifted the receiver.

She followed him, undecided. Should she let him or not? She watched Doug harden his jaw as he waited for the sheriff to answer. Her eyes moved automatically to his lips. Warmth suffused her. *I just kissed Doug Erickson.*

A pause and then he spoke, "Sheriff, Kir—Dr. Royston has been getting weird calls more than one or two a day. The line rings, there's breathing, and then the caller hangs up."

Kirsi reached for the phone. *This is my problem.* "I should be the one telling him this."

Stepping aside, Doug relinquished the receiver. But his expression warned her that he wouldn't let her fudge on how much she told the sheriff.

"Sheriff—," she began.

"I don't like to hear this, Doctor," Rodd said.

"It could be harmless, just kids . . ." She doubted her own words. But it might be.

In front of her, Doug grasped the back of a kitchen chair as though bracing himself.

"You mean kids like the one we talked to today?" Rodd said with a sardonic edge to his voice. "I want you to call the phone company tomorrow morning and request a new unlisted number. But first, you haven't seen any evidence of anything else we should worry about, right?"

"What do you mean?" she asked, beginning to untwist the long, snarled phone cord to avoid meeting Doug's gaze.

"Like someone following you."

*This isn't happening. But it is. I've been in denial too long.* She worried her lower lip. Should she tell him about the sedan that followed her her first Saturday in town? Of course not. It had just been her imagination. "No, nothing but phone calls."

"Okay, do you have a cell phone?"

"Yes." She concentrated on untwisting the cord. She felt Doug's breath on the side of her face. She leaned away, her shoulder propped against the wall.

"Tonight disconnect your phone and keep your cell phone at your bedside." The sheriff's voice became more stern. "And I'll have my deputies patrol your area all night—"

"That isn't necessary." Her nerves twisted with each word. She started picking apart an intricate knot in the telephone cord.

"I like to play things absolutely safe," Rodd insisted.

"What did you do about Matt?" she asked, trying to deflect the sheriff's interest in her.

Doug released his hold on the chair and straightened, staring at her.

"Matt's cooling his heels in jail overnight. I didn't want to let him go until I'm clear about what I should do with him. Would you press charges if I asked you to?"

Suddenly Kirsi felt exhausted. She dropped the knotted cord. *Not a time to make decisions, Sheriff.* "We can discuss that tomorrow. I'll call you. Good—"

"Will you do what I said about disconnecting your phone tonight?" Rodd cut in.

She mulled this over. Would disconnecting help? Or . . . or what? She didn't know.

Doug hovered near, so near.

"Doctor—," the sheriff prompted.

"Yes, I will," she conceded. *Anything! Just let me hang up, Sheriff, and let me get away from Doug!*

"Good. Oh, by the way, Jayleen Kainz called to say that she saw something she thought might be gang graffiti at the A&W. Burke went over to see what he thought. He's had experience with gangs in Milwaukee. This might give us something to go on. Give us something to follow up."

Kirsi wondered how gang graffiti would help them and

what it had to do with her. But after saying good-bye, she hung up.

"What did he say?" Doug said.

She repeated the sheriff's instructions while clearing the table, still avoiding eye contact with Doug. The pineapple upside-down cake had gone uneaten. Now the smell of its rich buttery topping made her queasy.

"That's what he wants you to do?" he asked, sounding as though he thought the advice woefully inadequate.

She frowned. "I know it feels silly to get excited over some prank calls." But from Doug's worried expression, she guessed what neither of them wanted to say aloud—that too much craziness had taken place since May. And there were too many unknowns to simply dismiss the phone calls. She'd been whistling in the dark for too long.

She headed toward the back hall, ready to say her thanks and leave. *I should have told someone, maybe the sheriff about the calls last week when they started increasing.* But she'd chosen to think that she couldn't suffer harassment in this small, innocent-feeling town.

She halted on the top step of the rear stairwell, wanting to leave, dreading to leave. *Doug, what did we start tonight with that kiss?*

"I'll follow you home," Doug said, right beside her.

She opened her mouth to object and then shut it. What if someone were watching her, waiting for her? *Dear God, this can't be happening again.*

"Kirsi?" Doug touched her arm.

She moved away. "Okay."

❖ ❖ ❖

Kirsi woke, the golden sunshine streaming in her windows. She glanced at her bedside alarm clock. It still had ten minutes before it sounded. *What woke me?*

Then everything that had happened the day before rushed back. Matt confessing to pushing her into the closet at the school, Doug kissing her . . .

She touched her lips. Closed her eyes. Her lips warmed as she imagined Doug's lips on hers again. The web of lush sensation threatened to snare her once more.

She pushed the comforter up and swung her feet over the bedside. "No time for regrets. I've got a busy day."

Her cell phone beside her alarm clock rang. She picked it up. "Hello?"

"Everything okay?" Doug asked, his tone diffident.

"Of course I'm fine. You followed me home, made sure no one was hanging around inside or out, and you saw me lock everything up tight."

*Kirsi, methinks thou protests too much.* "Okay. Just checking."

Silence.

What was she supposed to say: "Sorry about that kiss"? And what would he say: "Don't mention it"?

"I have to get busy. I'm doing a prenatal class in the church basement this morning, and I haven't prepared yet," Kirsi finally said.

"And you have to spend some time on the phone getting a new number."

"Thanks for reminding me. I love calling company menus: 'If you are right-handed, press one. If you want eight thousand free minutes, press three.' "

"Very funny. Catch you later. Bye."

"Bye." She hung up.

She walked out of her bedroom and went to the kitchen to make coffee. As she measured the coffee and water, she gazed out her window. Daisies and yellow yarrow had planted themselves in her wild backyard.

While the coffee perked, she headed for the shower.

Turning on the water, she checked to see if her razor needed a new blade. The razor wasn't in the shower. She looked down. Had it fallen?

No.

She moved the shower curtain. No.

After examining the small bathroom's linoleum floor and the shower inch by inch, she gave up. *This is weird. Too weird. That brush and now a missing razor?*

The hot water fogged the mirror. She opened the medicine cabinet over the sink where she had a spare razor. Her regular razor sat there next to her spare. Holding her misgivings at bay, she sighed loudly. "Kirsi, you're losing your mind."

�֍ ✖ ✖

Later, Kirsi knocked at Veda McCracken's back door and waited. The tall pines around the house rustled in the flamboyant summer wind. Kirsi knocked again. "Ms. McCracken! It's Dr. Royston! I've come to check your blood pressure!"

No answer.

Kirsi noticed that the windows were open. A car was visible through the very dusty window of the nearby detached garage, which listed to the right as though it might collapse. Kirsi tried the doorknob. Locked.

Had Veda gone for a walk? Kirsi looked around.

A red pickup pulled in and parked in front of the garage. Nick and Harlan got out. "Hi, Dr. Royston," the teen greeted her. Nick approached with a large grocery sack in his arms. Harlan waved as he ambled toward her.

Kirsi noted that Harlan moved more slowly than he usually did. "I don't think Veda's home."

"She's home," Harlan grumbled. "She just won't answer her door. Veda!" he called. "I'm leaving your groceries on the back step. There's ice cream. So don't let it melt!"

Harlan leaned close. "Wait here real quiet, and she might think you've gone, too, and open up."

Nick set down the bag of groceries and grinned at Kirsi. He and Harlan got back in the pickup and drove off.

Kirsi wondered if she should stay or go.

The door opened behind her.

Kirsi bent over and picked up the grocery sack. "Great. I just have time to take your blood pressure before I head off to the clinic."

Veda glowered at her. "I don't want my blood pressure checked! Go on to that clinic! I'm taking my medicine, and I don't want you checkin' up on me all the time." The woman snatched the bag from Kirsi's arms and slammed the door in her face.

Kirsi stared at the door, openmouthed. Then she tried the knob. It turned in her hand. She pushed the door open and walked inside. "Roll up your sleeve, Veda , or I'll be here all day. I'm not taking no for an answer."

Veda turned from her refrigerator, where she had been stowing the rectangular ice cream package. "I don't need you takin' care of me—"

"Roll up your sleeve." Kirsi returned Veda's glare.

Veda flounced over to the cluttered kitchen table and held out her arm. "Do it and get outta here!"

Kirsi hid her smile. Just another charming visit with Veda McCracken.

❊ ❊ ❊

A few days later while on duty, Kirsi glanced at the clock in the ER. Her shift was about over and now a rush. The EMTs should be here any—

The siren blared.

When the ambulance pulled up, Kirsi waited, poised just inside the ER doors with a nurse beside her. The EMTs hopped out, opened the back door, and slid out one stretcher, then another. They pushed through the doors. Blood soaked the shirt of the first patient.

"Fight at Flanagan's!" the EMT explained to Kirsi as he hurried the stretcher toward the examining area. "We have two for you, and then we have to go back for two more. It was a mess! Took the sheriff and three deputies to get things under control."

Kirsi hurried alongside the wheeled stretcher. "Where's the primary injury?"

"Stab wound to the chest area. I think it pierced a lung," the EMT huffed as he showed her the pressure bandage. Kirsi pressed a button on the wall and barked into the intercom that the second nurse was needed. Then she listened to the EMT recite the vitals before he left.

She peeled back the sodden bandage and watched sluggish blood seep from the gash. She'd need an X ray of his chest. Stat. Through the curtain, she called to the nurse in the area next to her. "What have you got? Do you need me?"

The nurse announced the other patient's vitals. Her patient also had been stabbed, but it looked superficial.

The ER doors swished open. "Hey! Anybody here?" a stranger called out. "My pal's been shot!"

Kirsi pressed the button on the intercom again. "Call the radiologist! And Dr. Doug at home!"

After that, the sudden rush of patients consumed Kirsi's and the nurses' attention. The radiologist bounced back and forth, shuttling patients to and from the X-ray room.

Doug swooped in with two strangers—a man and a woman—at his side. He introduced them to Kirsi while the three of them donned green scrubs and gloves. "Dr. Royston, Dr. Martin and his wife, Dr. Braun-Martin. They are going to give us a hand tonight."

Wondering who these people were, Kirsi nodded to them. She then filled them in on the patients she'd stabilized but who still needed further treatment. Then the EMTs arrived with another gunshot wound, and she was too busy to wonder who and why the two doctors were here and helping out. She was so busy that even Doug's presence didn't throw her.

Later, Kirsi slumped into a chair in the doctors' lounge. Holding a mug of strong, black coffee, she went over in her mind the patients she'd treated and asked herself if there were any symptoms she'd missed or anything that might lead to complications.

Doug entered, ushering the two doctors toward seats at the table.

Kirsi straightened up, pulling herself together for company. "Good. I was hoping you'd stop in here before leaving. I wanted to thank you for appearing at just the right moment."

Doug walked toward her.

Her heart did a jig.

The very feminine silver-haired one of the couple smiled and sat down across from her. "My husband and I were glad to help. We're up here at our cabin on Baker Lake."

"The Martins are old friends," Doug said, sitting down beside Kirsi. "They stopped by to visit Granddad this evening."

The hair on her neck prickled at his nearness. She took a nonchalant sip of her coffee. Too soon. It scalded her tongue.

"Yes, we've decided to retire a few years earlier than we'd intended," Dr. Martin, a tall man with a salt-and-pepper mustache, added.

Kirsi put down her coffee and rested her hands on the table. Showing casual indifference to Doug, she hoped.

"That's *semiretire,*" his wife put in. "I don't know how I could retire completely."

"Yes, Doug's grandfather understood that," Dr. Martin said. "And we're happy to see him taking it easier this summer. He's carried a heavy load for too long."

"Where will you be retiring?" Kirsi asked and began tracing circles with her right index finger on the smooth tabletop.

"Here." Dr. Braun-Martin smiled at her. "We're putting our house in Wauwatosa on the market, and we'll be living here year-round."

"You'll be practicing here?" Kirsi looked to Doug. *Two more doctors at the clinic. This is great news!* Why wasn't he smiling?

"Yes, and our friends the Nelsons, who are visiting us from Iowa, are interested in semiretiring here too. They've come up to visit us several times over the past few years and love this area as much—"

The door burst open. The nurse looked shaken. "Dr. Doug! It's Deputy Sloan! He's been shot!"

The next few minutes were a blur to Kirsi. Soon, law-enforcement officers crowded the entire reception area.

Unconscious, Burke lay on the examining table while the nurse reported his vitals and Doug examined the wound. "It looks like it missed any vital organs. I don't think it even nicked a lung."

"He is very lucky," Dr. Martin observed.

Kirsi hung back, not wanting to crowd the room.

Dr. Braun-Martin stood at her side. "Do you know the deputy well?" she asked Kirsi.

Kirsi shook her head. "I've only met him a few times. He's getting married this summer."

Dr. Braun-Martin turned to her. "He may be wearing an interesting sling to his wedding."

Burke's eyes opened. "Matt?" he rasped out. "Matt?"

"Burke," Doug replied in a clear even voice, "you're in the ER at the clinic. You've been shot. You're going to be all right—"

"Did someone get Matt?"

Kirsi moved forward, slipping in front of Dr. Martin. "Burke, do you mean Matt Witowski?"

"Yes, I found him . . ." Burke grimaced with each word as if it hurt him to talk. "He was . . . in parking lot at Flanagan's just like . . ." his voice trailed off.

"Just like that first body?" Kirsi asked, her nerves constricted with each syllable.

Doug made eye contact with her.

"Yes," Burke said. Pause. "I found him . . . shot . . . I opened my cell phone . . . called Rodd. . . . That's all I remember."

Kirsi and Doug exchanged glances, communicating shock without words. First, the unidentified man found at Flanagan's; then Weston disappeared, and now Matt!

She turned and hurried out into the reception area. "Which one of you brought Deputy Sloan in?"

A young deputy stepped away from the reception desk. "I did."

"Did you see another body near him?"

"Body?" the man looked at her quizzically. "No, I . . . should I have?"

"He says he found Matt Witowski wounded in Flanagan's parking lot—"

The deputy ran toward the ER doors while barking into his cell phone.

Less than half an hour later, Kirsi heard a siren just outside the ER. The Martins had left only moments before. She stepped out into the hallway and watched the deputy help Matt Witowski out of the backseat of his patrol SUV.

Calling for the nurse and Doug, Kirsi hurried forward, meeting the deputy inside the automatic doors. "Matt! What's happened to you?"

Matt's legs started to buckle under him.

The deputy gripped him to his side to keep him on his feet. "Come on, Matt. You've gotten this far, just a little farther."

Kirsi got under Matt's other shoulder and helped the deputy half carry Matt into the first examining area. The teen's weight pulled at her, threatening to take her down with him.

Matt gazed at her with eyes glazed with pain. "He kept calling," he mumbled. "He said he'd get me. He shot me." A weak sob slipped through Matt's lips.

Kirsi's heart pounded. What was he talking about? She hadn't seen Matt since that day at the sheriff's office. Matt had been let go. Rodd hadn't thought a prank on school grounds was sufficient cause to charge a minor.

"This doesn't make sense," Doug said as he hurried toward her. "Flanagan's doesn't serve minors. They take pride in being a real man's bar, not a teenybopper hangout. Matt, what were you doing at Flanagan's?"

"I . . . he must have dumped me . . ." Matt's eyelids drooped shut.

He became deadweight in Kirsi's arms. She swayed. Doug slid his arm between her and Matt and took the load.

With a nod of thanks, Kirsi rushed ahead.

The nurse caught up. Doug and the deputy lifted Matt onto the examining table. Then the deputy stepped back, letting the nurse take Matt's vitals and hook him up to an IV. Donning fresh gloves, Doug and Kirsi examined Matt's bloodstained shoulder.

"It just missed his heart," Doug murmured.

She nodded, fear pressing its spurs into her heart.

Doug called for the radiologist. "Where was he?" Doug asked the deputy who had brought Matt in.

"I missed him in the dark when I found Burke," the deputy explained. "Matt was off to the side beyond my headlights, and you know they don't light Flanagan's parking lot anymore. If Burke had been conscious, able to tell me about Matt, I would have brought the kid in at the same time—"

"We know," Kirsi replied as the radiologist arrived, ready to wheel Matt to the X-ray room. "Tonight's just been crazy."

She and Doug exchanged glances. She felt like burrowing into his arms. Who was doing these things? Why?

# CHAPTER ELEVEN

AFTER THE CRISIS had been dealt with, Doug waited outside the doctors' lounge as Kirsi took her turn changing out of soiled scrubs into shorts and a blouse.

When she emerged, Doug motioned for her to precede him. And for once, she didn't argue that he didn't need to follow her home or tell him she would be fine, thank you very much. He was steamed. Another life-threatening development had reached out and involved Kirsi. *None of this should have happened. It's bizarre.*

After trailing her home over the deserted dark highway, he jumped out of his vehicle and held the door of the cabin open for Kirsi. He wasn't leaving until he was certain she'd be safe alone here tonight and until she opened up and told him what she was thinking.

Silent, she led him inside. She switched on a lamp and a subdued glow gilded the room. The June night was unusually warm, and she opened the windows, letting in the night breeze.

Doug stood, looking around, stalling for time. What should he say? What good would words do, anyway? What was he going to do to protect Kirsi? *Whatever I do she won't like it or want to cooperate.*

"I can't take it all in," she murmured as she sat down on the sofa, sinking deep into its soft cushions.

Relieved at this opening, Doug eased down onto the armchair adjacent to her, the worn upholstery brushing underneath his thighs. The summer breeze billowed the curtains. Everything looked normal, but tonight nothing was normal.

"You're ready to admit then," he challenged her suddenly, "that something's going on, and you're in it whether you want to be or not?"

Kirsi looked at him.

He tried to read her expression, but most of all his arms ached for her, craved to hold her against him, protect her from the unknown evil that threatened her. *Kirsi, what's going on in your mind?*

"I told you—" she paused to clear her throat—"that a roommate of mine was harassed when we were in college."

Gazing into her somber face, he nodded, restraining himself from reaching to touch her.

"I lied." She cast her eyes downward. "I was the one who was stalked; it was during my first year of medical school. It was one of the main reasons I agreed to your grandfather's contract."

He gripped the arms of the padded chair. "Why did you lie?" *Why to me?*

She pulled her knees to her chest and looked over at him. "It was the most terrifying time of my life." She closed her eyes as though trying to pull herself together—but without success. "Whenever anyone finds out about it . . . everyone wants to know every detail. I don't like recalling every detail."

He stared at her, recalling their kiss. "I'm not—" he forced the words out—"everyone."

"But you've been upset with me and hovering over me at the same time ever since I came!"

"With just cause!" Doug slid off the armchair. "Ever since someone knocked you down in the clinic. Ever since that someone was murdered."

"How could we have known what would ensue? Don't you see I couldn't give in to the fear? Until the man in California was caught and imprisoned, he nearly destroyed my first year of medical school. I won't let it—the terror—take over my life, my mind again! He's still in a California prison, and I thought it couldn't happen here." She pressed her face into the tops of her knees.

He settled down beside her on the couch. *Lord, why does she always resist my help?* He rested his hand lightly on her shoulder, only the thin cotton of her blouse separating his palm from her warm skin. "You're not alone. We aren't facing this alone. God is here."

"Don't preach to me." She turned her face away from him. "When the harassment started in LA, I prayed and prayed. I came out alive—that's all!"

"That's a lot. And it didn't stop you. You're here, aren't you?"

She nodded her head like a puppet on a child's hand.

He slid closer to her. "God brought you through last time," he whispered, trying to console her. "He will this time too."

"It isn't fair! Wasn't once enough? Why is this happening to me again?"

Doug had no answer for her. He glanced at the small mantel clock. Nearly 1:00 A.M. Too late to phone the sheriff. "You're not alone," he repeated. He gazed at her, sensing that there was something more. If he asked, would she tell him now?

He tightened his grip on her slender, elegant shoulder. "Kirsi, is there something else you're not telling me? Did the stalker in LA actually assault you?"

"No." Again, she pressed her face into her folded knees.

Wanting to cup her delicately sculpted face in his hands, Doug waited. What was it? And would she tell him?

"My mother . . ."

Doug moved his restless hand to the nape of her neck as lightly as he could, saying without words that she could trust him.

She lifted her face but didn't look at him. "When my mother was a child, my grandmother's oldest brother visited her in California." Kirsi spoke slowly as though approving each phrase before letting it out. "He said that he had come to patch things up, that the family had forgiven my grandmother. She was thrilled. But it was a lie. When grandmother reneged on the marriage the family had arranged for her, she had disgraced the family. And he'd come to punish his sister."

Kirsi paused and swallowed with difficulty. "He was unbalanced. Later after he was convicted in California and then deported to India. His family had him institutionalized, and he died there. . . ."

"What did he do?" Doug fought to keep his voice calm, his hand gently massaging her neck. What had the man done that was so terrible to still affect Kirsi a generation later?

"My mother was only eight . . . he shoved her into the trunk of a car he'd bought and drove her through the night, through the mountains to Nevada." Her words began to rush, flowing together. "She thought she was going to die. He told her he was going to kill her and throw her body off a mountain and nobody would ever find her."

Unable to resist any longer, Doug encircled Kirsi's shoulders with both arms. "Dear God, no," he whispered.

"It was awful for her—careening over mountain roads in that trunk. . . ." Kirsi shuddered. "A gas-station attendant, listening to radio bulletins about the details of the kidnapping, noticed the car and got the license plate. He called the Nevada State Police, and they caught up with my great-uncle at a roadblock."

Doug rubbed his forehead against her satin hair. "That was your mother's horrible experience?"

She nestled against him. "It scarred her for life. She's never recovered fully. That's why she's claustrophobic. And why . . ."

*And why you are too.* He gathered her deeper into his embrace, breathing in the last of her cinnamon scent.

"It marked her," Kirsi began again. "Grandmother said nothing was ever the same. My mother couldn't live apart from my grandparents, so she didn't want to go to college. She married, but my parents' marriage didn't last. I hardly know my dad. He lives in Oregon. After the divorce, my mom couldn't take the pressure of being a single mom, even with help from my grandparents. All through my childhood, she has been institutionalized on and off with persistent depression."

Doug felt Kirsi trembling. He tightened his hold around her softness. In contrast to Kirsi's childhood, his had been the all-American ideal—almost a "Mayberry" experience. Even though his mother must have been unhappy living in a small town, it had never touched him because she loved his father enough to keep it from him and to stay—but only until his father died.

His mother's abrupt departure . . . her unhappiness here. The thought grieved him, more than ever now that he knew Kirsi would never be happy here either. *I can't keep her here.* Pain clamped hard over his heart.

"When I was being stalked," Kirsi went on in a defeated tone, "I couldn't tell my grandparents. They'd suffered enough over my mother's chronic depression. And of course I couldn't tell her. I've always had to make everything look perfect for her."

This last statement sliced Doug's heart in two. No wonder Kirsi always fenced with him! Always to hide her fear—even from herself. She'd always had to gloss over imperfection and make life appear fine for her mother's sake. *Now I see.*

Doug pressed a gentle kiss on her temple. Another. "We'll face this together." He kissed her cheekbone. "I won't let anything happen to you." He nudged her chin up so he could look into her eyes. *Believe me, Kirsi.*

She pulled back a few inches to stare into his eyes. "You can't protect me twenty-four-seven. You take too much onto yourself—"

Her eyes, always so mysterious, glistened in the low light. "Look who's talking?" he teased. He raised an eyebrow at her. "You face a stalker in LA without telling your family. And here you give the impression that you can handle anything, everything! Even when it's something like a vicious murder that the sheriff would even have trouble taking care of."

He studied her face. "You're not alone in this. And you're right. I can't be with you day and night. But the whole county is behind you—" he paused—"and God too."

She tried to give him a wry smile. "You sound as stubborn as I am."

Doug moved, closing the gap she had created between them, their warmth meeting. What could he say? He didn't have the answers. This wasn't like a difficult diagnosis, where he had to unravel the mystery of symptoms to find the culprit virus or bacteria. People weren't predictable like microorganisms. He had no vaccine or antibiotic against this threat.

"I still wonder where Weston is," Kirsi said in a fretful tone. "How could he just vanish? Why did he?"

"Granddad thinks he must have left the county and

headed for a big city, maybe Duluth or Minneapolis." Doug rested his chin lightly on her head.

"But why?"

"He must have been scared . . ." He shrugged.

"I can't help thinking that these things must all be related."

"That's just our human nature. Just because weird things—"

"Not weird things—dangerous ones! I know what you're going to say, Doug."

Their gazes met. "What am I going to say?"

"That just because these things have taken place around me doesn't mean that they are aimed at me. And I'm sure you're right. But I could be right, too. Weston's disappearing and Matt's turning himself in and everything else could have something to do with me."

Doug had no answer to that. He traced her cheekbone with his forefinger.

She shivered at his touch.

⊗ ⊗ ⊗

Kirsi heard the sound of an engine. She jerked upright. A car door slammed.

Doug sat up.

Kirsi stood, icy dread slicing through her. *This is foolish. I'm in my own home and Doug's here. God, don't let the fear take over again!*

A knock on the door. Fighting her jittery nerves, she strode to the door. Again, she heard her grandmother's distinctive voice reciting Scripture: *"The Lord is my light and my salvation; I will fear no one."*

Doug jumped up and tried to get in front of her.

*I will not be afraid.* Shouldering ahead of Doug, she opened the door—without first looking out the window.

Sheriff Rodd Durand stood on her step with his hat politely in one hand. "I'm sorry to bother you so late, Dr. Royston, but I had to go over what Burke and Matt said to you tonight."

He looked over at Doug whom she could feel bristling at her side. "Glad you're here too, Dr. Doug. That will save me from maybe waking up your grandfather to talk to you."

Kirsi's heart still thudded against her rib cage. "Is Deputy Sloan still in good condition?" Masking her inner riot, Kirsi motioned for Rodd to come in. Reluctantly, she had left the deputy in the care of another county doctor who took an occasional shift in the ER.

"The other doctor said he's going home in another day but will need several days of bed rest," Rodd said.

"Good." Kirsi rubbed her tense neck muscles. "That's what I thought."

Rodd nodded, one hand hooked in his belt loop.

"Please come in and sit down." Kirsi turned, pushing Doug toward the sofa.

Doug gave her a look but didn't resist.

She went back to her place on the sofa, tucking her legs under her. Rodd took the armchair. Doug positioned himself at the far end of the sofa.

His withdrawal from her was understandable since Rodd had arrived, but she felt . . . disconnected . . . solitary. She rubbed her arms covered with gooseflesh, trying to warm them with friction.

At all times serious, now Rodd looked at both of them, his expression dour. Kirsi understood that look. She'd felt the same way repeatedly in the past—whenever her mother had fallen prey to her depression once again and had to be hospitalized.

She sensed Doug's unhappiness filling the space that

yawned between them. Still, she fought the urge to slide closer to him.

"I need to talk to you about what Matt was mumbling," the sheriff said, hat still in hand.

Kirsi felt a denial springing to her lips. She pressed them together tightly, stopping it. *I can't distance myself from this. It's not possible—not now.* "I'll try to remember exactly what he said."

Doug shifted on the sofa, reminding her of his presence, his concern.

"I wish you would. It's important I hear it exactly as he said it, the exact words he used." Rodd stared at her while turning his hat slowly in his hands.

Kirsi closed her eyes, bringing up the image of Matt as he leaned against her inside the ER. She gathered her strength and let herself experience the scene again as it had happened. His hair had smelled unwashed. His solid body had weighed against her, testing her strength. His wet blood had stained her scrubs, smeared her arms. "I think he said 'He shot me.'"

Sliding forward, Doug cleared his throat. "He said something like 'He kept calling. He said he'd get me.'"

Unable to stop herself, Kirsi glanced at him sideways. The calling—was it the same person who'd called her? "He also said something about being dumped." She pushed Matt's battered image away. "But just because he said that, doesn't make it true" she argued. "He could have been confused. He was badly injured, shaken."

"Matt *thinks* it's true." Doug rested his elbows on his knees. "But you're right; that doesn't mean it *is* true."

His face drawn, Rodd set his hat on the floor and held up two fingers. "Two things are true." He touched one finger. "Someone shot Matt—" he touched the second finger—"and left his body at Flanagan's, where it wasn't detected until Burke decided to go over the parking lot with his flashlight."

"Why did he do that?" Kirsi asked, laying her arm on the sofa cushion between her and Doug. *Take my hand.*

Rodd gave a half grin. "Because he's a good cop. He remembered that May night when the unidentified body was found at Flanagan's after a brawl there. He'd just cleared up another fight and wanted to make sure that he hadn't missed anything this time."

"I don't understand why no one saw Matt." With one hand, Kirsi gathered her loose hair in a bunch at the back of her neck. The cabin had become warm or was it just her? "Why did Burke have to use a flashlight? Wasn't the parking lot lit?"

Rodd sat back and sighed with fatigue. "In some counties, law officers have been driving through parking lots of bars, jotting down license numbers and parking off-lot and waiting. Then when people come out and drive away drunk, it's easier to track them and catch them. So the bars have doused their parking-lot lights. That way police officers can't just drive through and jot down numbers so easily."

Kirsi grimaced and released her hair. "That doesn't make good sense to me. Don't the bars care that they are liable if they serve someone and then let them drive away drunk?"

Kirsi felt Doug's attention lingering on her.

"I've quit trying to make sense of what people do," Rodd said. "People do such stupid things all the time."

Kirsi couldn't argue with that. "So Burke went over the parking lot with a flashlight and found Matt wounded—"

"So who shot Burke?" Doug clasped his outstretched hands. "The same person who shot Matt? And do we know who shot the unidentified body?"

"The only lead I have on that is the bullets removed from

Matt and Burke—one each. I've sent them to the state lab
with a rush on it. I should have the results back tomorrow."

"That fast?" Doug said with a question in his voice.

Kirsi moved her arm on the sofa closer to Doug.

"When a lawman is shot, his case moves to the head of
the line." Rodd's sober expression slid into grim.

*This is hard for him—his friend wounded and a case that
won't let itself be solved.* Kirsi leaned forward, away from
Doug. "Do you have any news about Weston?"

"Confidentially?" Rodd lifted one eyebrow at her.

Kirsi folded her arms around her as though cold.
"Confidentially." She couldn't shake the feeling of vulnerability, a kind of nakedness.

"He's called his mom twice from pay phones in the
county. To tell her he's all right. Not to worry."

"Oh," Kirsi breathed.

"You traced the calls?" Doug asked the question that
flashed through her mind.

"Yes, but they led us nowhere," Rodd replied. "His mom
thinks that he's staying nearby because Carrie is due to have
his baby any day now. I will have your clinic under surveillance from the minute Carrie comes in to give birth."

"You think Weston will come out of hiding to see his
baby?" Restless, Kirsi slid her legs out from under her.

"Can you think of any other reason he'd be hanging
around?" Rodd asked.

"I can't figure out why he's still hiding." Kirsi mused
aloud. *Why can't this all end?*

"It has something," Rodd insisted, "to do with the man
who tried to disconnect his IV and was later killed. That's
too much of a coincidence for me to swallow."

"But haven't you proved that connection?" Kirsi asked,
struggling against the fear burrowing into the pit of her
stomach. *Doug . . .*

"Let's say that after years of dealing with criminals—" Rodd paused—"I have developed a sense of how their minds work. Usually people look for intricate schemes and motives when they think of criminals, but my experience has taught me that most criminals aren't masterminds like the ones you read about in suspense thrillers. Most of them have very basic motives. Greed, lust, and revenge being the most common."

Kirsi shivered, grateful that Doug was only inches from her.

"From informants, we know for sure that a new drug gang has entered the county and is marketing meth." Rodd's voice droned on inexorably. "We know that Weston had taken meth either by intention or accident and nearly died from the experience. We know someone tried to kill him at the clinic or at least make his condition worse than it was."

"And that person was killed within a week." Doug shifted in his corner of the sofa. "Why?"

Kirsi recalled being in the shelter of his arms. *I want Doug to hold me, but I can't let him. It would be dishonest because I'm not staying.*

"Because the person didn't succeed in harming Weston maybe?" Rodd suggested.

"Sounds logical," Doug muttered.

"That's where we lose the thread. We don't know if Weston actually could ID someone or not." Rodd exhaled deeply. "Now Matt is shot. And we don't know for sure if he is the one who pushed Dr. Royston into that closet at the school—"

"Or just claims he did." Kirsi wanted to know if anything ever rattled Rodd enough to ruffle his bone-deep calm. *I envy you, Sheriff.*

"You're right. All we have to go on is speculation, because no one knows if Matt is telling the truth or even knows the truth." Rodd paused again. "This case is enough to make a preacher swear."

So the sheriff just hid his frustration better than most. Kirsi couldn't think of anything to say in disagreement. She lifted her face, gazing at the beamed ceiling.

Doug and Rodd sat in tense silence. The low light illumined their faces faintly, showing nothing but intense concentration. The curtain at the window fluttered again. An owl hooted and the frogs from the nearby lake croaked. All this drama in this serene setting. *Lord, how can that be?*

Kirsi sighed. "I'm tired, Sheriff. I need to get some sleep. I have second shift again tomorrow or should I say today? And Doug's on duty at 7 A.M."

Rodd picked his hat up off the floor. "I had two more reasons for coming here tonight, Kirsi. First, I know that you came from Los Angeles. In the past decade, some LA gangs have 'franchised' parts of the Midwest drug trade. Did you have any history with a gang out in LA?"

Kirsi frowned. "I treated plenty of gang members over my residency. But I don't think I had any run-in with any particular gang or gang member. Do you think it's possible someone followed me here?" That outlandish thought had the power to make her spine freeze.

The sheriff shrugged. "I don't know. I just had to ask. It is a possibility—improbable but possible."

"What was your second reason for coming?" Doug asked as though trying to blot out the sheriff's concern.

Rodd pointed his hat at Kirsi. "I want you to move into town."

His deceptively calm words made her nerves vibrate. "What?"

Doug moved closer to her on the sofa.

*You don't think I'm safe here?* She wanted to shout this. She swallowed the words instead and looked to Doug.

"In Weston's case and in Matt's, you have been involved," Rodd went on, "and then you had those phone calls—"

"They've stopped now!" The words felt wrenched from her. "I'm unlisted and everything is fine."

But in the back of her mind, she thought of the razor that had been moved. *I just imagined it had been moved because of fatigue. I won't let paranoia set in. I won't end up like my mother!* This last thought shuddered violently through Kirsi's mind and body. *That's what I fear most of all.*

Rodd leveled his eyes on her. "I think you're too isolated out here, and we have at least one very dangerous person at large. He has a gun, and he isn't afraid of using it."

Kirsi's nerves leaped and twirled with tension. "But no one has done anything to me—except call me and hang up. And that might not have anything to do with Weston or Matt."

Doug squeezed her hand.

"I'm not in danger." Her voiced sounded shrill in her own ears. But she couldn't help her heart racing. "Nothing is going to happen to me."

Her final sentence summed it up. *There is no proof that anyone is trying to hurt me or planning to hurt me. I won't live in fear!* Her grandmother's voice came again: *"The Lord protects me from all danger. I will never be afraid."*

"I know I'd feel better if you moved," Doug ventured, rubbing her hand in his. "We have a bedroom and bath over our garage that no one's using now. Granddad had it fixed up for me when I first came home to practice so I'd have some privacy. Then when my dad died and my mom relocated to Minneapolis, I moved in with Granddad. He was rattling around in that big house. The suite's separate from the house but close and comfortable and you'd—"

"No." Kirsi stood up. "I'm not being stubborn." She

took a step away from Doug. "But there is no evidence that anyone is out to get me. None." *And I couldn't bear living that close to you, Doug. It would be a constant temptation to lean on you, to become dependent on having you around—not just for my safety.*

"I don't want you in harm's way." Rodd stood to object. "It's my responsibility to keep you safe."

"I am safe." A sudden urgency to put this all away made her adamant. "When you two leave, I'll lock all the doors and the windows if you like. I'm safe here. And I'm tired and I want to get some sleep." *If I can fall asleep after all this.*

Rodd shifted on his feet with obvious reluctance. "All right."

Doug stood also and opened his mouth as though to voice more objections.

Kirsi raised her hand. "Please we all need sleep." Her words came fast and smooth. "I know I do. We can talk about this more, especially after the test of the bullets comes back from the state lab and Matt is able to tell us more. If after that, it's obvious that I am in danger, I'll move. But not now. Not tonight." *I'm not in danger. This cabin is my refuge.*

After overruling a few more cautions from both men, she got Rodd and Doug out the door.

"Let me hear you lock up," Rodd said to her from outside.

*Fine! Anything!* "Yes, sir." She locked the button lock and turned the dead bolt. "And here I'm locking the windows." She went from window to window first in the great room, then the kitchen and finally, in her bedroom. She pulled the shades and went into her bathroom to get ready for bed. She switched on the light and stared into the bathroom mirror.

She felt bereft.

✖ ✖ ✖

Outside, Rodd and Doug stood looking at each other in the scarce moonlight.

"Don't worry," Rodd said in a low voice. "I'll have someone by here every hour for the rest of tonight."

"She's too stubborn for her own good," Doug groused. *Should I tell him about her mother, about the stalker in LA?*

"Good night." Rodd walked to his SUV and got in.

Feeling out of sorts, Doug followed suit. He sat in his car. *I should stay.* After Rodd had gone, Doug drove slowly away from the cabin, wanting to stay. Only imagining Kirsi's anger in the morning if she found him asleep in his car outside her door made him go. *Why does she have to be so prickly?*

But now he knew the answer to that. Kirsi wouldn't give in to fear because she didn't want it to linger long after this crisis was over. And ruin the rest of her life. As fear had destroyed her mother's life. And tried to damage Kirsi's.

✖ ✖ ✖

He watched the sheriff and that doctor drive away.

He'd let the kid dangle and watched him twist. Then he'd taken care of business with that little punk just like he'd intended.

But he still had a few more mind games he wanted to play with the woman doc. He'd turn the screws a little while longer.

He didn't want his fun to end too quickly.

✖ ✖ ✖

Kirsi yawned and opened her eyes. Golden sunshine leaked through the edges of the window shades. She stretched. Glimpses of the night before threatened to take over her thoughts. She pushed them aside with her covers and got out of bed.

Crows screeched outside. Noisy ducks were honking a loud quarrel at the lake behind her cabin. She smiled at the sounds so different from the horns, engines, and curses she'd heard from her apartment in California.

*I love this place. If mother and grandmother and grand-father didn't need me so . . .* she pushed this line of thought out of her mind. *Lord, let this reunion make the difference. My mother's suffered long enough.*

After putting coffee on, she went to the bathroom and brushed her teeth. She noticed that her razor was right where she'd put it. Dressed in sweats for a morning jog, she opened her front door.

And then she froze.

The door hadn't been locked.

*But I locked it last night. Both locks!*

Her heart galloped, making her feel slightly sick.

She grabbed her purse from the chair by the door, ran outside, and jumped into her Jeep.

# CHAPTER TWELVE

WHO HAD UNLOCKED Kirsi's door? The thought froze the marrow of Doug's spine. With his elbows propped on the table and his hands clenched together, he sat beside Kirsi in the doctors' lounge.

She'd entered the clinic at a trot and clung to him as she stammered a few words about her unlocked door. Then she'd subsided, trembling and silent. He'd called the sheriff and brought her into the lounge.

Now her shuttered expression scared him.

Doug considered putting an arm around her, but he couldn't bring himself to disturb her in the slightest way. Why wasn't she showing any emotion? Her outward calm felt as fragile as the first skim of ice on a pond. This worried him more than anything else.

Sheriff Durand burst through the door. "What's happened?"

"My door was unlocked this morning," Kirsi replied without looking at him.

Rodd thumped down on the chair across from them without voicing a reply.

Doug clenched his hands more tightly. When Kirsi had said the same sentence to him, he had blurted out, "But I heard you lock it last night." What a dumb thing to say. That had been understood. She'd locked the door last night, and it had been unlocked this morning. That was what had launched her straight to the hospital. Or had she come straight to him?

The sheriff spread both his hands on the table. "Now we have proof that someone is harassing you." And then he pronounced a quiet epithet.

Doug didn't blame him. A few had flown through his own mind when he'd heard the news himself. "What do we do now?"

Kirsi sat still and silent.

Doug held himself from leaning closer to her.

Rodd stared at them. "I think we'd better go talk to Matt again." He rose. "Come on."

Glad to be taking some action, Doug grasped Kirsi by the elbow, and the two of them trailed Rodd down the hallway to the first patient room. For a moment, Doug wondered if they'd find that Matt had vanished just as Weston had.

Looking past Rodd and Kirsi, Doug was relieved to see that Matt was still in his bed where he had seen him this morning when he'd arrived for duty.

He felt Kirsi resist slightly as they entered the room. He touched her arm, bolstering her.

She strode ahead as though unaware of him.

Matt did not look well. Still hooked to an IV and a morphine pump to ease his pain, the kid looked like he'd been through a war. Well, he had.

"Matt," the sheriff commanded, "I need to talk to you."

Matt's eyes met the sheriff's. "Don't feel good."

"Too bad." Rodd hovered over the kid, looking down at him. "Why'd you get shot?"

Matt brushed his head back and forth on the white pillow in denial. "Don't know."

Kirsi moved forward and touched Matt's forehead as if checking for a fever.

Matt glared at her.

Doug stayed close behind her.

Rodd put his hands on the pillow, one on each side of Matt's head. "I'm not leaving until you tell me everything."

"Don't know—"

Rodd's head was only an inch above Matt's forehead. "Do you have any idea what it means to have the county sheriff watch your every move?"

Doug had never seen this side of the sheriff. Rodd exuded an aura of power and menace.

Kirsi stepped back, bumping into Doug. He took a gentle hold of her upper arm. She didn't seem to be aware of him.

"I'm sick," Matt croaked.

"Next time you may be *dead.*" Rodd's voice rasped low in his throat.

Concerned for his patient, Doug took a step forward. No matter what Matt had done, he was Doug's patient. "Sheriff—"

The heated look Rodd gave Doug stopped him in his tracks.

Doug swallowed. *I need him to get the truth from Matt. Kirsi's safety may depend on it.*

Kirsi remained frozen beside him.

"Now, Matt," the sheriff insisted in an intimidating tone.

Doug was glad that Rodd wasn't talking to him.

Matt looked ready to cry. "I didn't know . . . I never would have done it—"

"Done what?" Rodd pressed him.

"I never would have stayed in the gym and saw him . . ." Matt looked toward Kirsi. "Then afterwards, I started

getting phone calls. Nothin' but breathin' and then sometimes he'd say, 'Gonna get you, narc.' "

"Why, Matt?" Rodd asked. "Why would you get calls?"

"That day, you know the day she got pushed into the
closet, I thought I recognized . . ." Matt's courage seemed
to fail him. He shrunk back into the bedclothes.

"Recognized who?" Rodd demanded.

"The guy with the guy who gave Weston the joint—
you know the one that nearly killed him."

Doug squeezed Kirsi's arm.

She looked at him, her eyes wounded.

"You were with Weston when he got the joint? Why
didn't you tell someone?" Rodd challenged, relentless.

Matt shrugged one shoulder. "I don't know. I just wanted
to get away from the guy—like Weston did!" Matt averted his
eyes. "Then on the phone, he said, the voice said . . ."

"Said what?" Rodd snapped.

"That I was gonna get it for sticking my nose where it
wasn't wanted. When I got the first call, I thought it was
someone's idea of a freaky joke. Then Weston called me
from the hospital. He said he had to get away. That someone kept calling him and that he knew a guy was going to
kill him because the guy had already killed Nail."

"Nail?"

"Yeah, the guy they found dead. You know." Matt
looked like he was on the verge of tears.

"You mean you saw the man you think is responsible
for killing this guy Nail?" Rodd asked.

Kirsi drew in a shocked breath.

Doug moved his arm to half circle her waist.

Matt nodded sullenly.

"Is that why you turned yourself in—for protection?"
Rodd asked.

"Yeah." Matt looked away. "I mean I talked it over with

my friends, and we decided that if I took the blame and got arrested or something, it might be enough payback and . . . whoever was going to get me might decide to let it go. And anyway I'd be safer in jail. But you wouldn't arrest me!"

The kid's fear-filled voice made Doug remember how awful being a teenager could be.

"You get no sympathy from me." Rodd rocked back on the balls of his feet. "You say you haven't done anything wrong, but at least twice you've been where you shouldn't have been! Once when Weston got the meth joint and once when Dr. Royston was pushed into the closet. If you'd been in class where you should have been, you wouldn't be lying here!"

Matt wouldn't meet Rodd's stern gaze.

"Am I right? Now tell me what you saw—all you know!"

Matt kept his mouth shut.

In one swift motion, Rodd grabbed the shoulder of Matt's hospital gown, wrinkling it in his fist.

"No," Kirsi gasped, turning to Doug who'd taken an indignant step forward.

Rodd ignored them. "Kid, you're not helping yourself—"

Matt's eyes flashed up at Rodd. "My mom's sending me away to relatives the minute I get out of this bed. I already got shot. You want me to get killed? I'm not tellin' you anythin' more!"

A glance at Kirsi made Rodd let go of the gown.

The nurse on duty walked in to check Matt's vitals. But she looked at Matt and then Rodd and back again.

Doug nodded at her. "Go ahead."

"Let's go talk to Burke." Rodd turned and marched out of the room.

Doug and Kirsi followed him, just two doors away to Burke's bedside. Kirsi retreated by taking refuge in reading Burke's chart.

"What's up?" Burke asked, looking and sounding tired.

"Somebody visited Dr. Royston's cabin last night, and he left her locked door unlocked for her to find this morning," Rodd said in a flat voice.

That point hadn't occurred to Doug. Someone had wanted Kirsi to know he'd been there. Doug turned to look at her, still standing beside him.

"That doesn't sound good," Burke said.

Rodd nodded and turned to Kirsi. "Have you ever had any indication that anyone has been in your cabin without your permission before this?"

The chart still in one hand, Kirsi looked down at the floor.

"Doctor?" Rodd prompted.

His heart aching for this woman who wouldn't give up, back down—Doug touched her arm. "Kirsi?"

"My razor," she said without lifting her eyes. "I think it was moved once. And . . ."

Doug stroked her arm, coaxing, reassuring.

Kirsi frowned. "And once I found my brush had been cleaned of hair, but I didn't remember doing it."

"Did you tell anyone?" Rodd asked.

Shocked, Doug wondered at Rodd's even tone. What Kirsi had just revealed—personally—gave him the creeps. Why would someone move a razor or clean hair from a brush? Creepy.

"No, of course not. I thought I'd forgotten and moved the razor or cleaned the brush myself," Kirsi explained. "I work long hours and . . . I mean it would have sounded ridiculous—'Sheriff, someone moved my razor, and by the way, someone also cleaned the hair from my brush without my authorization.' What would you have said?"

By the end of her comments, her normal determined voice had returned, but scarlet spotted each of her cheeks.

*Kirsi, you can't refuse help any longer.*

"You should have reported both instances," Rodd said. "Nothing has been normal since the day you arrived—"

"That's right," Kirsi snapped, "but I refused to let my imagination run wild. I don't give in to paranoia."

Doug could only feel relieved that she was bouncing back strong.

"Except for breather calls, there were no signs that anyone was stalking me," Kirsi railed. "How could I put any importance on such insignificant things as a razor and a brush?"

"Don't get angry with me," Rodd objected. "My point is that in light of everything, I probably would have at least given what you'd noticed some thought. But it seems to me that from the start, you've used denial to cope with this situation. And I'm telling you right now—denial has not worked and will not work for you. This is serious—deadly serious."

"Don't you think I know that!" Kirsi blazed at Rodd.

Doug brushed his hand down her arm, trying to jar her back to self-control. *Arguing with the sheriff won't do any good.*

Rodd held up both hands. "Hold on."

"Okay," Doug intervened, gripping Kirsi's arm, "let's all cool down. Anger won't accomplish anything."

Both Rodd and Kirsi turned disgruntled expressions toward him. Kirsi jerked away from Doug.

"Dr. Doug's right," Burke agreed from the bed, a cool voice of reason. "Now we know that someone wanted to harm Matt—for whatever Matt saw or whatever someone thinks Matt knows. And we know that someone unlocked Dr. Royston's door last night. We've got to figure out what to do to protect Matt and Dr. Royston."

"What can you do?" Kirsi asked, her tone full of frustration.

Doug took Burke's chart from her, his quelling gaze

meeting her fiery one. "You're going to move into the suite over our garage, and I'm—"

"No," she objected.

"Yes you are." Rodd put both hands on his hips and glared at her.

"*And* I'm going to hook up the intercom between the main house and the suite," Doug insisted, "so that you can contact me or Granddad any time of the day or night." *I'm not taking no for an answer.*

"And from now on," Rodd took over, "when you drive to and from work at night, I will have a deputy follow you."

Kirsi looked conflicted, torn.

Doug took her hand. "Sheriff, can you think of someone to help Dr. Royston move her things? I would do it myself, but I'm on duty today until three."

"Don't talk about me like I'm not present," Kirsi declared. "I'm upset but not helpless."

"Okay, but first," Rodd said, making eye contact with Doug, "I'll want to go over her cabin and dust for fingerprints. Her uninvited guest may have left some hard evidence for me . . . at last."

❖ ❖ ❖

Kirsi hated every step she took as she carried her duffel bag full of clothing up the stairs to her new suite. *I loved my snug, little cabin in the woods. Now I won't hear the bullfrogs in the evening or wake to the ducks quacking and go home and see deer and fawns strolling to the lake for water. . . .* She forced herself to hold this in. *I've been living a wonderful dream.*

Another thought intruded: *more like a nightmare.*

Huffing with the exertion, the senior Dr. Erickson followed her to the top of the steep steps. He carried a box of books for her. "We're glad to have you, but I'm so sorry you are facing this."

Kirsi nodded. *I've been through worse.* But that gave her no comfort. Why had everything gone so terribly wrong? She almost felt cursed. Kirsi felt fear churning inside her. She tried to come up with Scripture verses her grandmother had taught her, but her mind was blank.

The possibility that some unknown person had been in her cabin made her skin crawl. Had he stood over her last night and watched her sleeping? Did he want her to know that? Was that why he'd left the door unlocked? Had he left other clues of his presence before? Had she suppressed them even from herself?

"After his father's death, Doug had the intercom installed while he still occupied this suite." Dr. Erickson set the box of books on the floor. "I think that after his dad was gone, it made him feel that he had to protect me and his mother."

Kirsi wrenched her mind from her own agony and tried to decide if this was just a passing comment or if this good man was trying to tell her something about his grandson. She plopped the duffel on the stripped bed. A fine layer of dust covered everything. This was Doug's place. "Were Doug and his father close?"

Dr. Erickson sat on a Windsor rocker by the bank of windows. "Yes, they were. When his dad died, Doug felt very much the weight of his . . . heritage, the clinic. I started it back in the fifties; then his father joined me and then Doug. I think losing his father when Doug was so young put extra weight on him, as though he had to do the work of two. Sometimes I must say to him, 'Doug, you're not responsible for the whole world.' "

"I think I've said similar phrases to him." Kirsi found herself unexpectedly grinning. "He thinks he's supposed to protect me single-handedly."

"Yes, his sense of responsibility is his greatest strength and his worst flaw." Dr. Erickson began rocking rhythmically.

Kirsi nodded. Talking about Doug had lightened her load. Investing herself in others always did. Grandmother had demonstrated that to her.

"You were raised by your mother," Dr. Erickson said, "so maybe you understand. You feel responsible for your mother, don't you?"

These words brought it all back in a rush of fear, anger, frustration. *My mother was always the child. I was the parent.* Kirsi nodded and then looked away. *I can't think about her now.*

"Does Rodd think he found any clues when he went through your place?" Dr. Erickson asked.

Kirsi sat down on the edge of the soft bed. It creaked. "He dusted for prints everywhere he could. He watched me like a hawk when I was packing. I think he's still there poring over everything."

"Well, if anyone can solve this case, Rodd Durand and Burke Sloan will. Very little gets past them."

Kirsi held her peace again. Someone had gotten past them last night and into her cabin—even through a locked door.

▧ ▧ ▧

"Why is your number changed and unlisted now? Your cell phone was busy so I tried to call your home number to leave a message. Are you having problems with your phone again?" her grandmother asked over Kirsi's cell phone.

"I've moved a little closer to town, Nani," Kirsi hedged, watching the road as she drove.

"Why? I thought you loved that cabin you e-mailed us photos of."

"I do, but it's a long drive and we're shorthanded at the clinic. This is just temporary. How's my mother?"

"She's doing as well as she is able. I wish you wouldn't worry so! We knew she'd have difficulty adjusting to your being so far away. Don't worry."

*Thank You, Lord, for keeping things under control until I can get home and relieve my grandparents.* Intuitively, she knew Nani was putting a good face on matters, and Kirsi appreciated her trying to protect her from the truth. But it was her turn to assume her mother as her responsibility. Her grandparents had done their time.

"Now I don't want you worrying about us," Grandmother said. "We're fine."

How many times had she heard this and then later received an unpleasant and often teary phone call from her grandmother about her mother? "Okay. I've got to ring off. I'm on my way to a home-health visit before I go on duty."

"How wonderful!" Grandmother enthused. "I love it that you're in a place where you can do that. I'll tell your grandfather."

After loving farewells, Kirsi parked behind Veda's house. So what kind of welcome would she receive from Veda today? She mounted the back steps.

Veda waited for her behind the screen door. "It's about time."

Kirsi almost did a double take. Veda had never met her at the door before. "Well, aren't we chipper today?"

"Come in and get it over with. I've got to go into town." Veda opened the door.

Kirsi counted this as definite progress. Veda hadn't been to town for a long time.

Kirsi opened her medical bag and took out her blood-pressure cuff. "Are you taking your—"

"Yes, I'm taking my medicine!" Veda glared at her.

❊ ❊ ❊

A week later, Kirsi stood at the end of Carrie Walachek's bed in the clinic's labor room. To cheer up the room, someone had painted it pale yellow and stenciled yellow ducklings in a band around the four walls. Labor was going well; it had only been seven hours, relatively short for a first baby. But Kirsi didn't say this to Carrie, who wasn't in the mood to think that she was having a fairly easy time of it.

During labor, Kirsi had thought about Weston. Had Carrie? Or didn't she care that her baby's father was still missing? In the week since Kirsi had moved into the suite over the Ericksons' garage, nothing about drugs or gangs had rippled the surface of her life. She was afraid it was the calm before the storm.

She finished checking Carrie's dilation and then gave the soon-to-be mother a smile. "We can take you into the delivery room now."

"That's good news," Carrie's aunt Myrna said as she stood beside the girl's bed.

"Let's get this over with." Carrie panted. "I just want it to be over."

Wendy rolled Carrie's bed across the hall to the delivery room. Though Kirsi hadn't foreseen any complications, the surgeon was on call, a few minutes away, in case he was needed.

In the delivery room, Kirsi helped Wendy get Carrie onto the delivery table. The baby's head was engaged, and Kirsi bet that Carrie would be pushing for only a few minutes.

Eight minutes later with her fourth push, Carrie's red-faced baby slid into Kirsi's waiting hands. "It's a girl!" she crooned.

Carrie panted and lay back on the padded table. "Is she all right?"

"Looks good. All ten fingers and toes." Kirsi beamed.

"She's beautiful!" Myrna crowed.

Wendy received the squalling newborn from Kirsi and deftly went through the routine care. Then she showed Carrie her baby and put the little pink bundle into the new mother's arms.

Carrie began weeping, not an unusual reaction for a mother after intense labor and delivery.

Kirsi delivered the afterbirth, examined it, and motioned Wendy to take the baby away to bathe her.

But Carrie held on to her baby, tears streaming down her face. "I wish Weston were here. I've been so mean to him. Where is he? I want him here."

# CHAPTER THIRTEEN

LATER, KIRSI MET Wendy over an isolette where Carrie's baby lay. What would happen now? When Weston heard about his daughter's birth, would he come out of hiding? Had Matt told the truth about what Weston feared enough to send him into hiding? Would they find the answers to all the mysteries at last? *Lord, let it be so.*

"Well—" Wendy gently slipped a tiny pink knit cap on the baby's head—"I didn't expect Carrie to come to her senses and regret not including the father in the birth of their child. I'd given up."

"I'd hoped she'd take a step toward maturity when she gave birth." With one finger, Kirsi stroked the soft cheek. "You're too sweet and innocent," Kirsi murmured to the baby, "to be born into such a mess."

"Rodd hasn't given up looking for Weston." Wendy adjusted the newborn's flannel gown. "He'll be keeping the clinic under surveillance, and after Carrie leaves tomorrow morning at her aunt's home."

"Does that mean Carrie plans to live with her aunt?"

"Yes," Wendy said, "she's staying with Myrna because her father moved to Milwaukee. He used to work at the

Turner Mill, but he had to get a new job when it closed. He sends money to Carrie and Myrna every month."

"I hate to say it, but I don't think Weston will venture out of hiding."

"You can't assume he'll behave rationally. You have to remember Weston's just turned seventeen." With a light-weight blanket, Wendy swaddled the baby into a pink cocoon. "He's still thinking like an adolescent. But he's a good kid from a good family. It's terrible that they've had to suffer so over this. His mother's frantic."

Kirsi frowned, hesitating to sound judgmental, but Weston's part in this had begun voluntarily. Not like hers. Once again, the jolt of finding her door unlocked slashed through Kirsi like scalpel blades. She pushed the sensation down and went on with the conversation. "Weston shouldn't have bought or accepted drugs at school—"

"That proves my point," Wendy cut in. "He was acting out because of Carrie's pushing him away. He had to demonstrate to her what her rejection had driven him to. That's the kind of immature thinking that gets kids into drugs." Wendy pushed the wheeled isolette out into the hallway.

Kirsi followed her while turning everything over in her mind. But the chaos refused to make sense. And now, nagging at the back of her mind was the letter she'd received this morning. What effect would the letter have?

"You've had a rough time of it." Wendy looked over her shoulder.

Wendy's sympathy stung Kirsi's tender spot, and she had to tighten her defenses. "I'll be fine," she muttered.

"Everyone around here feels so bad about . . . everything that's happened to you. We wouldn't have worked so hard to bring you here if we'd known what you would have to face."

Kirsi shrugged, shaking off the vague what-might-have-been. "It's not anyone's fault. I mean, not anyone who brought me here. Life . . . just happens."

"Hi," Doug greeted them from behind. His voice reached out and soothed Kirsi's taut nerves.

Kirsi turned to look at him fully. His lean but powerful form, his brown hair curling around the tops of his ears, his prominent wrist bones and long slender fingers—Doug Erickson had become imprinted on her mind. How often did she close her eyes and find Doug's image waiting there for her?

The sudden thought of how much she would miss this man when she went back to California jabbed her and nearly brought tears to her eyes. She half turned so nothing would alert him to her feeling of impending, lifelong loss. "Hi." She kept her voice casual, but with an edge of irony to it. "I should have expected you. Nothing happens here without your knowing."

"News travels fast." He sauntered to her and nudged her shoulder with his. "So Carrie had a little girl?"

"You should be home asleep," Kirsi scolded, shielding herself from his assault on her senses. *You don't fool me, Dr. Doug. You came to follow me home, but you're trying to cover your tracks.* "You have duty at seven in the morning," she said. *Doug, I'm tired. I'm worried.*

"I know my schedule *and* yours, Doctor." Doug grinned. "I just wanted to see the baby and congratulate Carrie. By the time I'm done with that, your shift will be over and I can follow you home."

So she *had* nailed his motive. Conflicting emotions over the constant surveillance suddenly depressed Kirsi. *I don't want a bodyguard!* She bit her tongue to hold back hot words. *Lord, can't this be over? I'm sick of it.* Her answer came—her grandmother's voice quoting God's Word again: *"My grace is sufficient for thee."* Was it? It didn't feel sufficient.

And in an ironic move, God had answered her prayers. The letter was in her purse. Knowing she'd have to tell Doug the news very soon made Kirsi pass a tired hand over her creased forehead. *And it's not even summer's end yet.* "I'll go change."

❖ ❖ ❖

At the Ericksons' house, Kirsi permitted herself to be persuaded into Doug's den. Easing herself onto the love seat, she recalled the first time she'd sat in this room with the cool rain pouring outside and the cozy afghan over her.

Now she luxuriated in the languid, hot midsummer night. Wearing shorts, she stretched her bare legs out in front of her, the cotton slipcover sliding softly under her.

Being here so close to Doug in this peaceful setting tortured her, but going alone to her suite was impossible after the excitement tonight. Delivering Carrie's baby had aroused a tangle of feelings she didn't want to work loose. And solitude now would have forced her to try.

"You need your sleep," she stated perversely. "And I need mine." *And being this close and not touching you is an exquisite agony.*

Doug sat in the armchair beside her, his bare feet propped on an overstuffed ottoman. "What are you wanting to tell me but not telling me?"

His question caught her up sharply from her welter of longing. She pursed her lips. "Is it that obvious?"

"To me. I've started to catch on to your how-am-I-going-to-tell-him expression. Have you found a replacement?"

She nodded, her eyes downcast. "I got the letter today. That resident I mentioned is happy for a chance to come here—if your grandfather will have him. He wants to fly out in August to interview."

A heavy silence.

"So you did what you said you would." Doug crossed his ankles as if this news were unimportant to him. "You found a replacement before summer's end." His tone was light.

"Yes." She noted he didn't look her way.

"Why so glum then?" he asked.

Wave after wave of desolation washed over her, and she closed her eyes. "Can I tell you the truth?"

"Always."

She leaned her head back against the love seat, torn between speaking and remaining silent. *But I must tell him. I want him to know why I must leave here.* "It's been so wonderful, being a long-distance call away from my mom. When I was in LA, she often called me several times daily—even when I was on duty at the hospital." Kirsi shook her head at herself. "That's awful of me to say, but it's the truth." She opened her eyes to read his expression.

"From what you've told me, you and your mother carry a lot of baggage, as Granddad would say."

"Unfortunately." She read only concern in his face. Sighing long and low, she released the elastic band that held her hair in a tight ponytail. "But my grandparents are the ones who've carried the greatest load. I think my grandmother still feels so guilty about trusting her brother—"

"We're talking about something that took place over forty years ago." Sliding his feet to the floor, Doug edged forward and propped his elbows on his tanned thighs.

"To my mother, it's like yesterday." She ran her fingers through her hair, rasping her scalp with her nails.

"Then maybe it's not the act, but the person." Doug steepled his fingers and studied her over them.

"I don't know what you mean." The ivory afghan lay folded over the arm of the love seat. Kirsi ran her fingers through its fringe.

"I don't know how to express it exactly, but it makes me think of something I overheard my granddad say long ago when I was a child. He was talking to my mother and he said, 'There's nothing wrong with this town. You could like it here if that's what you wanted.' "

She stared at Doug. "I don't get it."

Doug drew in a deep breath. "My mother never wanted to live in small-town Wisconsin. My parents met at college. She was from the East."

Kirsi listened, hearing the shading Doug gave to each word. She sensed he'd never expressed this to anyone else.

"My parents fell in love, and after Dad finished his education and training, they came back to Steadfast—just as he had told her they would before they married."

Her fingers tingled with the yearning to brush back the waves of his hair that'd tumbled onto his worry-creased forehead. "But she was unhappy?"

He nodded. "Yes, she was a good wife and a good mother, but I suppose she must have been unhappy. Otherwise, why would she leave home a month after we buried my father? That says it all, don't you think?"

Kirsi heard his feeling of rejection in his diffident tone and felt it as her own. His mother hadn't wanted to stay with him and his grandfather. Only her love for her husband had kept her in Steadfast. Not her love for her son. Did his mother realize Doug felt this?

"She said she had to go right away in order to start her Ph.D. program that fall." Doug seemed frozen where he sat. "But she hadn't been planning on that before his death. Or if she had—I never heard of it."

Kirsi nodded.

"When she finished her doctorate, she took a job teaching at a small private college in Minneapolis, and she's been there ever since."

"She didn't go back East?" She glanced at his face.

"No, her parents—I barely knew them—passed away while she was writing her dissertation. So she comes on holidays and spends weekends here now and then."

"I'd give anything to have a mother that self-sufficient." The words bubbled up from deep inside Kirsi. "My mother barely holds down a receptionist job. She wouldn't have that if it weren't a small office owned by church friends. They have a married daughter who covers for my mother when she has a bad spell. And my grandparents still help my mother by paying her rent. They're in their late seventies, and their only child still isn't self-sufficient!"

"Is that why you have to go back to California?" He leaned toward her.

She nearly touched his face, so close, so concerned. "Yes, Mother can't be by herself."

"Why not bring her here?"

Kirsi shook her head. "Her psychiatrist said that such a large change might unbalance her even more. She's held her job there many years, and it's good for her to be out with people each day. Besides, if I brought Mom here, my grandparents would have to relocate too. They'll need me before long." She closed her eyes, losing herself in the night sounds—distant motors, the drone of insects, and from far away, the call of a loon.

"But your family is going to India this fall. Is your mother up to that challenge?"

"That's just a trip." Kirsi opened her eyes. "And we'd all be together—"

"And you're hoping that the reconciliation with your grandmother's family will finally put the past to rest for your mother."

"Yes, but how did you know?" Kirsi's voice sounded like a little girl's to her own ears. "But that's really just my grandmother. My mother's psychiatrist warned me against attaching too much hope in my grandmother's theory about the reunion finally turning my mother in a new direction. Now my mother is slipping into depression again. My fault for leaving, for trying to get away . . ."

Her defeated tone moved Doug. He couldn't stop himself. He went down on his knees in front of her and gathered Kirsi into his arms. Her own natural fragrance stirred his emotions, his desire to protect her. "I don't want you to go."

She quivered as if she were crying.

He buried his face into her long, long hair. "I don't want you to go," he repeated.

She turned her face to him. She was weeping. "I can't stay."

He kissed one of her cheeks, tasting her wet tears.

"Nothing ever turns out right," she murmured in a broken tone. "I came here to escape my mother, the stalker, everything. I just wanted to be free—finally free."

He kissed her other cheek, her skin smooth and soft under his lips. *Kirsi, I'd do anything for you.*

"But I'll never be released from this." Her quiet weeping overlaid her words. "Mother will need me until she dies. And when my grandparents die, I'll be left alone to shoulder the responsibility of her. I love her, but I won't ever be free—"

"I'll never be free either," Doug whispered, his lips beside her ear. "I have to stay and run the clinic. People depend on me."

She pressed her ear against his face and swallowed her tears, willing them away. She understood. Then she bent her forehead to his. "But you love the clinic—"

"Sometimes I hate it." His voice dropped low in his throat. "My grandfather sacrificed his whole life to provide quality health care to this county. If I left, that would mean that I didn't respect what he'd sacrificed his whole life to achieve. I can never leave the clinic. I don't want to really, but it's sometimes hard knowing that I can't ever leave. Do you understand?"

"Yes." She captured his mouth with hers.

He drew in breath, sealing their lips together. His skin blazed wherever her bare skin touched his. He gathered her flowing hair into his fist and pressed her face closer to his. He whispered her name again and inhaled her breath into his lungs.

She clung to his shoulders, tears falling from her eyes. "I don't want to leave you, but I can't stay."

"I want to go with you, but I can't leave." He felt her tears on his cheeks. He bent his head to her shoulder and took in her softness. He pressed a kiss on her neck and then bent his forehead down again. He wanted to say, "I love you." But that would be cruel.

She laid her head against his, heaving a sigh of pain, regret.

He echoed it silently. *Lord, is this some cruel joke? Where is Your hand in this?*

※ ※ ※

Early the next week, shortly after Independence Day, Kirsi sat at Harlan Carey's kitchen table for another morning prayer group. Doug sat next to her, and both of them kept trying not to catch the other's eye. Both failed repeatedly. When their gazes met, warmth ignited deep inside her— at first. Then frigid despair.

Kirsi felt no desire to pray. *I prayed for a replacement. I've got one, and now I don't want one.* And now Great-Aunt Uma . . . an early morning phone call from her grandmother had put even more pressure on her.

"We have some good news." Harlan beamed at them. "Bruce Weaver called me last night. It looks like their adoption of little Rachel will be final in a month."

"Great." Doug smiled.

Somehow Kirsi experienced in her own flesh how hard it was for him to tap his energy to bring up a smile. It was like mining gold from a deep pit.

She tried to smile herself and failed. *Should I give them my good news that I've found someone to replace me?* Like a needle in an open wound, pain pierced her. *Why can't I have a life of my own? Why does my mother's past hang around my neck?*

"Bruce and Penny will make great parents for Rachel." Wendy Durand high-fived her husband.

Kirsi tried to look pleased.

Doug touched her hand.

She let the current of sensation flash up the length of her arm. Then she broke their connection. *Doug, don't touch me. I can't bear it.*

Doug eased back in his chair.

"I'm happy for them," Rodd said.

Kirsi cleared her throat. "I need prayer for the health of my great-aunt Uma in India. She suffered a cardiac episode yesterday . . . Nani, my grandmother, might have to fly to India earlier than we had planned." *And I might have to fly to California to help with my mother. I'm sorry, God, but I don't want to go.* "Uma is her only remaining sibling, and Nani wanted to be with her one more time after all the years of separation."

"I understand that desire." Harlan folded his gnarled hands on the tabletop.

A moment of silence.

Rodd spoke up, "Harlan, I'm stymied about what to do about the meth invasion. We picked up two kids last night who had all the symptoms of taking meth. They were manic. We had to put them in separate cells in restraints—we were afraid they might hurt each other or themselves."

Kirsi propped her elbows on the table and rested her

chin on her hands. Across from her, Nick looked worried. She didn't allow her gaze to wander to Doug. He needed a haircut and all she wanted was to play with his errant curls and selfishly forget about India, about California.

Harlan looked grave. "I hate to hear that, but it's just why we are here. These problems are too big for us. But no problem is too big for God. Nick, open your Bible to Psalm 37. And read the first two verses."

*My problem is my mother's illness, her chronic depression— who else could carry this responsibility? And it's not that I don't love her. Or my grandparents. I love and want to help them.*

Nick did as Harlan said and read: " 'Don't worry about the wicked. Don't envy those who do wrong. For like grass, they soon fade away. Like springtime flowers, they soon wither.' " A dawning grin claimed Nick's handsome young face. "Yeah!"

Kirsi tried to take heart from this young man's lively reaction to God's words. Yes, in God's time, those who were set to do evil in this peaceful county would pay the price. She looped hair behind her ears and stared downward, seeing Weston as she had that first day at the clinic. But how many innocent or naive people would have to suffer before that day of judgment?

And how would she ever forget Doug's caresses?

Her grandmother's soft lilting voice played in her mind: *"This too shall pass, my dear child. Someday your mother will be well and whole. I believe that." But will you live to see it, Nani? Will I? Or will it happen in heaven?*

"If I'm going to apprehend the new drug gang," Rodd said in a gruff voice, "I evidently need God to give me something more to go on then. I can't seem to get even the shadow of a clue or evidence."

He'd called Kirsi with the lab results of the bullets test. Both Matt and Burke had been felled with bullets from the same gun as the one that had killed Nail, the unidentified body they'd found behind Flanigan's. But where did that lead them? Nowhere.

Harlan nodded. "As sheriff, you carry heavy responsibility, Rodd. I'm sure God will give you what you need—just when you need it."

Wendy touched Rodd's arm in that wifely way that spoke more than words of her support and understanding of the man who was her husband.

Kirsi envied Rodd and Wendy as they shouldered their load together. *How could I ever marry and weigh someone down with the responsibility of my mother? And when my grandparents and my mother die, I'll be all alone. I don't want that to happen, but I don't have a choice.* A frigid sensation settled into her . . . lower . . . lower.

Her unruly gaze found Doug's face. She stifled the words that wanted to pour out: "I love you, Doug." She looked away. *Why did I have to come to Steadfast—just so I could find the man I've always wanted to love but whom I can never share my love with?* Kirsi felt a physical ache that tightened around her heart and lungs, draining out her life, her hope.

"Dr. Royston?" Harlan drew her back to the meeting. "Will you read verses four and five of that psalm?"

She pursed her lips as Nick pushed Harlan's Bible in front of her. Without looking up, she read aloud: " 'Take delight in the Lord, and He will give you your heart's desires. Commit everything you do to the Lord. Trust Him, and He will help you.' "

"Have faith, Rodd." Harlan folded his hands. "He saved Matt and Burke. And Burke's already back on duty." Harlan looked to her. "Have faith, Kirsi. Now let's pray." The old man closed his eyes. "Lord, You give and take away. You hold all things in Your hands. Bless Kirsi's family in the U.S.

and in India. Here, we ask You to gather up the wrongdoers in Steadfast. Bind up their evil. Let them fall into the traps they have set for others. Protect Matt Witowski and his family.

"Bless little Rachel as she becomes Rachel Weaver. Bless Carrie Walachek's little girl, Amy. Bless her father and bring him safely back to Carrie and his parents."

Kirsi's sadness grew heavier inside her. She opened her eyes, trying to free herself of the pain. Her gaze met Doug's.

The anguish in his golden brown eyes matched hers. *Lord, how am I supposed to carry on here until the new resident takes over? If Dr. Erickson even approves this candidate. It's going to be a purgatory staying here. I should never have let Doug know how I feel.*

※ ※ ※

"I suppose you want to know if Weston has called me." Carrie challenged Wendy and Kirsi as they stood around Carrie's kitchen table. After the prayer meeting, Kirsi had decided to tag along with Wendy on her morning of calls. Being alone with her unhappy thoughts unnerved her.

"I'm sure that if Weston contacted you, you would do the right thing and let my husband know about it." Wendy lifted the infant from Carrie's arms.

The new mother slumped into the nearest chair in the red-and-white kitchen, decorated with matching gingham curtains.

Kirsi sat down beside her. "How are you feeling? Any mood swings or anything unusual?"

"I'm fine."

But Carrie didn't look fine. Her hair was bedraggled, and she had gray circles under her eyes. And she looked like she had slept in her shorts and T-shirt.

Kirsi wondered if she looked as unkempt as Carrie.

Certainly, the girl looked like Kirsi felt. "Nothing a good night's sleep wouldn't cure," she said, keeping up her end of the mundane conversation.

"You're right." Carrie yawned. "Amy got her days and nights mixed up for a while."

"Is your aunt working today at the café?" Wendy asked as she unwrapped the baby to lay her on the portable scale.

Kirsi swallowed a yawn of her own and gazed at the baby wriggling in Wendy's arms. She touched Amy's hand, and her tiny fingers wrapped around her finger. The sensation of wanting to protect this little innocent coiled through her.

"Yeah, but she'll be home for supper. I'm going to surprise her and grill a chicken." Carrie motioned toward a frozen chicken thawing on a plate on the counter.

"Sounds good." Wendy weighed the baby. "Amy's gained two ounces. Wonderful!"

Playing with Amy, Kirsi tenderly, bravely waggled her finger in the infant's grip. *I will never have a child.*

Carrie yawned again. "Sorry."

"You need a nap," Kirsi said on impulse, wanting to be a part of this child's life if only for a brief time. "Why don't I stay for a couple of hours and let you rest?"

Carrie looked surprised. "You mean it?"

Kirsi held out her arms. "Yes," she replied truthfully, "I can't think of a better way to spend the morning than playing with a pretty baby." Kirsi lifted Amy from the scale and cradled the child close.

Carrie snorted. "Wait till my pretty baby fills her diaper."

Kirsi chuckled, and it felt good, as though melting a layer of her sadness. "Are you done, Wendy?"

"Yes. Amy's doing fine. Now, Carrie, you'll be at the young mother's class tomorrow, won't you?"

"Yeah. I gotta ride already." Carrie looked over to Kirsi. "Would you mind giving Amy her bath, Dr. Royston?"

"I'd be thrilled." Kirsi stood up and danced the infant around the kitchen. "You'll be clean before you know it, sweetie pie."

Kirsi glanced at the clock. Carrie had been down for nearly an hour and a half. "I'll give your mommy another fifteen minutes, and then I have to go."

She kissed Amy's button nose. Baby-sitting had strengthened Kirsi. She'd lost herself in bathing, drying, powdering, dressing Amy in pink ruffles. Little songs Kirsi's grandmother had sung to her played in her mind, and she hummed them to Amy.

The phone rang. Not wanting to disturb Carrie, Kirsi grabbed it on the second ring. "Hi."

"Carrie?" a male voice asked.

"No, this is Dr. Royston. Carrie's resting and I'm taking care of the baby. May I take a message?"

"How's . . . how's the baby?"

Kirsi's spine tingled. Could this be . . . ? "Weston?"

"Is my baby okay?" he said, admitting who he was.

"Amy's beautiful and healthy. Weston, everyone's worried about you. Please come back," Kirsi urged. "The sheriff will help you. You aren't facing charges—"

"I can't risk it. Don't tell anyone I called. If I act like Carrie and the baby mean anything to me, they could be in danger."

"Weston, that doesn't make any sense. Come back. Please—"

"Tell Carrie I'll come back when I can. Tell her I'm happy about the baby—"

"Weston, please don't—"

He hung up.

"Weston!" she called into the phone in vain. The dial tone sounded. She hung up.

Carrie stood in the doorway. "Was that . . . ? Was it . . . ?"

Kirsi nodded. "He told me to tell you that he's happy about the baby and he'll come back when he can."

"When will that be?" Carrie slumped into the nearest kitchen chair, tears welling up in her eyes.

"I don't know, Carrie." Kirsi said as she dialed the sheriff's office.

# CHAPTER FOURTEEN

TWO WEEKS LATER in July, the gleaming white ambulance roared up to the ER doors. Her arms folded with tension, Kirsi waited at the curb, feeling heat roll up from the sun-baked pavement. As soon as the call had come in, she'd run to be at the ready.

Volunteering today, Ma Havlecek hovered beside her. "I've been worried about something like this happening to Harlan," Ma shouted. "I knew it would happen someday. That *woman* has wanted him dead since he married her sister in 1946."

Perspiration dripping down her spine, Kirsi shut out the older woman's anxious words. The litany of complaints about Veda McCracken—from almost everyone except Harlan—had been the one constant in Kirsi's brief stay in Steadfast. *Why don't people see how sick and miserable Veda is?* "Mrs. Havlecek," Kirsi said, raising her voice, "Veda is the one who called for the ambulance."

The siren cut off suddenly.

Ma humphed. "We know you think you can save that woman, but some people just like bein' mean."

Ignoring Ma, Kirsi stepped forward as the EMTs lifted

the stretcher out of the back of the ambulance. It jolted down on the cement, making Kirsi cringe. "Harlan!" She spoke loud and clear.

The old man looked gray with pain. The oxygen mask prevented him from speaking. But his eyelashes flickered and he looked up at her.

"Don't worry, Harlan," Kirsi reassured him. "We're going to take good care of you."

He blinked once as though in reply.

As the EMTs rattled off the information she needed, Kirsi ran alongside the gurney with her hand on Harlan's arm. After the heat, the air-conditioning inside enveloped her in gooseflesh.

Ma huffed behind her, speaking comfort and encouragement to her old friend. "Don't you worry, Harlan. You're gonna be fine. I'll call the church and get you on the prayer chain right away."

In the examining area, the nurse on duty quickly hooked Harlan up to the monitor and an IV. From what the EMTs said, Kirsi was already fairly sure that Harlan was in cardiac arrest, and the irregular pattern on the monitor confirmed the diagnosis.

Kirsi verbally detailed the instructions to stabilize his condition. She turned to Ma. "Call Dr. Erickson, please. I'm sure he will want to know—"

From behind Kirsi, Veda McCracken's unexpected voice came in gasps from what sounded like exertion. "Is he all right?"

"You!" Ma thundered, pointing a finger at Veda. "What did you do to Harlan?"

Veda struggled with tears. "He came with groceries. I heard him fall and he called me." Veda sobbed. "Is he going to be okay? Oh, Harlan—"

"Don't give us that pap!" Ma shouted. "You've wanted him dead for fifty years—"

"No! No!" Veda moaned. "I didn't!"

"Stop it!" Kirsi demanded. "Right now! I don't have time to referee you two. Veda, go sit on a chair in the waiting area. Ma, go call Dr. Erickson—now!"

Kirsi turned back to her patient.

"Full arrest!" the nurse called out.

"Begin compressions!" Kirsi whirled around and located the red crash cart. She switched it on and watched it charge. "Clear!"

*Please, God, help me—start his heart beating again,* Kirsi prayed silently. The next few minutes she fought for Harlan's life, repeatedly shocking his heart, trying to force it to beat again. "Come on, Harlan," she urged. "Come on. It's not your time yet. We need you."

*Beep. Beep.* The monitor sounded, signaling Harlan's heart beating again—weak, but beating.

Still holding the paddles in her hands, Kirsi stepped back—drenched with perspiration in spite of the air-conditioning. Her heart pounded like a kettledrum.

Harlan's eyes were closed, but he was breathing in the oxygen on his own.

"Stay with him," Kirsi told the nurse. "I'll get in touch with medi-vac. We'll transfer him to the Wausau Heart Center stat."

Kirsi turned and nearly bumped into Ma's solid form.

"Old Doc's on his way. Is Harlan going to be okay?"

Kirsi took pity on the older woman. She patted Ma's arm. "He's stable for now, but we've got to get him off ASAP for tests and whatever procedure he needs—bypass surgery or angioplasty."

Ma pressed her hand over Kirsi's. "Pastor Bruce is on his way over, and Harlan's on the prayer chain."

"Good. Then we've done all we can do for Harlan here."

After Harlan had been airlifted by the medi-vac chopper

to the heart center, Kirsi finally located Veda in her car in the clinic parking lot. Now, sitting beside Veda, Kirsi wondered how the impoverished woman could afford such a new car, but she didn't ask. More important was how Harlan's heart attack would impact Veda. Would this push her toward the help she needed or further away?

With her elbows propped on the center of the steering wheel, Veda was sobbing in the stuffy car. "I came out here because I don't want anybody to see me like this."

*You mean vulnerable?* What had it cost this woman to always look strong and invincible for the past fifty years? "This isn't helping Harlan, you know," Kirsi said in a soothing voice.

"You . . . you don't . . . understand. No one does."

"Try me."

Veda cried harder.

"Are you regretting the way you've treated Harlan?" Kirsi asked, trying to make progress now that Veda's surly veneer was beginning to crumble.

Veda gasped for breath and swallowed her tears. With the back of one meaty hand, she wiped her cheeks. "When I looked down at Harlan clutching his heart on my back step, I thought I'll really be all alone now." Another sob shuddered through her.

As the heat of the afternoon pressed down, Kirsi didn't know what to say. Veda was right. Harlan was the only one who had remained connected to her. *Lord, let me reach this woman's hardened heart.*

"You're leavin' too, I hear." Veda wiped her face again with her fists like a child.

"Yes."

"I can't ever remember being happy, not in seventy years. I've been a thorn in everyone's side since I was born."

With the heaviness only true regret could carry, Veda's

forlorn statement slid to the pit of Kirsi's stomach. "Why do you say that?"

"It's true." Veda's tone became harsh, ugly. "My mother didn't love me. She didn't even like me. I was her difficult child, her problem child. First, I had the colic and then I got the measles and chicken pox at the same time. That's why my skin looks so awful.

"And I never did do anything to suit my mother." Bitterness flowed in each of Veda's syllables. "But she always smiled at my sister and coddled her. She could do no wrong—ever! I wasn't pretty like my sister, and the kids taunted me. And then my sister married Harlan—he would never have even looked at me."

These revelations showed a crack had broken in Veda's hard shell. "I'm sure your mother loved you," Kirsi murmured.

Veda glanced at her. "If she did, she kept it a big secret. I don't know why I'm talkin' to you." Veda's normal venom leaked into her words. "I wouldn't talk to that psychologist you made me go to."

"Why not?" Time was short. Soon Kirsi would be going back to California, leaving Veda. And the woman needed so much help.

Laying her head back against the headrest, Veda sighed. "Talkin' don't make a difference. Things don't change—"

"That's not true. People can change."

"I won't—can't—change." Veda closed her eyes. "So what's the use of talkin' about it—to a psychologist or a doctor? It won't change me or anythin' else." Veda's sour tone was so familiar, so disheartening.

Kirsi wanted to speak of God, of Christ's power to change lives. But Veda had attended church all her life. She knew this as well as Kirsi did, but for some reason, Veda had never applied it to herself. Why not?

"Veda, I think you have already changed," Kirsi said, feeling her way through this. *Lord, help me help this woman. She has alienated everyone. She'll be all alone when I leave.*

*But God will still be here,* Kirsi thought. The thought sliced her in two. She nearly gasped aloud.

"I don't know," Veda went on. "I think . . . I think that I do feel better. I don't feel . . . heavy inside like I have for as long as I can remember. I think just sleeping sound at night . . ." She shook her head.

"Veda, you know who the Great Healer is. You've been to church enough—"

"Don't preach to me."

Frustration burned inside Kirsi. Her fuse was short today. "Fine. Then I'll do what a doctor does." She shook her finger at Veda. "Keep taking your meds and go back to the psychologist and talk this time."

Before Veda could object, Kirsi rushed on, "It's what Harlan would want. He's at Wausau by now. He'll do what his doctors say. So you do the same. Then when he comes back, you'll be able to talk to him and—" she turned to face Veda fully—"maybe now you'll be able to be a help to him."

Veda frowned. "I'm not much good to anybody—"

"Change that." Kirsi got out of the hot car. "Go home, Veda, and pray for Harlan. And for yourself."

※ ※ ※

*I want to remember everything about you, Doug. But don't look this way. I don't want you to know that I'm here.* The next evening, Kirsi stared at the back of Doug's head across the two sections of oak pews separating them. The distance between them seemed to expand before her eyes.

*Soon we'll be a continent apart. Maybe that will be easier to bear, to survive.* Aunt Uma was holding her own in India, but Nani called India and Steadfast, Wisconsin, every day now.

Pastor Bruce had called for this special prayer meeting for Harlan. She and Doug had exchanged shifts this week. She'd finished her shift at 3 P.M., and Doug wouldn't go in until eleven o'clock tonight.

Guessing that he'd come tonight, too, she'd slipped in late on purpose and sat in the far back corner. But she couldn't turn her gaze from the way his shaggy hair dipped and swirled on his nape. His tardiness in getting his much-needed haircut because he spent all his time at the clinic tugged at her. His selfless commitment to the hospital made her all too aware how hopelessly loving Doug was. He couldn't leave; she couldn't stay. Simple. Awful.

After the conversation Kirsi and Doug had shared in his den, they'd avoided each other except for passing each other at home and consulting at the clinic. She gazed across the width of the chapel now, recalling Doug's breath against her cheek and his lips caressing hers. Chiding herself for not focusing on the purpose of this meeting, Kirsi tuned in to what the pastor was saying at the front of the quaint country church.

"We all know how much Harlan has meant to this congregation over the years of his service." Pastor Bruce's golden hair looked blonder from the summer sun. Two oscillating pole fans batted the warm air back and forth. "Having him as an elder has been a great help in my own growth as a Christian."

"I'd like to shake that Veda McCracken!" Ma said loud enough to be heard by everyone.

Biting her lower lip, Kirsi held back a retort. Just because Harlan had his attack on Veda's doorstep . . .

Ma's dapper, silver-haired husband, Bruno Havlecek, patted his wife's arm. "Ma, she's her own worst enemy—"

"She doesn't have a friend in this county!" Ma exclaimed. "Except for Harlan—and did she ever appreciate him? No! I don't care what that new doctor thinks. Veda has gone too far this time."

Years of suppressed resentment toward Veda had poured out like so much acid. *I understand that, but it doesn't make it right!*

Kirsi stood up. "I don't know what you think Veda has done. Harlan brought her groceries as he does every week and collapsed on her back steps. She called 911 and she may have saved his life."

Doug turned and looked at her. Deep understanding passed between them. He read her heart as she read his.

"He shouldn't have been out in the heat yesterday," a woman Kirsi didn't recognize insisted.

Doug stood as though to come to her. She gave a shake of her head, warning him away.

"Nick had to work and couldn't take Harlan, so he went alone," the woman went on. "Harlan should have been home in his air-conditioning. We know that Veda wouldn't walk across the street to help Harlan."

Murmurs of agreement made Bruce frown. "We're here to pray for Harlan. Veda is in God's hands, and she needs our prayers too."

Olie Olson, a gray-haired man in his seventies, snorted. "He can have her."

"I think we're getting off track—," Bruce said.

Doug cleared his throat. "I think this would be an excellent time for me to give everyone some good news." He glanced over at Kirsi.

Did he have any idea how her love for him leaped higher and flowed stronger each time their eyes made contact? *Doug, I have to get away from you!* She sat down very still, holding everything in. What good news was he talking about?

"My grandfather has just signed contracts with a husband-wife couple who are both doctors. They are semiretiring here in the fall and will begin to cover the ER with Dr. Royston and me."

So the couple she'd met were really coming. *I'm so happy for you, Doug.* Tears threatened.

The disapproval of Veda was forgotten, and the room buzzed with excited whispers.

"What about Dr. Royston?" Olie asked. "Is she leavin' or stayin'?"

Kirsi struggled with herself and hoped she showed no reaction to this less-than-supportive question.

Doug assumed his protective stance. "Dr. Royston is staying—" he nodded toward her—"until she finds a replacement as she always said she would. My grandfather has talked with a resident Dr. Royston contacted who is interested in practicing here."

More chatter and a bit of clapping.

Kirsi tried to smile—as though the news were as joyful to her as she had once thought it would be.

"You mean we won't need Dr. Royston, anyway?" Olie asked.

Doug faced Kirsi, looking over Olie's head. "Family obligations she hasn't made public are pulling Dr. Royston back to California. But she would be welcome to stay if she could."

*But I can't. Oh, Doug . . .*

The next scorching day, on the way home from her shift, Kirsi decided to stop by Carrie's house and see how Amy was doing. Her morning with the infant last week had been the one bright spot in her week. She parked her car. As Kirsi stepped outside, beads of perspiration popped out on her forehead.

With Amy in her arms, Carrie opened the back door at

Kirsi's knock. "Oh, hi, Dr. Royston. Can you believe this weather?"

"Want a few minutes off? I need some cuddling-a-baby therapy." Kirsi smiled, though her emotions swirled through her like a stiff winter wind on the hot summer day.

"Sure. I thought you might have . . ."

Kirsi guessed the girl's thoughts. She shook her head. "I haven't heard anything from or about Weston."

Carrie pressed her lips together as though holding back emotions or maybe words. "Come on in."

Kirsi set her purse down on the kitchen table and sat in the chair Carrie motioned toward. Both of them wore shorts and tank tops. An oscillating fan buzzed in the quiet house. "So how's Amy?"

"She's finally got her days and nights right." The girl grinned, showing Kirsi a bit of her normal prettiness. "How is Mr. Carey?"

The mention of Harlan set a weight over Kirsi's heart. Her professional detachment had dissolved in this case. "Harlan had an angioplasty and a pacemaker implanted. He should be coming home next week." But Veda had locked herself in her house and wouldn't come out. Would Harlan's heart attack kill Veda? Kirsi wondered.

"I'm glad he's going to be okay. He always has something nice to say to everybody."

"Yes, Harlan is special." Kirsi nodded and held out her hands for the baby.

Carrie relinquished Amy but stayed at the table.

Thinking the girl might be lonely and want some conversation, Kirsi made herself look up and smile. *Okay, Carrie, let's talk. But not about Veda or my leaving.* "Is that coffee on the stove still good?"

"Sure." Carrie rose and went to the stove. She placed a cup of strong, black coffee in front of Kirsi.

"Thanks." Kirsi took a sip of the hot murky brew. Then she looked down at the baby and studied Amy. She frowned and touched Amy's forehead. "Carrie, bring me your baby thermometer."

"Is something wrong?"

"She feels a bit warm, that's all." Kirsi kept her tone even, although her pulse surged higher.

When Carrie returned with the thermometer, Kirsi pressed it into Amy's ear until it beeped. "One hundred and one degrees."

"I thought she was just hot because today's so steamy." With the back of her hand, Carrie touched her daughter's forehead. "Is she sick?"

Kirsi examined the child, taking inventory of her symptoms—fever, rapid respiration, slightly purplish tinge to the skin. Kirsi felt a chill go through her. *Should I have anticipated this?* "Carrie, go pack a diaper bag for her." Kirsi restrained her own leap to panic. "We've got to get her to the clinic."

"What's wrong?" Carrie's voice rose with alarm.

"I think Amy may have a Group B strep infection." Kirsi rose.

"Strep? You mean like her throat? Is that bad?"

"It's bad." Kirsi headed toward the door. "Get the bag and her car seat. I'm taking you both to the clinic now."

# CHAPTER FIFTEEN

"DON'T. DON'T." Kirsi pushed against Doug as he held her tightly in his arms. When he softly kissed her forehead, her cheek, she stopped struggling. "Hold me, hold me, Doug." His familiar scent made her weak. *I love you.*

A hand shook her shoulder—again. "Kirsi, wake up. Wake up."

Her eyes opened, startled by light. She looked into Doug's worried face. She touched his stubbled cheek. "Don't," she whispered and then realized she'd been dreaming. But she wasn't now. Doug was real.

"Oh!" She sat up on the bed in the dimly lit doctors' lounge. *Did I say his name? I hope not!*

"I wouldn't have wakened you," Doug apologized, looking uncomfortable, "but you were tossing and turning. I thought you might be having a nightmare."

*Yes, loving you and having to leave you. It's a nightmare.* She pushed her loosened hair back and swung her bare feet down onto the linoleum floor. She shoved her feet into her leather sandals. "I just lay down for a few minutes."

"When was that?"

She looked at the round wall clock that read 7:25 P.M.

and sighed. "Almost two hours ago." Stretching, she rose, fighting her awareness of Doug. His emerging honey-colored beard gave his face a fuzzy peach look that nearly turned her heart over. She almost leaned over and brushed her cheek against his. *Don't go there, Kirsi.*

Not giving her an inch, Doug stood his ground right in front of her.

*Doug, hold me and never let me go. No.* Eyes averted, she sidestepped him. "How's Amy?"

"She's still critical. But I think you caught it in time."

Kirsi folded her arms around herself, putting up her tattered defenses again. It was just like Doug to soften the blow. Even as she'd driven Carrie and Amy to the clinic, she'd noted the child worsening second by second. The baby's fever had spiked to one hundred and four degrees by the time they'd reached the clinic. Group B strep could cause brain damage from the high fever—could even kill.

*Please, Lord, no.* Regret, more regret. "I should have thought of this possibility," she admitted, hanging her head. "There's been so much debate about screening for the bacteria."

Doug moved closer still but didn't touch her. "Don't forget that she had leaked amniotic fluid for several hours before her water broke completely. Not enough has been taught about babies contracting Group B strep infections in the birth canal. And not every newborn develops the infection even if exposed."

Nodding, Kirsi chewed her lower lip. The few inches between them were charged with denied, pent-up longing. *I shouldn't be thinking about Doug and me. Amy's in critical condition.*

*Thank You, Lord, that I stopped by to check on Amy. Please let Doug be right, that we caught it in time. Save Amy without any long-term problems. Bless her parents. Oh,*

*Weston, where are you? Carrie needs you. She's too young to bear this all alone.* "How's Carrie?"

"Napping on a cot next to Amy's crib. At my insistence, her exhausted aunt just went home for the night. It's too bad Weston can't be found. Carrie could use his support about now."

Agreeing, Kirsi shoved her hands in the back pockets of her rumpled jean shorts. Hungering to press close to Doug, she kept herself in check. But the desire to feel his comforting touch crested in her, a tide of yearning. "I'll check on them and then I'll head home." *I have to get away from you.*

"It was good you stopped by Carrie's when you did. I think you caught it in time," Doug tried to reassure her once more.

Knowing it was too soon to know if this were true, Kirsi stared at the floor, simmering with sudden frustration. *Can't anything go right?*

"Kirsi?"

His soothing tone nearly swamped her with the desire to give in to her feelings. "Time will tell," she mumbled.

"You should get some real sleep in your own bed. I'll call you if Amy takes a turn for the better." He left unsaid, "Or for the worse."

*I didn't know I could feel more anguish than I do already.* "That's okay," she said shortly and snagged her purse from under the bed. "I'll just look in and be on my way—"

"You'll call the sheriff's department first and have them follow you—"

"Don't worry." She walked away from him, putting distance between them. "I'll call them on my way to Amy's room."

"Okay." Doug stayed where he was.

Sensing his gaze following her, she left the room and closed the door behind her. *I just want to be close to him. Lord, this is agony.*

As she made herself put one foot in front of the other down the hall, she took out her cell phone and punched in the familiar number.

"County Sheriff's Department."

"This is Dr. Royston." Kirsi sighed with fatigue and low spirits. Evidently her nap had sent her to a deep level of sleep, and wakened prematurely, she felt like the walking dead. "I'm going to be leaving the clinic in a few minutes, and I'll need my escort home."

"I'll let the sheriff know, Doctor," the dispatch said as usual.

"Thanks." She hung up and tiptoed into Amy's room. With an infant-size oxygen mask over her little face and hooked to two IVs, the tiny girl appeared even smaller . . . so very fragile.

Carrie was sleeping on a narrow cot beside the crib. Kirsi noticed that the young mother must have been holding on to the crib before she'd fallen asleep—one slender hand still lay between the crib railing.

*Lord, help this infant and her young mother. Please bring back Weston. All I've heard makes me think that he should have a chance to be a father to this sweet baby. Can't all this just end? Take away the threat that Weston fears and let Your power be felt in a mighty way in this.*

Right before Kirsi left the room, she peeked out to see if Doug was in sight, feeling like a pathetic weakling. *God, bring the new resident and the new doctors soon. I can't go on like this—torn in two.*

Doug was nowhere to be seen, so Kirsi scurried down the hall and out through the ER entrance. She would wait in her Jeep for a deputy to escort her home as she did every night after duty.

As she walked to her Jeep in the parking lot, she noted a car parked beside hers and recognized it as Veda's. Seeing

Veda sitting inside, Kirsi rushed ahead. "Veda, is there something wrong?"

Veda motioned for her. "Get in."

With a glance around the quiet lot to see if a police car had arrived yet, Kirsi got in on the passenger side. "What's wrong? Aren't you feeling—"

"I called Old Doc to see where you was." Veda's voice sounded funny, tense somehow.

Warning raced up both Kirsi's arms, raising the little hairs. "What is it?"

"I heard Weston's baby is sick."

How quickly news got around here. It had only been a matter of hours. "Yes, the baby—"

"Is it serious?"

"Yes."

Silence.

"Veda, I'm really tired and a deputy will be here soon to follow me home—"

"I see stuff," Veda broke in. "I drive around at night. I'm always watchin'. I don't want anythin' to get by me," she said with smugness. "I like knowin' things."

Kirsi had heard about Veda's propensity for having surprising knowledge of people's secrets. An innate snoop. But . . . "Why are you telling me this, Veda?"

Veda chewed her lip.

What was the old woman playing on her? "Veda?"

"I seen where that kid is."

Kirsi's heart sped up. "Kid?"

"Weston. I seen him—"

"Where?" Kirsi grabbed Veda's fleshy arm.

Veda gave her a sideways look, gloating. "Nobody else saw it. Not that Durand. Not that Sloan. But I did. Crazy Old Veda McCracken did." Her mouth curved into a self-satisfied smirk.

Kirsi clutched Veda's thick arm. "Where is he?"

Tugging her arm away from Kirsi, Veda ignored her question. "I was driving around one night after I got home from the hospital, you know . . . after the night he run away? I thought to myself, *I can find that kid.*" Veda leered at her in the dying light of day.

"Did you?"

"Sure I did," Veda boasted. "Everyone saying he might be hiding with a friend. They searched all the friends' houses, didn't they, and came up with nothin', right? And to my way of thinkin', he wouldn't want to spread trouble bad enough to make him run to any o' his friends, would he?"

"No," Kirsi had to admit it.

"And then people thinkin' he would hide out at some hunter's cabin somewhere in the woods or a lake cabin not bein' used. That's silly. It's summer!" Veda held out her palms. "People who stay away all year come for the summer. The woods and lakes are full of 'em." Veda turned to Kirsi and nodded once.

"Go on," Kirsi prompted. *Why are you telling me this, Veda? Can I trust you?*

"So I thought to myself—what's the one place within a few miles of the clinic where Weston could get to easy and be pretty sure nobody would be checkin' it out?" Veda gave her a triumphant smile.

"Please, Veda." Factual or not, Veda's story sounded true.

"You know the plant that shut down over in LaFollette?" Veda teased her along.

"I've heard of it." Kirsi's mind raced, trying to remember where the plant was. "Is he there?"

Beaming with self-satisfaction, Veda nodded.

"Why didn't you tell anyone?" Kirsi demanded, her clenched hands closing into fists.

The old woman shrugged. "Why? Nobody offered a reward."

Incensed, Kirsi felt like shaking Veda. How could the woman be so heartless? But, then, this was Veda McCracken. Her current behavior only reaffirmed how the woman had earned her unflattering reputation.

Kirsi still simmered but turned the heat down on her aggravation. "We've got to go get him," she said in what she hoped was a calm voice. "His baby's critical. Carrie needs all the support she can get, and she's been so worried about Weston."

"That's why I come. I knew you'd believe me. That sheriff—" Veda's words dripped with vinegar—"wouldn't believe me if I told him the sun rose in the east. They never believe what I say," she added darkly.

The sheriff! Kirsi fumbled in her purse for her cell phone. That deputy should be here by now. She punched the speed-dial for the sheriff's office. "Hello, this is Dr. Royston. I'm still waiting for my escort."

"I'm sorry, Doctor, but everyone is out of the office. An emergency."

*What emergency?* An ominous presentiment caught around Kirsi's heart. "Well, can't you call anyone or radio them?"

"No, Doctor, no one will be available until much later." The dispatcher paused. "You know, it's barely dark out. Why don't you drive home and call me when you get there?"

"I'm not . . . I-I . . . ," Kirsi stammered. The dispatcher had an odd tone in her voice. What was up? What had diverted the whole sheriff's department? Should she report what Veda had revealed? No. What if Veda was telling her a story—just to make herself important? If Kirsi mentioned it and it proved untrue, the anger toward the old woman would be even stronger. *I have to check it out myself first.* "Dispatch, okay, I'm going now."

"Be sure to call me when you get home, all right?"

"Will the sheriff be busy for long? What's going on?"

"I'm not at liberty to give that information."

Kirsi felt the same hesitance, pregnant with unrevealed information. Both she and the dispatcher had information they could not reveal. "Okay."

She snapped her phone shut and turned to Veda. "I want you to lead me over there."

"No problem."

"You're sure he's there?" Kirsi asked, jangling inside with warnings.

"He was today." Veda grinned.

Kirsi thought about running inside to tell Doug. *I can always call him on my cell phone if I find Weston.* Repressing her thoughts that screamed for caution, she jumped out of Veda's car and ran to hers. She still felt guilty for not preventing Weston from fleeing the hospital while she was on duty. *Oh, Lord, let me find him!*

Before Kirsi even got her seat belt hooked, she saw Veda speeding toward one of the lot exits. *No time to waste. Lord, help me find Weston safe and well!*

Following Veda's car the few miles to the plant was like a wild steeplechase. The older woman ran stop signs, sometimes drove her car onto the shoulder drunkenly, generally making Kirsi's heart beat and lurch in her chest. How did the woman keep her license?

Then from the veil of surrounding pines, the deserted plant stood out starkly on the dead-end road a mile from the highway. The large metal building with high dirty windows sat in the midst of the clearing, an empty parking lot spread out in front. A one-way access lane created an arc around the building. The entry along the right side of the lot led around to the back of the building, where the loading dock must be. Then the exit lane—one way out—continuing to curve around the other side of the parking lot and back out to the road in.

Dusk had settled over the sky above the treetops in bands of dark purple. Of course, Veda drove in the wrong way, entering the exit lane to the left. She pulled over to the side of the road into the deepening shadows under the cover of the thicket of looming pines.

Kirsi pulled in behind her. She got out and went to Veda's side of the car. She paused there.

"You walk around back and you'll find a door." Veda motioned around the right side. "The padlock's been unlocked. If you tug it, it comes open by itself."

Kirsi studied Veda's face.

"You don't believe me," the old woman grumbled. She made to open her door.

"No," Kirsi said in a low voice. Veda, with her precarious health, shouldn't be involved. "I'll go in by myself."

"I can go—"

"No." Kirsi didn't want Veda with her high blood pressure overexcited in this heat. "I'll go see if the door is still unlocked. If I can get in, I'll look for Weston. You stay here—"

"No—"

"Stay put. I might scare him out, and you can see which way he runs."

"Okay."

Her cell phone clutched in one hand, Kirsi walked close to the trees, taking cover in their long shadows. The night buzzed with insects; frogs bellowed from some unseen pond or creek. The humid heat pressed in on Kirsi, making sweat trickle down her spine. Her skin crawled as though someone was watching, following her. She glanced around uneasily. *I won't give in to paranoia. No one is here. Probably not even Weston.*

Edging around the large metal building, she spotted the door and its padlock. She ran to it, making her feet land softly. The padlock was just as Veda had described—Kirsi tugged it and it opened. She held her breath and pushed the door open.

Muggy, stale air roiled into her face. Her instincts shouted, "Go back! Do not enter!" Refusing to give in to nameless fear, she forced herself to step inside. Too many people needed Weston. And maybe if he was found, the awful chain of events that had started with his overdose would cease once and for all.

She stood inside in a small area near what appeared to be an office. She reached over and flicked on a wall switch. Nothing. The power was off. Humidity and heat that had built up from the sweltering day settled over her like a smothering damp wool blanket. Her nerves jittered. Had Veda set her up for some sick prank? *I can barely see my hand in front of my face. Weston, if you are here, how can I find you?*

She took another few steps forward beyond the entry-way. The interior looked murky. The charcoal shadows would turn inky black within minutes. She considered how she could get Weston to come to her, so she wouldn't have to go in farther or leave without him.

"Weston!" she shouted, desperate. "Weston, it's Dr. Royston! I need you! Your baby's in critical condition! Carrie needs you! Weston!"

The stillness and darkness closed around her, confining her as if she were in a cave, and triggered her claustrophobia. Her skin prickled. Her breathing came fast; then she couldn't breathe. Choking . . . she took a step backward, ready to bolt.

She turned and—

"Dr. Royston!" Weston stood before her. "How'd you find me? What's wrong with my baby?"

"Weston!" Relief roared through her, making her knees weak.

"What's wrong with my baby?" He clutched her arms. "The guys said she was all right."

"What guys?"

"I'm not tellin'."

The guys must be friends who brought him what—food, water, news? She smelled him. His sweat from spending weeks in this sweltering metal box. His eyes and teeth shone white against his grimy face. He was gaunt. Weak. "Amy, your little girl, has a Group B strep infection. She's in the clinic on oxygen and antibiotics."

"Is she dying?" He looked ready to faint. And why not, after weeks in this suffocating place?

"She's critical. You've got to come. Carrie wants you there. She needs you." Kirsi gripped his arms, letting him feel her insistence. *You're going with me, Weston.*

"How did you find me?"

Kirsi had to get out of here; the stuffy, heated air and the darkness were closing in on her. She shivered in spite of the heat. "Let's talk outside—"

"I can't leave. He might find me—"

"Who? Who exactly is after you, Weston?"

"I don't know his name, but I saw him talking to Nail that day—"

"Nail? Is that a real name?" She tried to make this fit in her mind. So much had happened since the day she arrived at the clinic and treated Weston for the overdose.

Weston nodded. "Nail was the guy out in the school parking lot who gave me the joint, the one I smoked and got so sick from."

Oh! Light dawned in Kirsi's mind. "Did Nail wear a ball cap and black sunglasses?"

"Yeah, the next thing I heard was that he'd tried to unhook me, kill me, and then I had a deputy guarding my room. Then Nail came up dead. Over and over, the sheriff described Nail and asked me if I'd seen anybody with Nail." Weston's voice shook. "I got scared. Why did someone kill Nail? I figured it might be connected to me.

"I mean I could ID Nail, so Nail tried to shut me up, but then he got killed. Everyone knows what happened to Nick's girlfriend when she got mixed up with somebody in a drug gang. And Nail . . . he had a gang tattoo on his neck. It was like the one Nick saw on the wall in the guys' bathroom at school. He showed it to me." The teen trembled.

"Why didn't you tell all this to the sheriff?" Kirsi shook Weston.

"I got scared. The sheriff wasn't able to stop Nail from getting killed." Weston's voice rose, shrill and emotional. Strain had taken its toll on him. "Why was Nail trying to hurt me in the clinic? All I could think of is it must be because I saw the other guy. And if I told about Nail and that guy, I might end up dead!"

Weston sounded near hysteria.

Kirsi gripped his shoulders and shook him again. "Nothing is going to happen to you. Come on. I'll drive you straight to the clinic, and then we'll call Sheriff Durand."

"No! Matt got shot, too, didn't he? I can't risk it!"

Kirsi pushed him back toward the door. "Out. I have to get out of here."

He resisted, but he was weakened probably by hunger and thirst. She managed to get him outside. She closed the door behind her and pushed the padlock up. "Come on." She started in the direction where she'd left her Jeep.

The sound of an engine came from behind her.

Still pulling Weston along, she turned her head. A car—a gray sedan. She began to run, her pulse speeding. "My Jeep's around this way! Hurry!"

From behind, a shot exploded in the stillness.

Kirsi screamed.

Another shot.

Kirsi turned her head.

Weston screeched and fell. He clutched his chest. Blood flowing.

*Weston!* She whirled around.

The car was bearing down straight at her.

She jumped to the side and stumbled, losing her footing. She skinned her knees on the loose gravel. *God, help us!*

The car screeched to a halt. The smell of burned rubber.

Frantic, she got up on her knees. *My cell phone—where is it? There it is!*

Footsteps running toward her.

She shrieked. Scrambling to her feet, she started to run toward the cell phone on the ground.

A strong hand swung her around and flung her up against the metal wall. She felt the wind swoosh out of her. Her head banged. She nearly went down.

"This is great!" a harsh voice snarled. "I came to take care of the kid, and I get you at the same time. This is my lucky day!"

Kirsi's ears roared. She shook her head, trying to clear it. "Who . . . ?" She gasped for breath, the hot air choking her. "Who are you?"

He slammed her backward again. With his body flush against her, he pressed her hard against the wall, his foul breath hot in her face. "They call me Spider. I like to see people squirm before I bite." Menace laced his tone.

Fear—freezing needles—shot through her. She raised her eyes, looking into his face. He was near her age, good-looking, but he had a brutal glint in his dirty brown eyes. He leered at her, pressing harder against her, nearly crushing the breath from her. She struggled, screamed, and tried to push him away.

He grabbed her ponytail, twisting her head back, and bent over her face. In her panic, she felt his evil like a physical force.

She cringed. *God, no!* Revulsion vied with horror. She fought to push him away again—her head aching from his twisting her hair tightly. Then she felt the muzzle of his gun pressed hard against her chest. She screamed.

He laughed and pushed her back harder against the wall.

She cried out again.

He slammed her head against the wall.

Her senses reeling, she felt him wrench her away from the wall and shove her forward.

"What are you going to do?" she demanded, staggering and tasting blood on her lips. "What—?"

He pushed her forward. "I'm going to tie up my last loose end—you," he said, a sneer in his voice, "as soon as I get us out of this county. The sheriff raided the lab. But I got the profits, and I took out that kid and now you. I've been watching you, Dr. Royston, playing with your mind for weeks." He laughed with a cruel inflection. "I'm going to take you far away. I don't want them to find your body. I don't want to be tied to your death. You'll just disappear and so will I."

Her insides congealed. Lessons in self-protection flooded her mind. *Never let an attacker take you to a second location.*

She suddenly twisted out of his grasp and started to run.

"Stop or I'll shoot you. You can bleed to death in my car. I don't care."

She ran.

A bullet hit the ground beside her.

She froze, reeling.

He grabbed both her hands from behind, pinning her wrists together with one of his large hands.

She let herself fall to the ground, deadweight.

He cursed.

The last thing she saw was the pistol butt coming down.

*God, save me!*

# CHAPTER SIXTEEN

KIRSI FOUGHT FOR BREATH, choked. She felt her eyes open, but no light came. She blinked. No light. Just stuffy, close blackness . . . and motion. The stifling hot air reeked of gasoline and what else? Ammonia? Alcohol? The sound of wheels under her. Her head splitting, she reached out farther into space. . . . Her fingertips touched metal overhead.

*I'm in a car trunk.* The ghastly revelation stopped her heart.

The gorge swelled in her throat. Screams coming from deep inside her couldn't get past it.

*I can't breathe!*

She panted, gasping for breath. Her arms and legs flailed, hitting the lid of the trunk—pounding.

The car slewed around a bend. Unable to stop herself, she rolled, bumping her throbbing head, her raw knees. Warm blood dripped into her eyes. *I'm hurt.*

*Help! Help!* Her screams never made it to her lips. She scrabbled at the coarse material beneath her, but still she rolled with every car motion.

She gagged. *God! God! God!* Her spirit wailed prayers

without words. The odorous blackness smothered her.
*Get me out! I can't stand it.*

She retched. Her mother's face flashed in her mind.
*Mother!*

She fought losing consciousness. She tucked herself in
the fetal position and tried to keep from reeling with each
movement of the vehicle. Panic flowed through her—a
rushing tidal wave. It threatened her sanity, her connection
to reality.

*I can't give in to this! I can't let it overpower me!*

*Oh, Father in heaven, help me. Preserve my sanity. Give
me Your strength. Mine is so pitiful. Help me. Help me
survive.*

❊ ❊ ❊

"Hello," a weak voice whispered into Doug's ear over his
cell phone.

Doug noticed Kirsi's cell phone number displayed on
the screen of his phone. "Kirsi?" Doug asked as he headed
out of the clinic into the hot night.

"No, it's . . . Weston." The faint voice faltered. "I'm at
. . . Turner Mill . . . I'm shot. Need help."

"How did you get Dr. Royston's cell phone?" Doug
asked, not believing what he was hearing.

"Dr. . . . she . . . dropped it. She had . . . number
program . . . I'm shot." Weston groaned. "He shot me."

The hair on the back of Doug's neck quivered. "Who?
Who shot you?"

No response. The line didn't click, but still no answer.

"Weston?" *Kirsi,why aren't you with your phone?* Doug
turned and ran back inside to the clinic's reception desk.

The receptionist looked up.

"I'm going with the ambulance to Turner's Mill," he told
her. "Weston's there—shot. Call the sheriff's office and tell

them to meet me there. No excuses. Dr. Royston could be injured!"

*Or dead! Dear God, forbid it!* His heart beating in time to his feet pounding the tile floor, he raced toward the ambulance bay.

※ ※ ※

With a police siren drawing nearer, Doug hovered over Weston, whom he'd helped strap to a stretcher and move inside the ambulance. The EMT had just finished hooking the teen to a portable IV.

Even in the dark Doug had found Weston lying in a pool of blood behind the shut-down Turner Mill. After assessing Weston's injuries and applying pressure bandages, he'd searched the surrounding area with the ambulance headlights. But he'd found no sign of Kirsi—except for her cell phone clutched in Weston's bloody hand.

A police SUV screeched to a halt near the ambulance. Burke, his arm in a sling, bounded out and over to Doug. "You found Weston?"

"He's been shot twice, both bullets lodged in the chest," Doug informed him, his hot blood surging with each beat of his heart, "but they missed an artery. We're rushing him to the clinic. But, Burke, Kirsi must have been here."

"I saw her Jeep on the way in, but how do you know she drove it here? Someone could have stolen it." One-handed, Burke hauled himself up into the ambulance and stared down at the unconscious teen.

"This is her cell phone." Doug indicated the second blood-smeared phone clipped to his belt.

"That doesn't necessarily mean that—"

"Weston used it to call me. When I answered the phone, it showed on the display that it was Kirsi's. So I asked him how he got it, and he said Dr. Royston dropped it."

Burke cursed softly. "We raided the meth lab tonight. We stirred up a hornet's nest—"

"We're ready to roll, Dr. Doug," the EMT announced.

Burke jumped down and snapped on a high-powered flashlight. "You go on, Doug." He began moving away, training his beam on the building and then the ground. "Take care of the kid. I'll comb the area inside and out and see if I can pick up any clue about what happened to her. Godspeed!"

※ ※ ※

In the clinic's ER, Doug stood over Weston, still lying on a gurney. Weston had suffered a punctured and collapsed lung. The other bullet had lodged dangerously near his heart.

Old Doc burst into the room. "You found him!"

"At Turner's Mill." Then Doug rattled off what he'd done to stabilize Weston. "The medi-vac is on its way."

Even as he spoke, Doug heard the thundering of chopper blades overhead. Doug and his grandfather, along with a nurse, pushed the gurney down the hall and out the door to the helipad.

The whirling blades beat the air—stirring up dust and small pebbles. Swirling hot air nearly choked Doug. Leaning close over Weston, he squinted as he guided the gurney to the side of the chopper. The pilot helped load Weston and secure him inside the helicopter beside the medi-vac nurse. Then Doug, his granddad, and the nurse bent over and ran back to the clinic.

As soon as they cleared the pad, the whine of the blades intensified. Doug clapped his hands over his ears. Then it was hovering in the air, clear of the building and rising higher, higher. The sound receded; the helicopter disappeared into the night sky.

Doug stood there—pummeled by the sound and vortex of hot wind.

"Where's Dr. Royston?" Old Doc asked, shading his eyes. "She never came home tonight."

"We don't know." Doug felt his stomach sinking. *I can't lose you, Kirsi. I love you.* "Weston used her cell phone to call me." The memory of Kirsi's softness within his arms hit him, forcing out a gasp. *Oh, Father.*

"Heavenly Father, bless us now in our hour of need," Granddad implored. He put his arm around Doug's shoulders. "Father, take care of our colleague and friend. Keep her in the hollow of Your hand. Defend her. Uphold her. Give her Your strength!"

*Where are you, Kirsi?* Doug pinched the bridge of his nose, holding back tears. *Dear God, let them find her. I could bear letting her go back to California, but I can't lose her like this!*

❋ ❋ ❋

*Lord, help me.* Kirsi moaned. Suffocating blackness wrapped around her. *I don't want to die. I want to see Doug again.* Then the memory of her kidnapper's hands striking her started her trembling again.

Terror worse than any she'd known ripped and shredded her deep inside, making her shake. *No! No! I've got to get away. I can't just lie here and wait for him to kill me. . . .*

The vehicle surged forward, throwing her against the rear. Her hands brushed against the key latch. She clawed at it in the utter darkness. The car sped up more. The momentum kept her pressed against the latch. *How do I get it to open? Lord, help me! Please help me!*

❋ ❋ ❋

Doug paced the floor at the clinic. Granddad was on duty and doing rounds. The phone rang at the reception area. Doug ran toward it.

The receptionist picked up. She nodded and handed the phone to Doug. "It's Deputy Sloan."

"Burke!" Doug exclaimed.

"I didn't find any sign of her at the scene of the crime. But I did find two sets of bloody footprints heading away from where Weston must have been shot and evidence of tire tracks. I checked her Jeep, abandoned on the shoulder in the cover of pines on the exit side. There were tire marks of a car parked in front of it, but it's long gone. How's Weston?"

"Airlifted. He's probably in Eau Claire by now at the Trauma Center."

"Good. I'm going to head back—"

"Burke—" The cell phone on Doug's belt rang. He looked down, hoping it was Kirsi. "Hold on, Burke." Doug lifted and snapped open his phone. "Hello?"

"He's got her in the trunk of his car!" a hoarse female voice screeched.

"Who is this?"

"Veda. It's Veda. He's stopped for gas. We're at that little station on 27 at Rushton Road in the next county south. I'm calling from the drive-up phone booth outside. He's driving a gray sedan, license number WHK 7709. WHK 7709. Got that?"

"Veda? What are you—?"

"He's coming out. Get the sheriff to call the state police. I'm afraid he'll pull off somewhere and attack her. He started to back at the mill. I'm trying to keep up with him, but not too close. I don't want—"

The line went dead.

"Veda!" Doug yelled into the phone. "Veda!"

No answer.

He turned to the other receiver. "Burke! Veda says Kirsi's in someone's car trunk."

Dead silence. "Veda! Veda McCracken? What's she got to do with this?"

"I don't know, but Kirsi's spent a lot of time and effort on Veda."

"Do you think we can believe her?" Burke demanded.

"I don't think we have a choice. She even got a license-plate number." Doug repeated the information Veda had given.

"I'll call Rodd right now so he can get the state police on it. They'll put out an APB. We can't take any chances. We didn't catch everyone at the meth lab tonight. Some nasty customers gave us the slip. I'll call when I have news." *Click.*

Doug felt like slipping to his knees. *Oh, God, this is a nightmare. There's nothing I can do, but You know where Kirsi is. Guard her. Save her. I love her.*

Then he ran for the door.

His granddad shouted after him, "Where are you going?"

"Highway 27!"

# CHAPTER SEVENTEEN

IN THE POSTMIDNIGHT HOUR, Doug zoomed past the gas station where Veda had called him from. He pressed down on the gas pedal. The arrow on his speedometer trembled at 71 mph, and he pushed his foot down harder. *God, protect her; protect my love.*

In the murky blackness ahead, he glimpsed red brake lights. Spanning the darkened state highway, rotating blue lights flashed against the dull pewter sky overhead and the pine-shrouded areas on both sides of the road.

Roadblock. He slowed. He swallowed, trying to bring moisture to his dry mouth. Had they found Kirsi? Had the APB worked?

Pulling over to the shoulder, he parked at a downward angle toward the roadside ditch. He got out, his heart pounding dully. Ahead, he heard the metallic crackle of police radios and glimpsed figures standing and moving around state-trooper cars.

He passed another civilian car parked on the shoulder. "Hey," the driver called from his open window, "don't go up there. They shot someone."

Doug took off at a run. "Kirsi!" he shouted. *Please, Lord, no.* "Kirsi!" He sprinted between two police cars.

State troopers in light tan uniforms shouted for him to stop. He ignored them. A warning shot fired. Then one trooper tackled him and held him.

"I'm Dr. Erickson from the Erickson Clinic in Steadfast!" Doug shouted as he struggled to get free. "Is Dr. Royston here? Is she all right?"

The officer didn't relax his grip. "Show me some ID." A second trooper came close, his gun at the ready.

Doug scrabbled in his hip pocket, pulled out his wallet, and flipped it open to his driver's license and clinic staff ID.

The second trooper trained a flashlight on both. "Okay, but—"

"Kirsi!" he shouted again, straining to pull away.

Kirsi leaned against a state cop, feeling as if her skeleton had dissolved. She couldn't stop crying. She felt ground down . . . sucked dry.

Then she heard his voice. "Doug?"

"Kirsi," Doug called back, "where are you?"

Was he here or was she imagining it? "Doug?" she whimpered.

"Kirsi, I'm here!" Then he was there in front of her.

She tried to move away from the officer, but he held on to her, objecting, restraining.

"Please, please," she gasped. "It's Dr. Erickson."

As soon as the officer released her, she fell into Doug's arms. Pressing her face against his shirtfront, she sobbed. "Doug . . ."

Doug crushed Kirsi to him, wanting to bind her physically to him always, forever, never to be parted, never to be in danger again. Words eluded him. Bending his head, he kissed her hair, her cheekbones and then found her mouth. He tightened his embrace. *My love, you're safe. Praise God.*

"I was afraid I'd never see you again," he was finally able to say. The words came from deep inside him, and he could barely make them heard over the voices, radios, and night sounds. "Are you all right?"

Kirsi nodded against him.

"Who kidnapped you? Where—?"

"I've already taken a preliminary statement from Dr. Royston," the state cop who had been supporting Kirsi interrupted. "But we will need to interview her again soon—when she's better able to give us information."

"Did you get him, get the kidnapper?" Doug asked.

"Yes, the information supplied by your local sheriff's department led us to set up a roadblock here. The kidnapper tried to break through it." The trooper motioned toward the gray sedan that was nose down in the ditch. Beside it, under the blue light, lay a crumpled form.

"Is he . . . did you . . . ?" Doug held himself from going toward it, even though he wanted to know more.

"We had to use deadly force. He didn't survive."

This formal-sounding account chilled Doug. "Do you have any idea who he is?"

The state cop shrugged. "Your local sheriff will probably get that from the meth manufacturers they arrested tonight. This perp had ID on him, but it might be an alias. We'll check it out, run his prints through our databases."

Doug smoothed Kirsi's hair back from her face. He wanted to turn and hustle her away with him, but he knew they would prevent him. "I need to get her back to the clinic. She's—"

"Good. I need to have Dr. Royston examined by a doctor." The state trooper hooked his thumb into his belt. "We haven't been able to get too many facts from her. She may have been sexually assaulted."

Filled with fear, sickened and incensed all at once, Doug

hated the way the lawman said this—to him, this was a routine matter. But not to Doug, not about Kirsi.

Then Doug felt Kirsi shake her head against him. His heart flowed with warmth. "She says no." Relief rolled through him. He pressed kisses into her hair again and again. Just holding her—alive—meant everything.

The trooper in charge told another officer to drive Kirsi to the clinic. But this changed when Kirsi refused to be parted from Doug.

Soon, Doug drove away from the roadblock with Kirsi on the front seat beside him. To get back to the crime scene as fast as possible, a trooper leading the way to the clinic had his siren and lights on.

She drew closer. He felt her warm breath against his neck. *I praise You, Father, for Your mighty and wonderful deeds.*

※ ※ ※

As the state-police car in front of them screeched to a halt, the siren cut off. Kirsi looked up, seeing the clinic through tears.

She felt the tightness inside her begin to loosen. Doug—the man she loved with her whole heart—was beside her. She wanted to tell him not to worry, that she was okay. But she had no strength. *Maybe I'm not okay. How can I be okay after everything that happened tonight?*

"Let's get you inside," Doug said. "I want to make sure you're all right." He helped her out of his vehicle and guided her toward the ER doors. They swished open. Cool air flowed into Kirsi's face. She looked up and saw Old Doc coming toward her. Too drained to run, she leaned against Doug and wept onto his shoulder.

"Praise God!" Old Doc opened his arms, and Kirsi let him hug them both as she stayed within Doug's embrace.

"Oh, Doc, I . . . Doc." She cried. She was at the clinic. *I made it, Lord. We made it.* She drew a shuddering breath before going on. "I wasn't assaulted." The cloying memory of the assailant made her shudder, but she pushed it away. "I'm fine. I'm home." *Home is where Doug is.* She clung to Doug. "I never thought I'd see you again."

Nodding, Doug now studied Kirsi in his role as doctor. Her face was smeared with tears, grime, and blood. Her scraped arms and legs were beginning to show bruising. But from his visual diagnosis, she needed only a cleanup and a few butterfly bandages. She might have a cracked rib or two and maybe a sprain, but nothing serious or life-threatening. Gratitude drenched him in a cool rush.

He turned to the trooper who had accompanied them into the ER and stuck out his hand. "Thank you. Thank you for finding her so fast."

The state cop shook Doug's hand. "I'll leave her in your care for treatment, but my superior will be back soon for more in-depth questioning." He touched his hat brim and turned away to hurry back to the crime scene.

Doug held Kirsi close as he walked her into the first examining area. He'd survived the past few hours. *But my ordeal was nothing compared to hers. Dear God . . .*

Desperate for action, Doug settled Kirsi onto the exam table and then jerked open several cabinets, collecting the materials he needed. He began by swabbing Kirsi's wounds—a split lip and a gash on her forehead that was already turning purple.

"Do you hurt anywhere else?" he murmured, trying not to show how much seeing her like this hurt him, filled him with outrage. *The man who hurt her is dead and I'm glad. I'm sorry, God. Maybe I can forgive him later but not now.*

Kirsi gazed at Doug. "I'm bruised all over—I bounced

around in that trunk. And I may be concussed—possible head trauma." She closed her eyes. "I can't take it all in."

Steaming, Doug dabbed antiseptic on her lip.

"How did you know I'd been kidnapped?" Kirsi asked, glad to feel the cream stinging. It made her feel alive. In spite of all that had happened tonight, the laws of nature still held.

"And where's Weston?" she asked. "I asked the trooper, but he only said that someone had called in the information. But how? I was all alone there. I'd left Veda back with the cars. She's all right, isn't she?"

Doug stopped swabbing. "Wasn't she at the roadblock where they caught up with you?"

"No." Kirsi's forehead creased. "Why would she be there?"

"Because she's the one who called in the information. She evidently saw what happened to you and followed in her car." Doug started swabbing again.

"But how? Earlier at the mill, I told her to stay with the cars." Doug's nearness tempted her to capture his hand and hold it to her cheek.

"Well, somehow she called my cell phone number." Doug gazed at her and then brushed her hair behind one ear.

Kirsi leaned against his hand. "I gave it to her a few weeks ago in case she needed help and couldn't get me on my cell phone. We need to call her and see that she's home safe."

Putting down the cotton swab, Doug dialed the number and listened until the phone was picked up. He handed Kirsi the phone.

"Veda, it's me, Dr. Royston!"

"I followed you at the mill and watched from behind some evergreens," Veda gloated. "Then I ran back to my car and followed him."

"Veda, how can I thank you? You saved my life!"

The line clicked. Dumbfounded, Kirsi handed Doug the phone. "She hung up on me."

"Well, if it weren't for Veda, you wouldn't have been found so quickly and unharmed," Old Doc declared with a chuckle. "And isn't that going to be something for this county to swallow!"

※ ※ ※

With Doug at her side, Kirsi walked in a kind of controlled stagger up the steps to her room. "I don't think I've ever been this tired before in my life, and that's saying something." She stumbled halfway up the stairs.

Doug gripped her arm. She swayed against him. He held her close and kissed her. "I can't let you go back to California. I can't."

"I don't want to leave you." She kissed his lips, lingering over them, drawing strength from them.

"So where does that leave us?"

"Caught in the middle." She rested her head against him, then pressed a kiss in the hollow of his neck.

He started up the steps again, drawing her along. "Come on. I want to see you in your own bed and sleeping before I go back to the house."

She let him pull her along until she stood inside her suite. Every particle of her battered body ached and begged for sleep. Every atom of her being ached for Doug to stay with her. *Hold me. Hold me.* But she had barely enough energy to fall into her bed and send Doug back to the house. "Good night," she mumbled, her eyes already closed.

"Good night. Tomorrow we'll sort this all out. I know just who can help us."

✖ ✖ ✖

The next day, with Doug beside her, Kirsi walked into Harlan's kitchen. She stopped a moment, noticing the homey details as if she'd never been there before. Was that what nearly dying did for you? Did it make everything new?

Last night Doug had kissed her good night, and she hadn't wanted to let him go. *I can't bear it, Lord. I love him.* Yesterday everything had changed. Nothing had changed.

Doug touched her arm. "You up to this?"

She nodded. "I am if you are." She wasn't surprised that Harlan was the person Doug wanted them to consult. Harlan's reputation for wisdom was notable in the small town. And his leadership of the morning prayer meetings held in this kitchen had proved that reputation to be well earned.

Nick was washing dishes at the sink. "Hi! You had a wild night last night, I hear. Are you okay? Is Weston all right?"

"Almost too wild." Remembering the night before made Kirsi cringe. Yet it almost seemed like it had happened to someone else. Except that her body ached all over, bruises showed on her arms, and she was tender everywhere. So it had all been real. *I could have been killed.*

"Weston," Doug said in reply to Nick, "is in fair condition at the hospital in Eau Claire. His parents are there with him."

"How's his baby?" Nick showed his concern with a deep frown.

"She's in good condition as of this morning." Kirsi had called the clinic upon waking. "Her fever is down and the antibiotic is working."

"Thank God," the teen said.

"Dr. Royston, is that you?" Harlan called from the living room.

The warm voice could not be ignored. Kirsi hurried in to Harlan and bent to hug him where he lay propped up in a hospital bed in the sunny room. When his frail arms embraced her, she began to cry.

"There, there, Doctor," Harlan comforted her. "You're going to be all right. Burke told us everything this morning. They've identified your kidnapper. An ex-con, a known member of a drug gang out of Milwaukee. God was with you all the way last night. He brought you through the valley of the shadow of death."

She straightened up, wiping her tears away. "I know. I'm here." *Alive!*

Doug came up and put his arm around her. She knew she should pull away, but she couldn't find the strength, the will. *I want Doug to hold me . . . always.*

"What a fine couple you two make." Harlan beamed at them.

Kirsi felt another tear drop.

Doug pulled her closer. "Harlan, we need your advice."

"Oh?" Harlan waved them to the sofa beside his bed.

Doug seated Kirsi, then sat down and took her hand.

"Nick, are those dishes done?" Harlan called.

"Yes. I gotta go now. I'm opening at the A&W today."

"Have a good day."

"See you later, Harlan!" They heard Nick leave by the back door.

"Now what's keeping you two apart?" Harlan asked.

"How did you guess?" Kirsi blinked back more tears.

Harlan shook his head. "You two were meant for each other. I knew it the first time I saw you together."

"You mean like half the gossips in the county?" Doug asked wryly.

Harlan smiled. "Now what *is* keeping you two apart? All the mysteries have been solved. Our prayers have been answered in full." He gave Kirsi a knowing look. "I know your mind has changed, Dr. Royston. I've sensed that you want to stay with us, don't you?"

"I do but my mother needs me." The last two words came out shrill. Kirsi cleared her throat.

"Tell me," Harlan encouraged softly.

Kirsi explained her mother's unstable mental condition and its cause, her grandparents' need for relief from the life-long burden of caring for their daughter, and the real reason for the trip to India. Then she gazed at Harlan, hoping he truly had the answer.

Harlan gave her his full attention until the end.

Kirsi wiped her eyes with the handkerchief Doug had handed her. "I don't want to be an unloving or ungrateful daughter or granddaughter."

Harlan smiled. " 'Honour thy father and thy mother,' " he recited. "The question is, what does that mean?" He looked to Kirsi. "Have you always exhibited respect for your mother and grandparents?"

Kirsi nodded, still sniffing back tears.

"Would you go to help them if they needed you?"

"Of course."

"Then you are honoring your mother and grand-parents," Harlan said with a motion of his hand.

"But—"

"Let me ask you another question," the elder said. "If you told your family how you felt about staying here, what would they say?"

Kirsi worried her lower lip.

"I don't think your grandparents and mother would ask you to return to California if they knew how your feelings had changed, do you? Do you?" Harlan insisted.

Kirsi was forced to answer. "No, but it would be easier on all of them—"

"Honoring doesn't include just making things convenient for your family," Harlan persisted. "Would your family ask you to return if they knew about your love for Douglas?"

Kirsi shook her head.

"Call your family and tell them. I think that you'll find that a parent's greatest wish is that a child be happy and well. Your family wouldn't ask such a sacrifice of you. And from what you've told me, your grandmother made a similar decision in her youth. She didn't think honoring her parents meant remaining Hindu and returning to India."

"I never thought of it that way."

"Trust me. They will want your happiness, for you to stay here with a fine man, Doug—if you really love him."

"I do." Kirsi squeezed Doug's hand.

"I don't want to make light of your family's situation," Harlan continued, "but love is too precious to waste. It's a gift from God because all good gifts come from Him. I think your mother and grandparents love you enough to want your happiness foremost. They will make adjustments and not resent it. Have some faith in them. Have faith that God can make up the difference for you."

Kirsi nodded, recalcitrant tears flowing down her face. "You make it sound so simple."

Doug kissed her cheek. "Thanks, Harlan. I knew you'd give us good counsel."

"Yes, and it's time I said something to you that I've been wanting to say for a long time." Harlan pinned Doug with a penetrating stare.

Doug looked into Harlan's eyes. "What's that?"

"Forgive your mother," Harlan pronounced sternly.

Doug's face burned with sudden shame.

"I know you hold it against her that she left Steadfast, left you right after your father's death. But maybe she was only doing what she thought was best for her *and* you."

"For me?" Doug felt his mother's rejection gnawing him afresh.

"Yes. Have you ever thought that she might have gone back to school because she didn't want to hover over you? She didn't want to be a burden to you?"

This alien thought shocked Doug. "Do you think so?"

"I think it's a strong possibility," Harlan said. "You need to discuss it with your grandfather, and then you need to make an effort to patch things up with your mother in any case."

Doug felt his forehead furrow as he mulled this over. Have I been thinking completely backwards on this? *Forgive me, Lord.*

"I'm tired," Harlan said, leaning back. "You young people, don't ever waste love! It's too hard to come by in this hard, cold, unforgiving world. Now, you two, let's see some love in action." He waved his hand.

Buzzing with a wealth of affection and passion, Doug turned Kirsi in his arms and kissed her. "I love you."

Kirsi returned Doug's kiss with warmth flowing through her. "I love you."

"Amen," Harlan intoned softly.

# EPILOGUE

WITH DOUG AT HER SIDE, Kirsi sat in a pew at the Steadfast Community Church. The contagious wedding joy had her beaming.

At the front, Pastor Weaver was leading Keely Turner and Burke Sloan in saying their wedding vows. The church overflowed with white satin ribbons and bows, yellow roses, and baby's breath. Keely was transformed from her usual high school principal look to a breathtakingly beautiful bride in a gown adorned with seed pearls. And though the groom wore a sling over his tux, no wedding couple ever looked more in love—especially to Kirsi, who was bursting with her own joy.

Doug held her hand. Kirsi felt as though she were a completely different person than she had been just a few weeks ago, the night she'd been kidnapped. She still struggled with nightmares, but she had gone to a psychologist and was working her way through the horrible spasms of vulnerability and flashbacks that hit her at least once a day.

Kirsi had taken strength from Harlan's advice and told her grandparents and mother about her love for Doug and her decision to stay in Steadfast. They'd been thrilled and were planning to fly out in the fall to meet Doug. When she'd tried to apologize to her grandmother about not returning to help with her mother, Nani had told her not to be foolish—her happiness was all that mattered to her family.

God had already intervened in amazing ways. Her mother was doing better on a new medication and was coming out of the latest downturn. And Great-Aunt Uma was stable and looking forward to seeing her sister after over fifty years of separation. Thinking of the upcoming reunion in India often brought tears to Kirsi's eyes.

At times, Kirsi couldn't believe that everything had fallen into place. Except for the trip to India, she was free to be with Doug.

The new resident from California had pleased Old Doc in his interview. The new doctor would be settling into Bruno's cabin while he and his wife looked for a piece of land. As a result of the meth-lab raid, arrests had been made. According to the prisoners, the man who'd stalked Kirsi had been the meth franchise owner from a drug gang operating all over the Midwest.

It was as if God had turned the page on all their worries, and she and Doug were now writing a new story. A happier one. One that trusted God more. Certainly seeing Weston here sitting beside Carrie holding little Amy proved this.

In the small, crowded church, Kirsi noted that another point of interest vied with the bridal couple for the congregation's attention. Wearing a new purple outfit, Veda McCracken sat beside Harlan.

Veda's part in Kirsi's rescue had astounded the county. When Kirsi had gone to thank Veda in person for saving her life, Veda had surprised her by bursting into tears. Then she had mumbled, "I want to be happy now. I never wanted that before. I only wanted everyone else to be as miserable as me."

Kirsi had hugged her and whispered, "That's God softening your heart. That's a good thing."

Though Veda still had a long way to go to make a real change in her life, her shunning had ended. Kirsi prayed that with this new acceptance Veda's feeling of having accomplished something of true value by saving Kirsi's life would make a difference. Medication and counseling could also be used by God to change the woman's life. Veda still needed the Lord and Kirsi prayed for this daily. Now she felt many more were with her in this, too.

When Pastor Bruce asked for the ring, Rodd Durand, Burke's best man, pulled it from his pocket and gave it to Burke. Burke slid the gold band onto Keely's finger and began, "With this ring. . . ."

Little Rachel Weaver stood up on the pew beside her mother, Penny, and clapped her hands. The congregation chuckled while Bruce beamed at his little daughter.

"Shoosh," Zak, Rachel's five-year-old brother, cautioned with his finger to his lips. "We're in church."

Wendy, the bride's matron of honor, turned toward Rachel, smiling. It was fortunate that Keely had chosen high-waisted gowns, because Wendy had just started showing. Harlan was bragging all over town: he would soon be a great-grandfather!

*A Note from the Author*

Dear Reader,

I hope you enjoyed this final book of my Northern Intrigue series set in fictitious Steadfast, Wisconsin, the county I created for my characters.

Each book explored the challenges that any of us might face in life. In each story, my hero and heroine had to work out their relationships to their parents and how it affected their relationship to others and most importantly to God. This is a universal struggle and it doesn't end when we're eighteen—though many teens think it will. "It's my life!" they say. Until they need family again and they realize no life is separate from others.

In his poem "For Whom the Bell Tolls," John Donne wrote, "No man is an island." This theme was revealed in the lives of the patriarchs of the Old Testament, such as Abraham. Actions they took shaped the lives of their descendants and still have impact on our lives today.

I hope you will treasure your family and be willing to entrust your relationships to God. None of us can be the perfect parent or perfect child, but with God's help we can strengthen our families, be glad we have each other, and give our descendants a good foundation for their lives, especially when we bequeath them a heritage of faith.

*Lyn*

## *About the Author*

Born in Texas, raised in Illinois on the shore of Lake Michigan, Lyn now lives in Iowa with her husband, son, and daughter. Lyn has spent her adult life as a teacher, a full-time mom, and now a writer. She enjoys floral crafts, classical music, and traveling. Lyn and her husband of over twenty-five years spend their summers at their cabin on a lake in northern Wisconsin. Lyn writes and her husband telecommutes for his company. By the way, Lyn's last name is pronounced "Coty."

*Summer's End* is the sequel to *Winter's Secret* and *Autumn's Shadow* and book 3 in the Northern Intrigue series. Lyn's novella "For Varina's Heart" appears in the HeartQuest anthology *Letters of the Heart*. Her other novels are *Finally Found, Finally Home, Hope's Garden, New Man in Town,* and *Never Alone* (Steeple Hill); *Echoes of Mercy, Lost in His Love,* and *Whispers of Love* (Broadman & Holman).

Lyn welcomes letters written to her in care of Tyndale House Author Relations, P.O. Box 80, Wheaton, IL 60189; on-line at l.cote@juno.com; or through her Web site, www.booksbylyncote.com.

Visit www.HeartQuest.com for lots of info on
HeartQuest books and authors and more!

www.HeartQuest.com

HEART
QUEST

*Coming Soon*

WINTER 2003

*Catching Katie*

Robin Lee Hatcher

∽⊘∾

*Patience*

Lori Copeland

## HEARTQUEST BOOKS BY LYN COTE

*Autumn's Shadow*—A suppressed scream vibrated in Keely's throat. Frozen in place, Keely heard footsteps. Sloan grabbed her, shoved her behind him, and hustled her sideways the few feet to his Jeep. He pressed her down behind his vehicle. "Don't move," he ordered. Still crouching, Keely bent her head against the back of Sloan's neck, seeking his protection. She gripped the shoulders of his jacket with both hands.

High school principal Keely Turner is not prepared for the dangers that await her in a small town in Wisconsin. As teenage pranks escalate, she must turn to Deputy Burke Sloan for help. But as they join together to protect their community, they find their hearts in jeopardy. . . .

*Winter's Secret*—Standing to the side of the battered door, Sheriff Rodd Durand eased out his gun in the icy stillness. "Police! Come out with your hands up!" He expected no answer. This lowlife criminal preyed on the most defenseless—the elderly who lived out in the country and alone. Righteous anger swept through Rodd like flames.

There's only one unlikely link to the crime spree in this sleepy Wisconsin county: Wendy Carey. But the threat to the community is nothing compared to the threat Wendy poses to Rodd's heart. . . . Book 1 in the Northern Intrigue series.

*For Varina's Heart*—What says romance more than a handwritten letter from the one you love? Suddenly finding herself tied to a man she does not know, Varina treasures her heart's dreams while hanging on to each letter that arrives from Gannon Moore. This historical novella by Lyn Cote appears in the anthology *Letters of the Heart.*

## CURRENT HEARTQUEST RELEASES

## MOVING FICTION

### OTHER GREAT TYNDALE HOUSE FICTION

- *Safely Home*, Randy Alcorn
- *The Sister Circle*, Vonette Bright and Nancy Moser
- *'Round the Corner*, Vonette Bright and Nancy Moser

- *Out of the Shadows*, Sigmund Brouwer
- *The Leper*, Sigmund Brouwer
- *Crown of Thorns*, Sigmund Brouwer
- *The Lies of Saints*, Sigmund Brouwer

- *Looking for Cassandra Jane*, Melody Carlson
- *Armando's Treasure*, Melody Carlson

- *A Case of Bad Taste*, Lori Copeland
- *Child of Grace*, Lori Copeland

- *Into the Nevernight*, Anne de Graaf

- *They Shall See God*, Athol Dickson

- *Ribbon of Years*, Robin Lee Hatcher
- *Firstborn*, Robin Lee Hatcher

- *The Touch*, Patricia Hickman

- *Redemption*, Karen Kingsbury with Gary Smalley
- *Remember*, Karen Kingsbury with Gary Smalley
- *Return*, Karen Kingsbury with Gary Smalley

- *Winter Passing*, Cindy McCormick Martinusen
- *Blue Night*, Cindy McCormick Martinusen
- *North of Tomorrow*, Cindy McCormick Martinusen

- *Embrace the Dawn*, Kathleen Morgan
- *Consuming Fire*, Kathleen Morgan

- *Lullaby*, Jane Orcutt

- *The Happy Room*, Catherine Palmer
- *A Dangerous Silence*, Catherine Palmer
- *Fatal Harvest*, Catherine Palmer

- *Blind Sight*, James H. Pence

- *And the Shofar Blew*, Francine Rivers
- *Unveiled*, Francine Rivers
- *Unashamed*, Francine Rivers
- *Unshaken*, Francine Rivers
- *Unspoken*, Francine Rivers
- *Unafraid*, Francine Rivers
- *A Voice in the Wind*, Francine Rivers
- *An Echo in the Darkness*, Francine Rivers
- *As Sure As the Dawn*, Francine Rivers
- *Leota's Garden*, Francine Rivers

- *First Light*, Bodie and Brock Thoene

- *Shaiton's Fire*, Jake Thoene
- *Firefly Blue*, Jake Thoene

- *The Promise Remains*, Travis Thrasher
- *The Watermark*, Travis Thrasher